Summer of Deception

Elva Cobb Martin

SUMMER OF DECEPTION BY ELVA COBB MARTIN
Published by Lighthouse Publishing of the Carolinas
2333 Barton Oaks Dr., Raleigh, NC, 27614

ISBN: 978-1-946016-34-8
Copyright © 2017 by Elva Cobb Martin
Cover design by Designs By Rachelle, LLC
Interior design by Atritex, www.atritex.com

Available in print from your local bookstore, online, or from the
publisher at: ShopLPC.com or LPCBooks.com

For more information on this book and the author, visit:
http://www.elvamartin.com or
http://carolinaromancewithelvamartin.blogspot.com

Library of Congress Cataloging-in-Publication Data
Martin, Elva Cobb.
Summer of Deception / Elva Cobb Martin 1st ed.

Printed in the United States of America

Chapter One

Charleston, South Carolina

Rachel York gasped when the taxi headlights pierced the stormy night and illuminated Barrett Hall in all its southern grandeur. Her travel fatigue faded, and she leaned forward, energized, as the cab crunched its way up the tree-lined shell drive to the entrance. At the gate, she exited the auto with her umbrella extended, and the taxi driver placed her large bag and tote at her side. Rachel thanked him, paid him, and hurried up the front walk, pulling her valise behind her. The vehicle disappeared down the drive, and darkness closed in as she made her way up the front steps.

On the wide porch, she propped her umbrella beside her suitcase, took a deep breath, and tried to ignore a shiver of disquiet that traveled up her spine. She would discover the truth. This summer job in Charleston was her first step.

The rain pounding against the slate roof stopped as quickly as it began. The moon angled out from behind a cloud, and Rachel glanced around the plantation's wide portico with its six imposing columns and rocking chairs bathed in shadows. The brass horse-head knocker adorning the entrance added to its aura.

She held her wristwatch to the moonlight and grimaced. Ten o'clock. She'd arrived five hours late and with her cell phone dead. How early did the elderly Mr. Barrett retire? Did he think she would change her mind about his job offer? *No way.* It was an answer to prayer.

Rachel breathed in the moist air. The sweet smell of gardenias delighted her. Swinging her thick hair behind her shoulders, she lifted the knocker and let it go. The sound broke the quietness like a pistol shot.

A sharp bark from behind startled Rachel's already antsy nerves. She whirled around. A gray German shepherd the size of a calf stood on the steps. She grabbed her umbrella and pointed it at the beast as if it were a sword.

"Gabriel, what are you growling about?" A tall man stepped into view from a path beside the house, shaking rain from his cowboy hat. The moonlight revealed his strong build and rich tan. He wore an eye patch and an olive green T-shirt etched with the word *Marines.*

When he caught sight of Rachel, he commanded the dog in a strong low voice, "Come, Gabriel." The animal obeyed, and he snapped a leash on its collar. "Sorry if this big mutt frightened you. He's not ferocious, but we don't broadcast it. And the umbrella wouldn't suffice for your defense if he wanted to attack—which he doesn't." The man chuckled, a pleasant sound in the shadows.

Was he a farmhand or some kind of security patrolling the grounds? Rachel breathed easier and lowered her umbrella. She opened her lips to speak, but the porch flooded with light and the door opened. Rachel turned.

A gray-haired woman in a wilted apron stood in the partial opening. She glared at Rachel with narrowed blue eyes that rounded as she spied the luggage.

"I'm Rachel York. Mr. Barrett's expecting me. Sorry I'm so late."

"Mr. Barrett, eh? He didn't tell me he was 'specting nobody, 'specially for overnight." She frowned and pursed her lips. "And I'm the housekeeper. What did you say your name was?"

"Rachel York." *Not expecting me?* And not just for overnight—but the whole summer.

The woman opened the door wider, and her eyes fell on the man in the shadows. "Oh, there you are."

Rachel glanced back at the man and dog.

He spoke to the housekeeper. "Mrs. Busby, show our guest to the game room in about two minutes."

"Yes, sir."

Obviously not a farm employee. Or a guard. Rachel pulled her luggage into an elegant entrance hall lit by a grand chandelier. A delightful fragrance wafted up from roses on a side table. She propped her suitcase upright and dropped her carry-on beside it. Glancing around, she tilted her chin and smiled. What a place to have a job for three months. Even a nanny job.

Just who *was* the striking man?

The housekeeper disappeared down the hall, and Rachel tried to still a flutter in her stomach. How could her arrival be a surprise to the help? The woman soon returned and gestured for Rachel to follow. They turned past a curving staircase and down two steps into an enclosed patio dotted with plants and white wicker furniture. Rachel's metal-capped heels clicked across polished brick.

The house appeared to be exactly the kind of historic residence she expected a southern plantation owner like elderly Charles Barrett to own. That day in the college office, Dean Woods described it perfectly as a *Gone with the Wind* setting. Her future employer laughed and nodded at them both.

The woman gave a brief knock at a door and opened it. She motioned for Rachel to enter and came in beside her.

Rachel inhaled the delightful woodsy scent of cedar chips and turned at the sound of the masculine voice she recognized from the porch.

"Hello, again." The man and the dog stood in front of an unlit fireplace at the far side of the room. He wore a towel around his neck and Levis tucked into army boots. The German shepherd wagged its tail and started to move forward. But its master spoke a command. "Sit, Gabriel."

The dog obeyed.

Rachel found it difficult to breathe as the man glanced from her hair to the stilettos peeking beneath her jeans. She resisted the urge to smooth her curls or straighten the blazer.

He cast aside the towel and strode toward Rachel and the housekeeper. His boots clunked on the hardwood floor.

Mrs. Busby spoke with a stiff voice. "Mr. Barrett, shall I place her luggage in your room, sir? Or a guest room?"

Blood rushed to Rachel's face. In *his* room? "No—this is not the person I'm here to see."

The housekeeper turned to her. "You said Mr. Barrett expected you, Miss York."

"I would like to speak with Mr. *Charles* Barrett, if you please. He should be expecting me."

The housekeeper's mouth fell open, but the man

waved her out the door. She left without a word.

He turned to Rachel, a corner of his mouth quirked up. "You mean my uncle invited you here to spend the night? That'd be a first."

Speechless, Rachel stared at him, her cheeks hot enough to fry an egg. Raindrops glistened on his short black hair, and brown stubble darkened his chiseled face. The hint of a mustache floated above thin lips now stretched into a grin. Surely she was the victim of a joke—and by a most handsome man, even with the patch across his left eye.

He propped on the edge of the desk, folded his powerful arms, and met her burning glance. "Sorry, let's start over. It's been a long time since I've seen an honest-to-goodness flush like the one lighting your face."

Some apology.

"I'm Luke Barrett." A smile showed even white teeth, and he leaned forward and extended his hand. The low, rich timbre of his voice vibrated through Rachel, and the scent of spicy aftershave tickled her nose. She took a needed breath and shook hands. Luke's calloused palm swallowed hers, and their gazes met. A tiny shock coursed through her.

"Rachel York," she said, surprised at the tightness in her throat.

She tried not to stare at the patch and disengaged from his handshake.

He reached up and adjusted the black oval. "Won't you sit down and tell me why you're here?"

She moved to a chair and perched on its edge.

Luke sat behind the desk. A small, half-finished woodcarving lay in front of him. He swept the shavings into a trash basket and dropped the wooden piece and pocketknife into a drawer. Leaning back in his chair, he cracked his knuckles twice and gazed at her.

Rachel started to speak, but a grandfather clock nearby struck the hour, making speech impossible. Luke cocked his head until the chimes stopped.

"I'm sorry I'm late," Rachel said when silence again reigned, "but my plane was delayed by the storm, and I couldn't get a phone connection. Has your uncle retired already?"

Something like shutters closed over Luke's face. And he sat up straight, alert, similar to a tiger ready to pounce. "You might say so. You claim he was expecting you?"

Rachel's empty stomach knotted. What was going on? First, the housekeeper, now this nephew. Not the welcome she hoped for. She shook off her uneasiness— everything could be cleared up in two seconds. "Mr. Barrett offered me a summer position caring for a child. Would you like to see the note?"

Luke's brow rose, and he reached a wide palm across the desktop. "Definitely."

Rachel opened her handbag. As she searched for the paper, his rapt attention reminded her of her stepfather Lester's interrogations. A lipstick plopped out onto the floor, and she bent to retrieve it. Finally, she found the missive and passed it to Luke.

He unfolded it and read it.

Relax. Never again would she fear Lester Black and his stifling control. When he discovered she'd left for a summer job states away, he might become furious, but he could do nothing about it. She was in the midst of a new beginning, like her brother Ron surely enjoyed in his earlier move to Charleston. A pain crossed her heart. But she couldn't think about Ron. Not yet.

She studied the man before her. Thank God there was nothing else about him remindful of her stepfather. A calm strength emanated from Luke Barrett evocative of Ron and his Drug Enforcement Administration associates, who kept in top physical condition.

Luke glanced up at her.

She squirmed and blinked. He'd caught her staring at him.

An uneasy silence settled in the air as he reexamined the note. A frown creased his brow. Rachel's travel weariness returned, and a dull pain began to throb behind her eye. She inspected the room to avoid gazing at him. A padlocked gun case on the left displayed an assortment of rifles, pistols, and revolvers. She scanned titles in the bookcase behind Luke. Her jumbled mind made out "Marines" etched on a manual. A Bible sat in a corner with some framed pictures. Two of them featured a dark-headed little girl. Her charge, perhaps? Some of Rachel's tension evaporated.

She stole a glance again at Luke still bent over the letter. A muscle worked in his jaw. Obviously, he did not know about his uncle's job offer to her. Mr. Barrett's gentle face the day she talked with him in Dean Wood's office floated across her mind, and her confidence recharged.

Luke dropped the letter on the desk and sat forward. "Where did you get this, Miss York?" His challenging demeanor startled her.

She stood and swallowed. "From your uncle, of course. He can explain everything."

"Uncle Charles died two weeks ago."

Chapter Two

Luke Barrett moved to the edge of his desk, concerned. He stared at the young woman, who had dropped back into her chair like a limp rag doll. Quite an attractive one. "Are you okay, Miss York?"

A pleasing fragrance emanated from her. *Musk or lavender?* But what was this beauty up to? Was she the first of several who might show up at Barrett Hall—with its tea production and history—with unlikely stories of job offers from Charles? But this request was no small matter relating to plantation work.

His lips tightened. "I'm not sure what this is about, Miss York. If it's some kind of act, I'll take my hat off to you. This note does appear to be in Uncle Charles's handwriting. But I can't figure out how or why he would have written it."

If her story proved to be true, was this attractive girl before him another of his uncle's attempts, even from the grave, to whittle away Luke's vow not to remarry?

Rachel York appeared glued to her chair. Her words came out almost in a whisper. "Mr. Barrett left it in my college dean's office with my plane ticket"—she swallowed—"about a month ago. He was in a hurry to catch his flight."

Luke folded his arms across his chest. "Do you expect me to believe my uncle made this offer to you regarding my daughter's care and didn't even mention it to me?"

~*~

His daughter? No, Rachel found it hard to consider the elder Mr. Barrett not clearing her job offer first with the child's father. What was going on here? She averted her face and blinked away moisture. *God help me.* That brief prayer ignited her tardy faith, as well as her Scottish-Irish blood. She was meant to come to Charleston, regardless of this turn of events. She took a deep breath and lifted her chin. Before any response formed in her brain, a brisk knock sounded and the door opened.

A silver-haired woman in a blue silk robe glided into the room. A violet fragrance came with her. Her gray eyes, bright with intelligence and concern, swept from Rachel to Luke. She clicked her tongue. "Luke Barrett, why are you frowning at our visitor like one of your Marines caught absent without leave?"

Luke lowered his head under the heated question, and a grin played at his mouth until he pressed his lips together. He stepped behind his desk. "Aunt Jessica, this is Rachel York. Rachel, may I present my aunt, Jessica Buckner?"

Rachel swerved her attention to the kind face like a drowning victim spotting a lifeline. She managed a smile.

The woman came closer and gazed at Rachel. "Are those tears in those lovely blue eyes? Luke, do you owe this young woman an apology?"

"I might, if she's on the up and up about this job offer." Luke's face turned firm. "But if she's not, we're being made fools of by a pretty Yankee who knows how to shed a tear at will."

Rachel's toes curled in her shoes.

Jessica's eyes flashed toward her nephew, but she smiled when she glanced back at Rachel. "Job offer?"

Luke waved the note. "This young lady says Charles gave her this."

Jessica took it and read it. "This is definitely my brother's handwriting—and what a lovely idea for the summer."

Rachel breathed easier.

Jessica met her gaze. "But, my dear, Charles did not mention anything about this to me." She turned to Luke. "And he never spoke of it to you?"

"Nary a word." Luke eased into his chair and stared at both of them.

The woman tapped a slippered foot. "But I am positive there's an explanation. Luke, why don't I sit down with Miss York and report back to you." A statement, not a question.

"All right, Aunt Jess. I'm not going anywhere."

Rachel rose and found her normal voice. "I'm so sorry about Mr. Barrett. I had no idea."

"Of course you didn't," Jessica said, laying a small, soft hand on Rachel's arm. "Come along and I will ask Mrs. Busby to get us something hot to drink. You must be exhausted after traveling in this weather."

Luke stood and strode to the door, opening it for them. Rachel willed herself to ignore his gaze and the slight bow he gave as they passed. The pain behind her eyes faded as he closed the door behind them.

She and Jessica proceeded down the hall and into

a formal sitting room. Jessica turned on a lamp and gestured toward a sofa. "Please take a seat, dear. Now I'm a tea drinker, but would you prefer hot chocolate?"

"Chocolate sounds wonderful."

After Jessica left, Rachel strolled over to an antique piano with its petite Victorian stool. The scent of lemon oil rose from its polished surface. She reached to touch the yellowed keys when a portrait over the mantel caught her attention. A young, blonde woman in a rose gown surveyed the room with a contented smile. Pearls shimmered around a slender neck. Her pale green eyes were long-lashed, her cheekbones high, and her lips delicate.

Rachel walked back to the flora loveseat and sat. She ran her hand over the satiny fabric, and a quiver of pleasure flowed over her. To be surrounded by such beauty, even for a summer.

Luke's handsome, suspicious face broke into her thoughts, and her shoulders stiffened. Would the man honor his uncle's offer to her?

Jessica reentered the room. "I've roused Mrs. Busby—or riled her, as the case may be this time of night—and asked her to bring our tea and chocolate."

Rachel suppressed a smile. Mrs. Busby had been irritated since she opened the front door. Jessica sat down beside Rachel and adjusted the silk folds of her robe over her knees. "I'm glad you appear more at ease now. Please forgive my nephew's reception tonight. It is Rachel, isn't it?"

"Yes, but I'm not offended. I managed to show up so late in the evening and, apparently, unexpected."

"He is not excused." Jessica's voice softened as she continued. "Luke was in the Marines' Special Ops in the Middle East for ten years, and some dreadful things came his way, including his eye injury. I'm afraid he's suspicious first and trusting later."

Rachel relaxed, listening to Jessica.

The door opened, and the rich aroma of chocolate drifted across the room. Mrs. Busby set a silver tray before them with two small teapots. She was not smiling.

"Thank you so much, Mrs. Busby." Jessica gave the woman an appreciative nod.

The housekeeper grunted and left.

Rachel's hostess raised her brows and poured a steaming cup of cocoa and another of tea into exquisite cups. She handed Rachel hers.

The sweet chocolate infused Rachel with warmth and helped calm the butterflies in her stomach.

Jessica leaned back and sipped her tea. "Now, please tell me a little about yourself and how you came to know my brother Charles. I do believe he wrote that note."

Rachel explained she'd met Charles Barrett in the college dean's office at Ohio State University. She worked for Dean Wooten part time her senior year.

Jessica nodded and smiled. "I remember Charles did visit his old college friend shortly before he passed. And this offer to you sounds so much like him." She drank the rest of her tea. "After Georgina, Luke's wife, died—and Luke went back to the Middle East—Charles took care of everything and seldom said howdy-do to anyone about it."

Rachel finished her chocolate and set her cup down.

A shadow passed over Jessica's face. "My brother had a stroke right after he returned from his trip north. He was paralyzed and died quickly. Otherwise, he would've told us about his offer to you, Rachel." Jessica lifted her chin. "And I think it's a great idea."

The hall clock struck the quarter hour. Jessica smiled at Rachel. "It's late, and I'm sure you must be weary, my dear. You'll certainly need to stay the night, no matter what Luke decides tomorrow. Did you miss dinner?"

"Yes, but please don't bother. This drink has hit the spot."

"No worry. A sandwich will be the right thing and fast." Jessica stood and tightened the sash of her robe. "Let me go speak to Luke. Meanwhile, we'll need to show you to a guest room upstairs. I guess I'll annoy Mrs. Busby once more."

They both chuckled.

A few minutes later, Rachel surveyed a lovely bedroom decorated in royal blue and bright yellow fabrics with ecru walls. She thanked Mrs. Busby for her help, and the woman mumbled something and left.

Rachel cast off her blazer and stepped out of her heels. Relief flowed from the small of her back to her neatly painted toenails.

Shuttered French doors framed by white Priscilla curtains lined one side of the room. She sauntered over, opened them, and took a deep breath. Warm, moist air laced with lilac filtered into the room. She stepped out onto the balcony and welcomed the cool dampness of the wood against her bare feet. The song of crickets filled the night as she peered out on a shadowed garden. Her Aunt Ruby, an avid gardener, would love the view. As soon as everything was settled about her summer, she'd call her mother's sister, who served as Lester's housekeeper. And Raven, her college roommate and best friend, who was already probably dialing Rachel's dead cell phone hourly.

A firm knock on the door interrupted Rachel's musings. The roused and riled Mrs. Busby with the promised sandwich, no doubt. She stepped back inside. "It's not locked. Come in."

The door opened, helped by a large black boot. Luke Barrett strode in carrying a covered tray. His presence made the room shrink and almost hid Jessica following him with a tall, lemon-fringed glass.

"Where do you want this?" Luke's bold gaze moved from her face to her ruby-tipped toes. She folded her arms across her snug silk pullover. She would not let this man disconcert her again, no matter what he decided tomorrow.

She moved to the coffee table. "Right here will be fine, Mr. Barrett, and thank you, but you shouldn't have bothered."

"No bother." After setting the tray on the table, Luke ambled to the door and paused, turning back to glance at Rachel. "Aunt Jessica says I owe you an apology, and she might be right."

Surprised, Rachel dared to scrutinize his handsome face.

"But I'll decide after I do some checking tomorrow. Good night, ladies."

Jessica clicked her tongue and sat the drink on the table. "Enjoy your supper, dear, and rest well. I've talked to Luke, and I think everything's going to be fine."

Casting off frustration at Luke's arrogant suspicion, Rachel thanked Jessica and locked the door when she left.

Check for what? The last person on earth she'd want

Luke Barrett to talk to would be her stepfather. But Lester Black was out of town—in fact, out of the country—on one of his mysterious trips. Luke could not inform him of her whereabouts.

She lifted the cloth on the tray and found a triple-decker turkey sandwich. She hurried to the bathroom sink, scrubbed the day's travel off her hands, and stared in the mirror. Her thick, black hair flew out from her chin to her shoulders in a tangle of curls, thanks to the humidity. Suddenly, Luke's rugged face and mocking words came back to her.

A pretty Yankee who can shed a tear at will.

A stab of guilt pierced her. Everything she'd told him was the truth. What she didn't tell him really wasn't his business. Was it?

Besides, Luke's arrogance reminded her of a certain law-student-turned-lawyer her stepfather introduced to her. She pushed all thoughts of Easton Watkins and her stepfather from her mind and enjoyed the sandwich.

Later, before turning out the bedside lamp, she pulled her Bible from her luggage and opened to the bookmark she'd placed earlier at Psalm 24. *The earth is the Lord's and everything in it, the world and all who live in it; for He founded it upon the seas and established it upon the waters.*

Even Barrett Hall and Luke Barrett.

Slumber pressed against her eyelids. She set the Bible aside and fell asleep.

~*~

A droning, clanging sound filled her ears, loud and horribly familiar. The struggling plane emerged from the clouds, erupted in billowing orange flames, and plunged into dark waves below. *Ron!*

She sat up, gasping for air. The dream again. Had she screamed out his name? Grief threatened to choke her as words in the Drug Enforcement Administration report flashed across her mind. *Fiery plane crash over the Atlantic. Assumed dead.* Rachel held on to the word "assumed" like a lifeline. It drew her to Charleston, the city of her brother's last assignment.

Her anguish mingled with guilt as she recalled her arrival hours before. How could she tell suspicious Luke or his trusting aunt her real reason for coming to Charleston? She turned her face into her pillow.

~*~

Luke walked into his room at the end of the hall, musing over the lovely surprise visitor. Jessica was pleased at this turn of events and the promise of summer assistance with Kristina. "Luke," she'd told him, "Miss York has graduated with a degree in elementary education. What better help could you find, if you'd looked? Kristina will have a head start for school this fall."

But there was another reason Jessica was probably happy about Rachel's arrival. Like her brother Charles, his dear aunt would love for him to marry again. He walked to the mantle and picked up the framed photo of his wife. Sitting astride her white mare on the beach, Georgina's golden hair formed a halo around her lovely face. He propped the picture back in its place of honor. No one could ever replace the love of his life. No worry there. He sat on the bed, unlaced his boots, and threw them aside.

A muffled scream sounded from somewhere on the second floor. He lunged up and into the hall, every muscle taunt. First, he went to Kristina's bedroom and eased the door open. She slept peacefully with her teddy bear clutched in her arms. He crossed toward Jessica's suite and listened. Gentle snoring.

He was headed back down the corridor when he remembered their guest. He stopped before her entrance and cocked his head. Nothing. He ambled toward his room, flexing the tight muscles in his arms to normality. *Maybe a tree limb scraped across the roof, old boy.* Or one of the crazy peacocks on the plantation lost its perch.

He removed his eye patch and laid it on the dresser, undressed, and stepped into the shower. Tomorrow, whether Jessica liked it or not, he would run a full check on Miss Rachel York.

Chapter Three

The next morning while showering, Rachel prayed for God's will to be done. Was she to stay or leave Charleston?

The thought of leaving the beautiful plantation, finding out nothing more about Ron's death, and having to return to Ohio made her heart sag. As she finished her toilette, a tap sounded at the door.

"Give me a minute, please." Rachel moved to her unpacked suitcase and withdrew a fresh pullover. She slipped into the same jeans she'd worn the day before and strapped on her yellow heels. When she opened the door, a pretty girl about five years of age gazed up at her. Rachel noted the gray eyes like Luke Barrett's. Her hair, dark as his and plaited in two braids, hung down her back. But the fair, oval face and tender lips must have come from her other parent.

"Hello," the child whispered.

Rachel smiled and reached out a hand. "Hello, I'm Rachel, and you must be Kristina."

The child nodded and took Rachel's hand. They walked down the hall. The aroma of coffee and country ham wafted around them as they descended the stairs.

Jessica Buckner stood at the bottom of the stairs with a pregnant miniature dachshund at her feet. The dog barked at Rachel.

"Good morning, Jessica. What a sweet little dog."

"Good morning. Yes, and her name is Sadie Grace."

Rachel bent to pet Sadie. "We used to own a red mini similar to you, little mother, and I helped deliver two litters of puppies." Sadie sniffed Rachel's hand and wagged her tail.

Jessica smiled. "I think Sadie understands you like dogs."

"I love dogs," Rachel said.

Jessica led the way to the brick-tiled loggia, with Kristina skipping ahead of them. "Kristina has already eaten, and I usually eat a light breakfast. But I've an idea you're going to get the works."

They took places at the wicker table set with gleaming white china and silverware. Kristina knelt on the floor to pet Sadie, then climbed onto a stool and observed Rachel.

A tall woman with cocoa-colored skin entered. Streaks of gray lined her dark hair pushed under a blue kerchief. She set a steaming platter of ham, eggs, and grits before Rachel. A basket of biscuits, a bowl of sliced cantaloupe, and an antique glass pitcher of orange juice sat nearby.

"Maggie, this is Rachel York. Rachel, meet Maggie Sims, our excellent cook." Jessica poured Rachel a cup of coffee.

"Hi, Maggie, and thank you so much. I'm not positive I can make a dent in this delightful spread, but I plan to try."

"Sho' is nice to meet you." Maggie's soft, full lips spread into a smile.

Rachel unfolded the lace-edged linen napkin across her lap, noting the interest sparkling in the woman's dark eyes. The whole plantation probably buzzed about Rachel's unexpected arrival by now.

Jessica turned to the child. "Kristina, would you like to say grace for our guest?"

Kristina bowed her head and repeated a memorized blessing, skipping over several words. In the same breath with the word "amen" she blurted out, "Aunt Jess, you 'pose Daddy'll let her stay wid' us?"

Jessica lifted the child's chin in a gentle gesture. "I'm sure I can't say what your father might decide. And its *sup*-pose and w*ith* us. Why don't you go on the patio and play with Sadie and your dog, Judge? Perhaps Rachel can join you after she finishes eating."

"I'd love to come outside in a few minutes—if there's time." Rachel glanced at Jessica.

"No problem. I am almost sure Luke won't be back before lunch. He's usually up at the crack of dawn and either hopping on his black stallion or into the jeep with Cade before the rest of us are awake."

Kristina clapped her hands and ran out the patio door with Sadie barking at her heels.

When she finished eating, Rachel touched her lips with the napkin and laid it beside her plate, conscious of the older woman's thoughtful gaze.

Jessica sipped her tea and set her cup down. "I don't know what decision you and Luke will come to, Rachel, but personally, I'd love for you to stay the summer. Charles's idea was good. We need your cheerful face here, and Kristina needs a younger woman to gad about with—and help prepare her for school."

They both stood.

Rachel didn't know how to respond to Jessica's kind words. How could she admit wanting to stay when Luke must first offer her the position? "Thank you and Maggie for a wonderful breakfast."

Jessica walked to the glass patio door with Rachel. Sadie pushed in as soon as it opened and nudged Jessica's leg. "My, my, what is it, Sadie?" Jessica asked.

Rachel stepped into bright sunshine. Her heels clicked on the rain-washed brick patio. Azaleas and lilac bordering a low wall glistened with blossoms of red, white, and purple. Beyond them, outbuildings and green bushes in rows stretched toward the horizon. She took a deep breath of the scented air and smiled. The scene before her and the possibility of summer at such a place dissolved the anguish of the previous night. What a blessing it would be to work at Barrett Hall. *But Your will be done, Lord.*

Kristina threw a small rubber ball for a collie at her side. When her pet chased it, she came running up and took Rachel's hand. "Kin I call you Rachel?"

"Please do. What is your dog's name?"

"Judge, and he's mine since he's been borned. Daddy's got Gabriel, but Judge belongs to me." Kristina skipped away.

Rachel moved to the shade of a pear tree filled out with new pale leaves and watched the child play. Luke Barrett's promise to check her story invaded her thoughts. How would he do it, and what did he expect to find?

A tall, lanky man in a cowboy hat, faded Levi's, and western boots stepped over the wall onto the patio. He pulled off dark glasses, gave Rachel the once-over, and emitted a low whistle.

"Dakota!" Kristina's face lit up in a wide smile, and she ran toward him.

The man's strong, brown arms lifted the child easily. His hat fell off and revealed thinning dark blond hair. "You're about to get too big for this, dumplin'," he said and ogled Rachel again. He tweaked Kristina's braid before setting her down. She ran to romp with Judge.

The man replaced his hat and reached out a broad, tanned hand. "Dakota Busby, farm manager."

Rachel introduced herself and shook hands. She pulled away from his lingering handclasp. Something hard glinted in his amber eyes.

"York, you say? Now where did I hear that name?" The man propped a leg against a section of the wall, pulled a pack of cigarettes from his shirt pocket, and lit up. Soon smoke permeated the morning air. Rachel stepped aside and glanced at Kristina and Judge playing. The child's cherub-like voice and the collie's answering barks cascaded across the patio.

The farm manager took a long draw from his cigarette but didn't take his eyes off Rachel. "So you are the mystery lady who showed up late last night?"

Why was the man staring at her? "I guess I am."

"Why are you here?"

Rachel sighed but answered the question. "Charles Barrett offered me a summer job caring for Kristina. It was sad to learn Mr. Barrett had passed since his offer to me."

"Yep, that deadly stroke shocked all of us. Went fast. How did you meet Mr. Barrett?"

"I met him in my college office back home. He was a friend of the dean's."

"So you're here to help with our little girl—*if* Luke honors his uncle's offer?"

"Yes." Rachel moved farther away from his smoke and more questions, she hoped. "It was Charles Barrett's idea, but things are different now."

The man's face tightened, and his eyes narrowed. He leaned closer. "Yeah, lots of things are changed here, dear lovely lady." He smiled into her face. She could smell his alcohol breath. "You're one of the good things."

"Busby!"

Luke and a large African-American man walked up from the garage. The two of them made quite a picture of brawny strength.

Dakota dropped the cigarette on the stones, ground it with his boot, and sauntered toward them grinning and adjusting his hat.

"I thought I told you to go into town this morning and pick up fertilizer." Luke's words cut the air like a sword.

"Sure, Capt'n, sure. I was only introducin' myself to our visitor." He nodded at the two of them and hurried away.

Luke, dressed in khaki slacks and a yellow shirt, turned to the man beside him. "Miss York, Cade Gant, my assistant."

Cade whipped off his cap and nodded. "Glad to meet you, miss." Strength emanated from the man's thick neck and bulging arms, but his eyes spoke gentleness and respect.

Rachel smiled. "Hello, Mr. Gant."

"I'd like to talk to you in the game room, Miss York." Nothing about Luke's face or voice revealed whether she would be offered the summer job or not. He turned on his heel and headed toward the patio door. Cade stared after Luke. Something like sadness flickered across his brown face.

Rachel bit her lower lip and followed Luke. They passed through the loggia with its table already set for lunch.

In the room that passed for Luke's office, Rachel eased into the same chair as the night before, and Luke sat behind the desk. He lifted a legal pad and addressed her. "I'm at a loss to understand why a young woman like you, fresh out of college—magna cum laude even—would agree to come to Charleston for what amounts to a summer babysitting job."

Rachel's eyes widened under his probing stare. So he'd called the college.

He flipped another page of the pad. "I understand you and a brother were raised by one Lester Black—your stepfather—and an aunt, I believe, after the loss of your parents. You are well thought of by the community, and recently your brother, Ron, who worked for the Drug Enforcement Administration—"

Rachel gasped. "Excuse me, what are you reading from?" She had not told him or Jessica anything like this. Although her stepfather's name should be on her college records, nothing about Ron should be.

"Miss York, before I'd consider hiring you to care for my daughter, you must know I would do some investigating. Does it bother you?"

"No, but how did you find this information this morning? I mean, if I've had a criminal record, I can understand your discovering that."

Luke smiled. "Believe me, I checked that the first thing. You're clean. But there are ways and means of getting more information." He studied her a moment, with his fingers steepled in front of him. "Why not find something in your home town, even like the place you worked for the past two summers, since I assume you have or are hoping to find a fall teaching position?"

Rachel's head spun. How did he get all this

information?

She met his scrutiny head on. "I do have applications out, but…no, Mr. Barrett, I don't yet have a contract. I accepted your uncle's kind offer because I didn't want to work another summer at the drugstore. I love children, and I admit I wanted to check out a working southern plantation."

"Perhaps you're running away from something. Or someone?"

Her heart sank to the pit of her stomach. "What do you mean?" Did he somehow find out how horrible Lester was, or did he discover about Easton?

"You've got the same demeanor I've seen on soldiers, the young ones, who came into the military to find—or get away from—something."

His intense gaze pierced her. She struggled to collect her wits. "I understand you spent ten years in the Marines. Did you find what you were looking for?"

He surprised her with a direct answer. "No."

He stood and walked to the window. His silence caused her to wonder if he'd forgotten her. Ten years was a long time to search for something without finding it.

Luke turned and came toward her. He stopped within a yard of her. Rachel blinked up at him—his firm, tanned jaw, the strong blue eye, and the patch—and resisted something like a power source that drew her toward him like steel dust to a magnet. She tightened her lips and leaned back in her chair, willing her heart to slow down.

When he spoke, his deep voice was strictly businesslike. "Miss York, I am prepared to make good on my uncle's offer. Same salary and responsibilities with my daughter, Kristina, if you think you might like it here for the summer. You've probably met the best and the worst of our crowd. Jessica can tell you our schedule and Kristina's. Anything different you'll need to pass by me." He walked behind the desk and continued. "With your training, I believe you can help prepare Kristina for school. What is your answer?"

Rachel's heart did somersaults. "I accept. With pleasure."

"You're hired. Weekends off, of course, and I will make a car available to you if you want to drive into Charleston."

Rachel stood with a new vision of Luke Barrett in her head. Even an automobile for trips into Charleston? She smiled and headed for the door, but Luke's next words arrested her.

"About Dakota Busby, Miss York."

Stiffening, she turned back to him. What was on her new employer's mind?

"Take a word of advice. Don't encourage Busby. Ever."

What? The smile faded from her face.

He stared at her. Waiting.

"I assure you, Mr. Barrett, I did not, and I *have* no inclination to encourage your farm manager."

Luke shrugged, strode to the door, and opened it for her. He glanced out into the loggia. Appetizing smells wafted toward them. "I believe they are waiting lunch for us."

Rachel sauntered out, careful not to brush against him as she passed. Jessica and a somber-faced Kristina waited on the nearby sofa. Their eyes searched her face and Luke's.

"They want the news, whether you are staying or leaving, Miss York." A smile tugged at his lips. "Why don't you put them out of their misery?"

Rachel lifted both hands and grinned. "I'm here for the summer."

Kristina squealed with delight as she ran to throw her arms around Rachel's waist. Jessica's face brightened. Luke pulled out chairs for the women while Kristina crawled up on a stool.

Rachel found it difficult to relax and enjoy the lunch of she-crab soup, flounder, salad, and fresh bread with Luke's unsettling presence across the table—his strong, tanned hands passing food, his deep voice rolling over them. She tried not to meet his glance. Nothing like dining with Easton.

Lord, thank You for this wonderful summer position, but I'm going to need Your help big time to sit at table with this man every day.

Jessica exhibited a penchant for reading her thoughts. "It's a real treat for Luke to have lunch with us, Rachel. He usually eats lunch at the plantation kitchen with the workers or with Cade in our kitchen. And we only dine with him at dinner, if he makes it back in time."

"Not tonight, Aunt Jess." Luke wiped his mouth with his napkin. "Cade and I will be busy till dark getting ready for the first flush cutting. Gotta run up and change after I make a couple of calls."

He pushed his chair back and headed toward the game room.

Rachel relaxed and began to enjoy the meal. "What is the cutting Luke mentioned?"

"It has to do with the tea harvest. The first harvest of the leaves after the winter rest of the bushes." Jessica sipped her hot drink. "And it's a rather big deal, as the new leaves are supposed to make the best brew of all. I expect you will enjoy learning about tea harvesting this summer, and I hope you'll grow to love our favorite drink."

"Oh, yes. I would like to learn all I can, and I am open to the love of tea."

"Luke or Cade will tell you the harvesting side of it. My understanding is limited, although I certainly recognize a good cup of tea when I drink it." Jessica's eyes sparkled. "And you may be interested to know we usually enjoy tea at four each afternoon."

"Wonderful. I've always loved reading about afternoon tea time in British literature."

Jessica served a dessert pear to Kristina. The child's eyelids were droopy, but she soon devoured the fruit.

"Did you meet Cade Gant, Luke's assistant?"

Rachel laid her napkin beside her fork. "Yes. He's a physically powerful-looking man. But there is something tender and gentle about him at the same time."

Jessica lifted her brows. "A good description of Cade, Rachel. Luke was Cade's captain in the Marines. In fact, I understand Cade carried Luke to safety after he was wounded."

"Does he have his own family?"

"Cade is not married, as far as I know. However, he is part of a close-knit church group, a little inner city congregation somewhere in Charleston. He helps there on his days off, I believe."

Kristina slid off her stool, her brows knitted. "Must I take a nap, Aunt Jessica?"

Jessica stood. "Yes, dear, you need a nap. And Rachel can go up with you to tuck you in. Would you like that?"

"Yes, ma'am, if I have to go." Kristina ran to pet Sadie, stretched out in her corner bed.

Jessica turned to Rachel, who also stood. "Sadie is restive today. She won't let me out of her sight. I wonder if I should call the vet. Her puppies are not due for another week or two according to him."

Rachel walked over to observe the pregnant dog. Large brown eyes lifted toward Rachel. "She doesn't appear to be in labor."

"Good. I am glad you're here, Rachel, for several reasons." Jessica led the way upstairs to the child's bedroom. She pulled the shades above the half shutters as Rachel spread a light blanket over Kristina.

"Will you go to my secret place with me after I get up?"

Rachel leaned down and kissed a soft cheek. "Certainly. Can hardly wait."

Long, dark lashes closed over contented eyes. They fluttered open again as Rachel turned at the door to glance back.

In the hall, Jessica asked, "Wouldn't you like to unpack and change out of your traveling clothes into something cooler while we're on this floor?"

Rachel smiled. "Oh, definitely."

"I'll wait for you downstairs."

Rachel hurried toward her room and unpacked her tennis shoes and a yellow sundress. She tackled her thick tresses. She brushed and braided her hair into one plait at the back. Ignoring the tiny curls refusing to stay in place around her face and neckline, she clasped a small yellow bow at the end of the braid. Now she was ready to explore with Kristina after her nap.

At the bottom of the stairs, she ran into Luke, dressed in faded denims, an army shirt, and work boots. He muffled a sound of surprise when she came into his view. "Miss York, if I didn't know you were twenty-one, I'd think I'd hired a teenager."

Rachel's cheeks turned pink. How was she supposed to respond to that remark?

"It's a compliment, Miss York, not a criticism." Luke tossed the words behind him as he walked out the front door.

He probably didn't even catch her soft, "In that case, thank you, sir."

Lord, how do I relate to this man who surprises me at almost every turn and does something to my peace?

She twisted a slip of paper in her pocket with its hastily written number and swallowed a knot in her throat. Where were the phones in this house? Unfortunately, her cell was not going to be of much use in Charleston. She'd left her charger in Ohio.

Chapter Four

Rachel entered the loggia. She glanced out the window. Luke and Cade paused at the barn entrance, with Gabriel bounding and barking around them.

"My, how pretty and cool a dress." Jessica patted the loveseat beside her.

"Thank you." Rachel sat and chewed on her lower lip. "I left my cell charger at home, and I really should call my Aunt Ruby to let her know I've arrived safely. Is there a phone I may use?"

"Certainly. There's one in the hall under the stairs. Want to call now? Afterwards, if you'd like to tour the rest of the house, we've got a little time while Kristina naps."

"That'd be wonderful." Rachel smiled and headed for the hall.

Ruby answered on the second ring. "Hello."

"Hello, Aunt Ruby, I am calling from down south."

"My goodness, young lady. I read your cryptic note saying you'd call me in a couple of days and not to worry, but when I could not get an answer when I tried to call the cell, I was about to get desperate. Where in the world are you? Down south, you say?"

A twinge of homesickness flowed over Rachel at the delight as well as scolding in the affectionate voice. "I left my battery charger at school. Sorry. Is Lester back?"

"No, Lester isn't, and you can speak freely. Don't worry. I won't spill the beans, as long as you're safe, dear child."

"Dear Ruby. I've found a lovely summer job at a tea plantation in Charleston, South Carolina, caring for a little girl, and I'm perfectly secure and happy. Trust me, please."

"For heaven's sake, child! Charleston, South Carolina? How on God's green earth did you find a job down there?"

"My college dean helped me." The sound of an automobile made Rachel turn toward the open front door. A farm truck munched its way up the long shell drive. "Aunt Ruby, I need to hang up. I'll write you all the details later. Please don't worry. Believe me. The Lord definitely worked this out. And I left a note for Lester telling him I'd found a neat summer job but didn't tell him where."

"Okay, if Dean Wooten is in on this, it must be okay. I'll keep mum here, Rachel, but you be sure and write and call when you can. I guess I understand why you wanted to get to Charleston. But don't you go searching for trouble, young lady."

"Only for the truth, Aunt Ruby." Her aunt sighed, so Rachel added, "Besides, you wouldn't believe what a wonderful place this plantation is. Right out of *Gone with the Wind*. I'm going to enjoy this summer, for sure."

She told her aunt goodbye and hung up. Glancing out the front door, she watched the truck head down the side road to the barn. Later, she had another call to make, but not while a tour of the house with Jessica awaited.

In the loggia, the elderly woman stood ready to lead. "I bet your aunt was happy to get an update from you, Rachel. Please use our phone any time you need to make calls. We are not charged for long distance, and there's a more private telephone in the second floor sitting room you're welcome to employ also."

"Oh, wonderful—I mean, how convenient. I shouldn't disturb anyone. Thank you."

Rachel followed Jessica into the wide hall, trying to contain her eagerness to learn more about Barrett Hall. Somewhere in the house, kitchen sounds echoed. Pots and pans clanged, and glassware tinkled. From the back entrance, birdsong and the distant grind of a tractor flowed through the screened door.

Jessica stopped in the middle of the hall under the lovely chandelier. "The original Barrett, whom Luke is named after, received a land grant for nine hundred acres in the 1700s. At the time, Major Barrett was a respected gentleman, but it has been pretty well documented in his earlier years—before he took the king's pardon—he sailed the Atlantic as a pirate," Jessica confided. "There's even a legend of buried pirate gold on our beach, and Maggie's mother, Granny Eller, loves to embellish that story."

A thrill ran up Rachel's spine. Barrett ancestors sailed pirate ships and stashed gold, perhaps on this coast? A vision popped into her mind of Luke, with his eye patch, dressed in a waistcoat and breeches of crimson velvet and polished black boots, swinging a cutlass on a schooner's deck. Her breath stopped in her throat.

Jessica continued down the hall to the front rooms. "I believe there is still a painting of Major Barrett as a pirate in the house somewhere. He planted the first live oaks lining the drive and built the original house in the mid-1700s, I think. It escaped burning during the Revolution because the son who inherited it remained a loyal Brit until the latter months of the war. I suspect he discerned the tide coming in and joined the Patriots in time."

"So Barretts always owned the plantation?"

"Yes, although I understand they almost lost it after the Civil War, when the whole way of life here altered. Somehow, they managed to hang on and shift from rice to other crops not requiring intensive slave labor."

Jessica stopped and turned to Rachel. "Kristina may one day be the first woman to inherit and change the Barrett custom of male ownership. However, Luke could still marry again and father a son." With a lowered voice she added, "I know one interested person who is hoping Luke will marry again."

Rachel waited to be further enlightened, but the older woman clicked her tongue and continued the tour.

Thirty minutes later, back in the hall, Jessica gestured toward an open door under the stairs. Cooking sounds were more prominent, and the aroma of baking bread and cinnamon made Rachel's mouth water. "The kitchen is in the basement and down the steps. I don't think I'll tackle it today, if you don't mind."

Rachel agreed. "By all means, let's skip it." Did Jessica usually nap when Kristina did?

They walked into the loggia and sat on the wicker sofa. Sadie crawled out of her bed and lay down at Jessica's feet.

Rachel asked a question she'd wanted to ask since

her arrival. "Why is Luke's office called a game room?"

Jessica smiled. "Because the room was originally used by the gentlemen after dinner when the ladies withdrew to the drawing room. The men played cards, smoked, discussed the crops and politics, and shared drinks. There's an entrance to the wine cellar there. But since Luke doesn't drink alcoholic beverages, it's never used now."

Luke didn't drink? Interesting.

The thudding of the front door knocker echoed through the house.

"Now who would be calling this time of day? Would you answer it before it wakes Kristina? Sadie and I both are comfortable, and it's probably a farm supply salesman for Luke. Tell him Luke is out. I try to be courteous. After all, they come some distance to find Barrett Hall, but I am in no mood for it today. Tell them they can leave a card."

Rachel reached the entrance as the knocker sounded again. She pulled the door open and gazed into the brown eyes of a handsome blond man dressed in white trousers and a blue knit shirt. An older man in a dark business suit stood beside him.

"May I help you?"

"Wow. Who are you? Man, I hope Captain Luke hasn't pulled a fast one on us!" The blond man grinned at Rachel.

"I'm sorry, I don't understand what you mean. Are you...selling something?" Rachel glanced beyond them at a low, red sports car in the drive.

"Who is it, Rachel?" Jessica came up from the loggia with Sadie waddling behind her.

"It's Archer, Aunt Jessica," the visitor called through the doorway, his eyes still on Rachel, "and

James Sanders is with me."

Rachel's gaze fell beneath his bold inspection.

Jessica stood beside Rachel. "Hello, Archer, James. I suppose you hoped to find Luke, and he is somewhere on the plantation and will be back heaven knows when." Following Archer's gaze, she said, "I'm sorry. Rachel York, please meet Archer Pennington, our neighbor, and our solicitor, James Sanders. Rachel is here to help care for Kristina this summer."

"In answer to this beautiful lady's original question, I am not selling anything, except perhaps good graces. Glad to meet you, Miss York."

Humor danced in the solicitor's dark eyes. "Same here."

Jessica rescued Rachel from a reply. "Won't you two come in for a cool drink or something?"

"No, but thank you, Jessica. We are headed to the house and decided to swing by. Will you ask Luke to call me or Morgan when he gets in?" Archer's eyes returned to Rachel.

"Certainly, Archer, but it may be late before he returns."

"No problem. Tell him it's about the new museum in Charleston. He has community obligations since he's become master at Barrett Hall, and my dear sister will not let him off the hook."

Archer flashed one more smile at Rachel and added in a low voice, "And do I have some news for sis." He and James headed off the porch.

The solicitor turned back. "Oh, and do tell Luke to give me a call too…about an entirely different matter." He bid them good day and rejoined Archer. They got into the car and roared off.

"If Morgan has Luke on a hook…" Jessica said as

she closed the door. Rachel glanced at the older woman.

"May I get up now?"

Both women turned toward the stairs. Kristina, fresh from her nap, stood on the landing holding her sandals.

"I think your job has begun." Jessica patted Rachel's arm and spoke to the child. "Yes, you may get up, young lady, but now it's my turn."

Kristina bounced down the stairs. "Will you go to my secret place with me, Rachel?"

"I'm standing ready."

Jessica started up the stairs. "I'm going to lie down for a nap while you two gallivant. Kristina, if you're planning to show Rachel the attic, don't play there long. Your father will not be happy if you do. I'll meet you both for tea."

Rachel gave way to the pressure on her hand and went with Kristina up the staircase toward the third floor. Why would Luke not be pleased? And who was Morgan?

At each step, the warmth and staleness of the air increased. They finally walked out onto a landing covered only by a faded runner.

Unlike the smooth walls below, paint cracked and peeled in several places. Rachel wiped beads of perspiration from her upper lip and noted the tightly bolted windows at each end of the hall.

"Hurry, Rachel!" Kristina ran ahead and stopped at an oak door.

They entered. A disarray of boxes, trunks, and odd chairs filled the room. Several mirrors and pictures in ornate frames leaned against walls. The smell of age and dust permeated the warm air. Moisture slid down

Rachel's back. She walked over to a window and tugged at it until she raised it.

Kristina knelt down beside a small brass-trimmed trunk next to a larger green one. She turned a tiny silver key stuck in the trunk's lock and reached inside. "Look! Pictures of my mother."

Rachel sat in a faded wing back chair, and the child proudly handed her several snapshots of a young woman, less mature than the portrait downstairs. "Your mother was pretty, Kristina." Rachel meant it. Childhood memories of treasuring pictures of her own mother flooded her mind.

But a pout twisted the child's lips. "I wish my hair was gold like hers and Morgan's and my Barbie doll."

"Morgan?" Rachel asked.

"Daddy's friend who buys me dresses, but I really don't like her."

Rachel ignored the child's last remark. "It's nice of her to buy you dresses, Kristina. And do you know what? I've always liked my dark hair, and besides, Snow White has dark hair."

Kristina's pout evaporated. "Like yours?"

"Similar to mine and yours." Rachel patted the child's head. "Do you come up here often?"

The sulk returned. "No, daddy doesn't want me to."

"Perhaps we'd better go explore somewhere else." Rachel started to stand.

Kristina pulled a small bound book from the trunk's depths. "But not 'fore you read me this, please."

Rachel accepted the small book and wished she'd talked Kristina out of staying. The book was a diary. "I really think we need to be getting back downstairs."

"Please, Rachel, please. Read one page?"

Rachel gave in to the insistent voice and to her own curiosity. She opened the thick, embellished cover. Immediately, she regretted it.

An inscription read simply, "Poem from L."

"Read out loud," Kristina pleaded, tugging at Rachel's skirt.

Rachel glanced at the first line and sighed in relief. She recognized it as a poem by Edgar Allan Poe. What harm could come from reading a famous verse to the child?

It was many and many a year ago,
In a kingdom by the sea,
That a maiden there lived whom you may know
By the name of Annabel Lee:
And this maiden she lived with no other thought
Than to love and be loved by me.
I was a child and she was a child,
In this kingdom by the sea,
But we loved with a love that was more than love,
I and my Annabel Lee;
With a love that the winged seraphs of heaven
Coveted her and—

Kristina gasped, and Rachel twisted around. Luke stood in the doorway, his face like a thundercloud.

Chapter Five

The diary slipped from Rachel's hands. A pale-faced Kristina caught the volume, dropped it into the trunk, and closed the lid with a thud.

Rachel's heart echoed the thump. Out of the corner of her eye, she detected a furtive movement from behind one of the mirrors. She gasped even as her mind registered the fact it was only a tiny brown mouse. It scurried across the room and behind another object.

Luke pulled off his cowboy hat and swiped sweat from his brow with the back of his hand. "Miss York, surely you can understand this is not a pleasant place for a child to play. Did I need to spell it out?" Luke's gaze bore into her face before moving to Kristina. "But I did tell you, didn't I, Kristina? Go to your room."

Kristina's countenance fell. She scrambled to her feet and squeezed past Luke, her chin low.

Luke's heated stare turned again to Rachel. "I am telling you now, Miss York, this floor is off limits."

Rachel fought a ridiculous urge to snap her heels together, salute, and report, "Yes sir, Captain Barrett."

Luke slapped his hat back on his head and wheeled around. His heavy tread pounded down the stairs.

Rachel sighed and moved to close the window. He'd actually said *off limits*. Probably runs the whole plantation like a platoon. Perhaps he hadn't given up the military, after all. His face was so gray. Was he still fighting a war of memory? Such a war could catch his daughter in the crossfire, especially in her need to remember her mother.

Entering Kristina's bedroom, Rachel found the child sobbing into her pillow. She comforted the little one with the promise she would begin to teach her to read the following day and they'd plan a picnic. Soon the tears dried, and she left Kristina happy with two of her favorite picture books.

Rachel walked to her own room and lay across her bed, waiting for teatime. Did Luke discern what a sweet, sensitive daughter he had? Didn't he understand her curiosity about her mother's keepsakes was only natural? Whatever the case, Rachel understood she needed to encourage Kristina to abide by her father's wishes.

A few moments later, a thought jolted Rachel. Archer Pennington and James Sanders left a message for Luke to call them. Had anyone told him?

She sat up on the edge of the bed. Every cell in her body dreaded facing Luke again, but she stood, tidied her hair, and walked to Jessica's room. Perhaps she spoke to her nephew. But through the half-closed door, Rachel observed the elderly lady napping on a chaise lounge, her Bible on her lap.

She waited in the hall, indecision plaguing her. A new idea popped into her mind, and relief bubbled up inside. Mrs. Busby or Maggie probably heard the visitors and relayed their message.

She found the two women in the basement kitchen, flour up to their elbows. The delicious fragrance of baking bread and cinnamon filled the room.

Mrs. Busby glanced up from her work kneading dough. The corners of her mouth lifted, indicating a better mood than the night before. "Oh, hello, Miss York, you've come at a good time. Monday is baking day, and I help Maggie. We will be serving tea shortly, but would you like a cup and a scone or cinnamon roll now?"

"No—thank you. I—I wonder if anyone has told Mr. Barrett Mr. Pennington wanted him to call. He dropped by this afternoon."

"No, we were busy baking. Would you mind telling him if he's in his office? We can scarcely turn loose here."

Rachel went back up the steps, chewing her lower lip. She stopped in front of the Game Room door and finally knocked.

"Come in."

Luke turned his attention from the papers on his desk to her with a scowl he made no effort to conceal. His face was no longer gray but its normal tan.

He adjusted the eye patch. "What is it, Miss York?" His voice was barely above abrasive, but his glance flickered over her and spread warmth to her limbs.

"A Mr. Archer Pennington dropped by after lunch today and would like for you to call him or his sister. And Mr. Sanders with him also asked for you to contact him, Mr. Barrett." In spite of her determination to appear collected, her voice came out edgy.

"You don't need to be so nervous, Miss York. Thank you for relaying the messages." He turned back to the documents before him. A shadow of a grin crept across his lips.

Righteous anger rose in Rachel like a tide. She should turn and walk out, but his smirk infuriated her when she recalled the banished child upstairs.

Father, give me the right words.

Luke glanced up. "Why don't you go ahead and spit it out, Miss York? Whatever it is you want to tell me. I can discern it from those flashing blue eyes of yours."

Shocked, Rachel blinked and swallowed. "If I have anything to say, it's simply that I find I must sympathize with your daughter and her natural interest in her mother's keepsakes."

Thick cords of muscle in Luke's neck bunched up, and to Rachel's alarm, he stood, passed behind her, and kicked the door shut with his boot. Rachel jumped when it slammed.

"Sit down. Please."

The please sounded like an afterthought to Rachel.

She dropped in the chair Luke pushed toward her and folded her hands in her lap. What possessed her to speak of Kristina's mother? Poor child. She promised her she would teach her to read, and now Luke was probably going to dismiss her. His silent scrutiny as he sat behind the desk made her draw up in a knot.

"Don't pass out on me, okay?" His countenance and voice softened. He leaned back in his chair and cracked his knuckles. "But I guess we better straighten a few things out, Rachel. And you can call me Luke."

She nodded. Her given name on his lips pleased her. Somehow.

"Obviously, coming here like you did, you have no way of understanding certain things." He ran his hand over his dark, cropped hair.

Rachel's eyes widened. She noted a total absence

of arrogance or cynicism in his voice. Had he finally stepped out of his military role? Was she about to meet the real Luke Barrett?

"Kristina's mother is gone, and I don't want my daughter dwelling on the past. It wouldn't be good."

Rachel leaned forward. "But every child needs a mother, if only a deceased one to remember and love." Memories of Rachel's own mother still warmed her heart. At the right moment, she planned to share them with Kristina.

"Every child should be blessed with a *living* mother," Luke corrected her.

"Oh, yes, if that were pos— " Rachel stopped too late. Warmth climbed up her neck.

A condescending smile flashed across Luke's face. He stood up, came around the desk, and sat on its corner close to her. She caught a scent of tangy aftershave.

"I hear your unbelief, and I think you discredit me. There may be one or two qualified women who would be willing to become a mother to Kristina, as well as my wife."

Heat spread over Rachel's cheeks. The conceit of the man was amazing. *Let me out of here.*

She stood to leave but, to her dismay, found her face in close proximity with his. Her heart twirled in riotous dance.

He reached out and touched her hot cheek. "A blush like this is refreshing these days."

Something similar to an electric shock passed through Rachel. She turned away, determined to escape.

His deep voice stopped her at the door. "Remember, let's major on the present with Kristina.

The past can't be relived."

Would you want to relive it, if you had the opportunity? But she asked him a different question. "I plan to begin Kristina's studies tomorrow. Is it permissible to take her on a picnic once in a while, for fun or a field trip?"

"Now those are constructive ideas, and they should fill the days." Luke reached for the phone but turned back and regarded her. "But do prepare to avoid chiggers, fire ants, and snakes. You are in the South, Rachel."

Brushing the tingling spot on her cheek, she walked to her room. His touch and the warm sound of her name on his lips kept her heart waltzing. She really must get hold of herself.

The afternoon teatime drew Rachel downstairs with high expectations. Jessica and Kristina waited for her in the drawing room. Mrs. Busby brought in a silver tray boasting an exquisite steaming teapot and three delicate china cups. Maggie carried a second tray with mouth-watering dainties. Rachel chose a chair and feasted her eyes on cucumber sandwiches, scones, pastries, and thin slices of chocolate cake.

She followed Jessica's lead and filled her small plate. Soon she could not take another bite. Delighted with her first tea experience, she turned to Jessica. "How did such a fabulous custom start? I assume it began in England."

"Yes. I understand one of Queen Victoria's ladies in waiting started the English tea tradition, which consisted of a small meal of thin sandwiches, tiny cakes, and various kinds of the hot beverage to help overcome what she called the 'late afternoon sinking feeling.'"

Supper was a light affair, and Jessica dined with Kristina and Rachel since Luke did not come in. Later, Rachel read a bedtime story to the child and went to her own room. Going to bed early and sleeping clear through until seven or eight in the morning tempted her. First, she wrote a brief entry in her prayer journal:

Charleston, May 10.

Father, thank You for this wonderful summer position on a tea plantation. I believe I am in for one of the most exciting adventures of my life. I already love little Kristina, and I have an idea why you sent me here. Jessica is wonderful. This place is way beyond my expectations. She hesitated before writing her next thought and swallowed. Finally, she penned her last sentence. *Moreover, I am sure I will learn more about whatever happened to Ron.*

Drowsiness overtook her, and she closed the notebook. She would write Ruby tomorrow and Raven, her college friend. Both were probably chomping at the bit to get a full report. Rachel fell asleep almost the moment her head touched the pillow.

Much later, a soft knocking on her door awakened her. She flipped on the lamp, grabbed her robe, and opened it a crack.

Jessica stood in the hall, her face tight with worry. "Rachel, I am so sorry to awaken you, but it's Sadie. She's having her puppies. It's not yet four o'clock. I can't call the vet at this time of morning, and I would hate to awaken Luke. He gets up at six and works so hard these days. He needs his rest."

The puppies! Rachel pulled Jessica into the room and closed the door.

"Don't worry, Jessica, I've been through this twice. I believe you and me and Sadie can handle it. Not to mention our major help, Father God."

Relief spread over Jessica's face.

Rachel tore off her robe, slipped into jeans and a T-shirt, and pulled her hair back into a ponytail. In three minutes, she was bending over a padded crate at the foot of Jessica's bed. Sadie, lying on her side, emitted soft grunts. One puppy, already born, nosed around for a nipple. Another larger puppy struggled in the birthing process. Rachel got down on her knees and spoke softly to the dog. "Good girl, Sadie, you're doing fine. Everything's going to be okay. Get me a clean, soft washcloth, Jessica."

Sadie barely wagged her tail in response, turned trusting eyes up to Rachel and Jessica, and pushed again.

Rachel placed the cloth around the puppy's exposed body and gently eased it free. Two other puppies soon followed without help. Sadie licked each one. The palm-sized babies, red like Sadie, sniffed the air with tightly sealed eyelids and rooted toward the mother in search of their first meal. Once the hungry little mouths found a nipple, tiny velvet paws began to push and knead.

Jessica pulled a chair near and sat beside Rachel. "Oh, they are so sweet. Birth of any kind is such a miracle to me."

Rachel plopped cross-legged on the floor, enjoying the whole scene of new puppies, sleep forgotten. "Yes, it truly is."

Every pup filled its little tummy.

"Rachel, I can't tell you how glad I am you were here and knew what to do. I want to give you a gift.

Take your pick of the puppies. Only three are promised to friends in Charleston, and Sadie has four."

"Oh, Jessica, are you sure? I admit I would be delighted to raise another miniature dachshund."

"I am sure. Which puppy might you prefer? It's fine to pick now. Before my friends come to see them."

Rachel touched the tiny, soft ears of the largest puppy in the litter, the one she'd helped deliver. "Well, my pick is this fellow, the fat one I gave a helping hand." The puppy fell over on its back, rooted away by a hungry, whimpering sibling. "Oops, it's not a fellow."

"What will you name her?"

Rachel smiled. "Oh, now naming is a big deal. But 'Penny' comes to mind since she's copper red."

A light knock sounded at the door. Jessica and Rachel turned toward it. Early beams of sunshine now crept under the window shades, and crowing roosters echoed in the barn.

"Is that you, Luke?" Jessica tightened the sash of her robe. "Come on in."

Luke pushed the door open and walked in, freshly shaven and dressed for plantation work in his usual Levi's, boots, and army shirt. The sight of him made Rachel's heart bump against her ribs.

"Good morning, Luke. We have four precious puppies Rachel helped Sadie birth."

Rachel shook her head. "Oh, I did little. Miss Sadie did all the hard work."

Luke came close, glanced at the newborns, and studied Rachel a moment. She smelled his now familiar aftershave and remembered her lack of makeup and hastily done hair. She reached up and smoothed her ponytail, thankful for the dim morning light.

Luke stooped down on his heels. Rachel ducked her head as he beamed a glance toward her. "So you are a lady of many talents."

His lowered voice vibrated through the room and along Rachel's nerves. She studied the puppies and tried to breathe normally. "Not really."

"Rachel, show Luke the one I've given you. Your little Penny. Sadie is too tired to mind."

Rachel reached into the box and lifted the sleeping Penny. She couldn't resist pressing the warm, furry body to her cheek before handing the puppy to Luke.

It curled up on Luke's palm and still slept. He gently brushed its velvet back with a thick finger.

"Yep, you are like a copper penny." He laid the pup back down next to its mother and stood. He glanced at Rachel again and walked to the door. "Kristina will have a fit over these puppies, Jessica, but remember she already has a dog. And I am planning to get her a pony for her birthday."

Luke left the room. His booted tread echoed down the stairs.

Rachel stood. "When is Kristina's birthday?"

"The third of June, right before our Saturday tours begin. She'll turn five. She's wanted her own pony for about a year since our neighbor's child got one."

"Saturday tours?"

"Oh, yes. Morgan talked Luke into receiving tour buses here on Saturdays from two to five. And, I understand, it does augment the plantation income nicely during the summer months. I sometimes go into my town house in Charleston on Friday nights, and you're welcome to come with me any time you like, Rachel. You're also welcome to hibernate on the second floor those few hours visitors are here. We only open the first floor for tours."

Rachel made a mental note. A Saturday afternoon after the tours started sounded like a good time to make her important phone call. But could she wait so long? Perhaps an earlier opportunity would present itself.

Kristina did get excited over the puppies. Twice, Rachel reminded her they were too young for much handling. She gave up her plan to start lessons.

That evening, she put Kristina to bed with the Bible story of Jonah. Luke worked late again, but he came in as Rachel closed the book. Dust and sweat covered his shirt and Levis, but his damp face, hands, and wet hair gave evidence of a washing. Kristina reached out her arms. Rachel stood and moved to the door.

"Daddy, why do you work so hard and get so tire't?" Kristina asked as he hugged her.

"Because this is a big place, and there's lots to do, baby." The fondness in Luke's voice touched a chord in Rachel.

So there was real tenderness under his hard exterior.

In her room, Rachel brushed her hair into loose curls, pinned it back from her face with combs, and sauntered downstairs. Jessica invited her to view the sunset with her on the front porch.

A lovely twilight cast rosy shadows across the white-columned porch. She and Jessica sat down in woven-bottomed rocking chairs. The song of crickets and fragrance of flowers filled Rachel with a peculiar peace. A person might never want to leave Barrett Hall.

"Don't you love old rockers like this? Many years

ago, servants originally wove these seats from wet corn shucks. Now they are sweet grass like our baskets."

Rachel listened with interest, but a part of her mind kept straying to the bedroom upstairs. Was Luke able to relate to his child, mend the unhappiness from yesterday?

Jessica stifled a yawn. "I believe I've about rocked myself to sleep, especially after our early hours this morning. Would you excuse me, Rachel? Feel free to stay on the porch as long as you like. And check on the puppies whenever you like. You won't disturb me."

Rachel sat for several minutes without rocking, entranced by the dusky, southern twilight and lulled by the humming of the insects.

With an effort, she stood up and strolled to the porch's edge. The massive oak trees and their drapery of silver moss delighted her. The departing sun cast an apricot glow over everything and lingered in the shadows.

Ron, did you come to love these long, southern evenings? Would you have come back to us?

On impulse, she stepped off the porch onto the winding garden path. A familiar floral fragrance enticed her steps down the narrow walkway bordered by camellia bushes.

Near the base of a tall oak, she discovered the gardenia bush whose fragrant white blossoms drew her. She stepped off the path, plucked a snowy blossom, and brought it to her nose. The intense, sweet scent almost dizzied her. Her hair brushed against the cords of gray moss hanging from the tree limbs, and a curl caught. When she reached to untangle it, the tough dryness of the plant surprised her. It appeared soft and flowing. A movement on the path behind startled her.

She whirled around, entangling her curls further.

Luke came out of the shadows and gently pulled her hair free. "There's a legend about this moss."

Rachel's heart pounded against her ribs so hard she dared not speak.

Luke stepped back, fingering a piece of the plant, and gazed at her.

She cleared her throat, glad he probably couldn't read her face in the twilight. "A legend?"

"It's called Spanish moss. The legend says an enemy killed a Spanish prince and princess on their wedding day. The two families buried them beneath a tall oak, but not before they cut the bride's long hair and hung it in the branches of the tree. The hair turned gray in grief and continued to grow and spread to other oaks." Luke tossed the twig to the side and crossed his arms over his broad chest.

Aware of the descending darkness, along with his presence, Rachel found it hard to breathe. She shouldn't have come into the garden so late.

"Of course, it's only a legend. The stuff's neither Spanish nor moss. It's an air plant." His eyes still searched her face.

She took a deep, shaky breath and turned toward the house. "Interesting. I wondered about the plant that drapes so many trees here." She started to move past him.

He shifted his stance and blocked her way.

Her eyes rounded, and her mouth fell open. He was so close she was sure he could discern her ragged breathing, her pounding heart. What on earth did he think he was doing?

"I saw a look like that once before in a doe's eyes when I walked up on her in a clearing while hunting."

"And what did you do?" Rachel couldn't move or take her eyes from his face. His glance moved across her face and hesitated on her lips. Her breath stopped.

"Nothing. It wasn't doe season." He unfolded his arms and stepped aside.

Rachel ducked her head and hurried past him.

"Rachel."

His authoritative voice halted her, but she did not turn back to face him. "Yes?"

"It may not be wise for you to walk around the place after nightfall. We hope we are safe. But we employ many workers who come and go on the plantation, some of whom might care less about doe season or anything else."

She turned in time to see him disappear down the path.

He must think her a child. She shook her head and darted up the walkway to the front door and upstairs to her room. Perhaps the laborers weren't the only ones she should take warning about.

Later, lying beneath the blue canopy, she mulled over what happened. Luke almost kissed her. She was sure of it. Few guys she met in college would have let the opportunity pass without trying. What was the magnetism from him that held her against her will in those strange moments? Thank God she'd finally broken away. Why she was thinking about Luke Barrett at all? He was hardly a man for her to be interested in, other than as her employer. He was arrogant and cynical—the exact opposite of the type of man she found attractive. His temper and his ability to confuse all her senses distracted her. Only the latter made him different from the men at college, including Easton. She always managed to exert control over romantic situations. When she'd met a tall, intense law student, she'd thought it might be the real thing. For a time.

But all that was over. *Don't even go there.*

She tossed in the bed. Immediately, Luke's face loomed back into her sleepy brain, troubling her. She punched her pillow. Was she was misjudging the man? She remembered his gentleness with his motherless child earlier. And his anger may have more to do with his wife's death than the loss of his eye in the war. She turned over to sleep but whispered a prayer first. *Lord, You understand Luke's problems and needs. Does he know You? Is he angry at You because of what happened to him? Help him find Your peace and hope.*

She shook away the memory of Luke standing so close in the garden. Tomorrow she must try the phone number her brother secretly gave her. Even half-asleep, Ron's earlier words and their seriousness rolled over her.

Rachel, if anything happens—I don't expect it to, but if it should, like I don't contact you for more than two months—here is a number you can try. It's my DEA partner, Joseph, and I give you permission to call him. I've given him a couple of secrets only you have the answer to, so you'll be sure you're talking to the right person and vice versa. Be careful not to blow his cover or mine by sharing this with anyone.

Sometime later, she awoke with the hairs standing on her arms.

A sound still reverberated in the darkness—the grinding, buzzing of a low-flying plane, so close to the top of the plantation house it almost shook the rafters. She sat up, her mouth set in a hard line. Was this part of her recurring dream, like the previous evening?

Another sound, not an echo, struck her like a cold shower. Galloping hooves pounded away from the barn. She cocked her head as they grew more distant. Why would anyone be riding out so late at night? Perhaps there was an emergency. Or…could something sinister be going on at this beautiful plantation?

Chapter Six

Luke walked from the garden into the house and the Game Room. He slumped into his chair without turning on a light. Moonlight cascaded from the windows across his desk. He sat there silent, a hollowness in his chest. Suddenly he slammed his fist down on the desktop and dropped his head into his hands.

What was happening to him? Was he losing his mind? He'd almost taken Rachel York into his arms. But there could be no other woman for him. And what woman would want a one-eyed jack? He jerked the patch off and threw it across the room.

He left the house and entered the barn. Stopping at Haidez's stable door, he fumbled the key into the lock. The stallion gave a welcome nicker and stamped to him. Luke's mind cleared as he threw the blanket and saddle on the silky black back. The night breeze cooled his hot brow as he galloped to a far pasture and the family cemetery. For weeks, he'd not even driven by the grave. He needed a good reminder of what he and Georgina had enjoyed and could never have again.

His inner eye traced back through happy memories. The day Kristina was born with his black hair but Georgina's sweet lips and heart-shaped face. Georgina with her golden hair blowing in the wind, riding her white mare on the beach.

His "Annabelle Lee" an angry God let die.

He spurred the stallion forward and stopped beneath the pecan trees surrounding the cemetery, close to the newest stone monument. The song of crickets filled the humid air. He sat there a few moments. Haidez swung his head and pawed the ground, snorting. The horse desired to fly across the fields as they often did. It did help, flying like the wind, until they reached the ocean's foaming barrier and a measure of peace. But tonight, a strange stillness flowed over Luke without racing to the ocean. Finally, he reined the tossing head toward the plantation house and rest for them both.

A thought settled in his being. He could be cordial to Rachel York, as he was to Morgan Pennington. What danger was there of anyone replacing Georgina? None.

He walked back into the house and flipped the light on in his office. He searched in the corner for the patch, found it, stuck it in his shirt pocket, and headed for the stairs.

Tomorrow promised to be a busy day. He and Cade would go into Charleston to meet with the solicitor at four o'clock. Luke wouldn't ever make an appointment during the first flush cutting, but James Sanders insisted. He dropped into bed and fell asleep as soon as his head relaxed against the pillow.

The enemy came over the hill like ants toward him and his reconnaissance team. He hit the ground with his Colt automatic exploding and all hell broke loose. The dying scream of the young lieutenant beside him seared Luke's soul and blood splattered his arm. Cade? Cade was still beside him, wasn't he? Feeling and sight abandoned him in the loud explosions. He kept firing into the darkness. He needed to kill them for what they'd done.

A loud groan awakened him—his own. Every muscle in his body clenched, sweat dripped off his torso and his chest pounded. He sat up, swung his shaking legs off the bed, and stumbled to the bathroom. He sluiced cold water over his face, dried off, and swiped the damp towel down to his waist. Back in the bedroom, he dropped into a chair. Post-Traumatic Stress Disorder the docs called it, but Luke had his own name. *It's been a while, you nightmare werewolf, but I'll beat you yet.*

He waited for the tremors to stop. Finally, his heartbeat slowed and the usual headache began to throb. He returned to the bathroom and drank a glass of water, and fell into bed.

The next afternoon he and Cade, still in their work clothes, walked into the solicitor's office at four o'clock. What was so important to bring them out of the field?

"Hello, Luke, Cade. Glad you made it. I understand it's a busy time of year for you. Pull up a chair." Sanders, impeccable in a blue suit and white shirt, stood behind his desk. He reached a hand out to both men. Another person stood near the window.

"I want you to meet Bill Deeson. He's head of the Charleston DEA." The man came forward. Dressed in a nondescript suit and with salt and pepper hair he appeared middle-aged, but he moved as if much younger. He grasped Luke's hand in a firm grip and Cade's. His blue eyes glowed with intelligence.

Everyone sat.

Luke took off his hat and twirled it in his hand. "What's this all about, James?"

"We'll get to that, but first, would you like something cold to drink?" James pushed a button on his desk. "Sally, we're ready for the drinks." A petite blond in stiletto heels came in balancing a tray of frosty canned drinks and bottled water. Every man claimed a can but Luke. He reached for the water. The young woman's lingering stare pinned him to the chair. Had she never seen a patch before?

James spoke to her as she left. "Hold all calls and visitors, Sally." He popped the top of his Pepsi. "Luke, I'm going to let Deeson explain why I called this meeting."

Deeson took a deep swig of his soda and sat forward in his chair. His bright eyes settled on Luke.

"Barrett, I need to tell you up front, I happen to have proof you and Gant here were part of the Special Forces, and you managed to pull off some pretty tidy ops in the Middle East."

"Not smart enough to save my eye."

Deeson glanced at Sanders before continuing. "Hated to learn about your eye, Luke." He gestured toward Cade. "But I understand the good Lord has given you an extra set of eyes as well as a second strong arm."

Cade lifted his eyes to the window and flexed his hands before turning his attention back to Deeson.

Luke nodded. "You got that right."

"And that's what we're looking for."

Luke's brows shot up. "For what?"

"Some extra eyes and hands."

Sanders leaned forward. "All this is under wraps at this time, Luke, but we believe there's a new drug smuggling operation going on in our coastal waters."

Luke quit fingering his hat. "Along Barrett Hall's coast?"

Deeson answered, "Might be. We're not sure. But cocaine's coming in. Lots of it and these sleaze balls, whoever they are, mean business. Big business and big bucks. And I'm going to share something else." He took another swallow of his drink and stood up. "The only reason I'd do it," he said, and cast a quick look at the solicitor, "is we believe you two are trustworthy, given your war records and reputation."

He paced to the window, turned to face them, and dropped his bombshell. "We think there's some well-to-do Charleston folks involved in this, not your ordinary drug pushers." He stopped as if considering his next statement. "In fact, we have some evidence to prove it. We, uh, lost a first-rate man getting the information."

Luke exchanged glances with Cade. "You got names?"

Deeson shook his head. "Let's say we've some good ideas, but no proof to hold up in court. Yet."

"So what are you asking us to do?"

"Keep your eyes and ears open."

Luke slapped his hat on his knee. "Hey, man, I run a plantation from sunup to sundown. I'm a little busy to patrol the coastline day and night."

Sanders stood up and walked over to Luke. "No, no, my man. Deeson's not asking that. They'll be doing their job. But you happen to be one of our coastal plantation owners we fully trust, and we wanted to let you in on this." He turned to the agency head. "What exactly can you tell these two to be on the lookout for?"

"Low-flying planes. Lights on the beach. Strange boats in your waters."

Deeson came back and sat down. "And one other thing, don't you start Saturday tours soon?"

Luke almost groaned, thinking about it. "Yes."

"You probably know the sort of characters to

watch for, with your investigative background. And, hopefully, you'll discern the difference between them and one of our agents we might send on tour occasionally."

"Are you saying drug pickups or drop offs could take place during our Saturday tours?"

"Maybe. We want to cover all the bases. This thing is going to come to a head sometime this summer. But we don't know when." Deeson ducked his head and tapped the arm of his chair for a moment before glancing at the solicitor.

Sanders nodded. "Go ahead and tell Luke. I'm sure it's safe."

Deeson continued. "We've reason to believe the operation so far has been a practice run for the big one. I'm talking about a literal white gold load of cocaine, worth millions, to come in here for distribution over the southeast."

Luke sat forward. "And you say this summer?"

"Probably in the next month, perhaps two."

Luke cocked his chin at Cade who gave an almost imperceptible nod. "We'll be glad to cooperate any way we can. You understand I hire many day workers who come and go. Any one of them might slip in or out with drugs, and we'd never discover it. But, as you said, we'll keep our eyes and ears open."

"Good, good. That's all we want. I'm relieved we now have an informed plantation owner we can trust. And before you go, I'm sure I don't need to tell either of you, this must be kept in strict confidence until it's over." Deeson pressed his lips together.

"Over?" Luke sat his empty water bottle on the corner of the desk.

"If we are right and get our job done, there will be

a number of arrests before the summer is out. It's all I can tell you for now."

Sanders and Deeson thanked them for coming and Luke and Cade left.

Walking back to the car, Luke turned to Cade. "How's that for making you distrust every stranger as well as your neighbors? By the way, you were mighty quiet in there."

"I had my eyes and ears open, boss. Taking it all in."

Luke stopped with his hand on the jeep door. "You've guessed why they've brought us in on this, haven't you, Cade?"

"Sure. They're zeroing in on your coastline."

"Yep."

The two climbed into the jeep and headed back to the plantation. Luke mulled over the meeting as they drove across the Cooper River Bridge. Rachel York lifting the gardenia to her face in the garden floated into his mind. Did he make a mistake bringing her on the plantation in the middle of a drug sting operation? A thought hit him in the gut like a fist. Rachel York had not been one hundred per cent truthful about coming to Charleston. Yes, for a neat summer job but there was something else. He knew people too well. She held something back. Would such a lovely, innocent young woman be involved in some way in the drug operation the solicitor was investigating? *Rachel, what are you hiding from me?*

Chapter Seven

Mindful of Ron's caution for secrecy, Rachel searched in vain for a good opportunity to make her call to her brother's DEA partner without someone being around. Why did she leave her cell charger at college? She'd never have luck trying to replace it with something that would work on her old phone. She'd tried before at college when she'd left her charger at home.

The first week passed swiftly. Rachel tried hard not to appear anxious or preoccupied.

Jessica moved Sadie's crate down to the pantry area, near the back door in the kitchen, and Rachel enjoyed checking on the puppies two or three times a day.

Kristina found learning her letters and numbers exciting. The child possessed a ready mind and surprised Rachel at how fast she caught on.

One morning Kristina recited her ABC's to Jessica and counted to fifty without hesitation.

"You're doing well, Kristina and I am proud of you." Jessica turned to Rachel. "Luke plans to send her to a private boarding school in Charleston in the fall. We are so far out to drive in every day. I think Morgan Pennington picked out the school. But when it gets right down to it, I wonder if he'll be able to send the child off."

Luke sauntered into the kitchen when Rachel sat with Penny in her lap while Kristina ate supper. Since the garden encounter, Luke hadn't crossed Rachel's path. Warmth rose in her cheeks when she spied him standing inside the doorway. His fresh camouflage t-shirt and combed damp hair, as well as his spicy scent alerted her. The man had something on his mind.

Luke glanced at her and the puppy trying to chew her fingers. He inclined his head slightly, sat down beside Kristina, and tweaked her pigtail.

He turned to Rachel. "Would you care to see a little of the plantation, Rachel? I think we have enough time before dark and this young lady's bedtime."

Kristina gave a delighted squeal and jumped up to hug him.

Luke's steady gaze caused Rachel's heart to skip. "Oh, yes. Thanks for offering."

He glanced at her sundress and hair. "You might want to get a scarf. We'll be in the jeep. Come on Kristina." He and the happy child walked out the back door.

Rachel placed the puppy in the crate with Sadie and hurried up the stairs. She met Jessica in the hall and couldn't keep the excitement from her voice. "Luke has offered to show me some of the plantation."

The older woman nodded. "Well, it's about time he took an evening off. Have a nice tour, dear. It's lovely outside, even if hot."

Luke and Kristina sat in the jeep. Rachel joined them, now in jeans, and a pink shirt tied at her waist with her hair clasped in a ponytail. The fragrance of freshly cut grass wafted over the windshield as Luke headed toward the distant outbuildings. Cultivated fields, pastures, and rows of green bushes stretched into the distance.

Kristina's eager voice rose over the grinding noise of the jeep. "Daddy, let's go visit the new calves first, please! Let's show Rachel the pecan orchard and the tea barn and Granny Eller's. Let's take Rachel to see Granny Eller, Daddy!"

"Whoa, Kristina, we can't get all that done in one evening. Here's the first stop. Baby calves, watch out. Kristina is coming."

The child giggled with excitement.

"What are your crops here besides tea?" Rachel asked

"Vegetables, pecans, and we raise a few beef cattle."

"How big is the plantation?"

Luke stopped at a large barn. "Seven hundred hardworking acres."

Rachel no longer wondered what kept Luke so busy. This place made the small farm she called home appear miniscule.

"Kristina, don't even think of going into a stall without me," Luke cautioned as the child climbed out of the jeep. "And remember, no loud noises or quick movements around these animals."

"Yes, Daddy, I remember."

"This building," Luke told Rachel, as they walked to the entrance, "houses pedigreed, at risk, Angus cows with new calves." The mooing of cattle and the pungent smell of hay and feed greeted them as they entered the cool shadows of the long barn.

Luke enticed a cow into a neighboring stall with grain in a bucket so Kristina and Rachel might visit her velvety, soot-black calf. The baby animal tried to follow its mama, but came on wobbly legs to investigate the visitors and Kristina's outstretched hand.

Thankful she'd changed to jeans, Rachel dropped on her knees to pet the calf with Kristina.

"What a beautiful baby you are, and, oh, so soft, little one," she whispered to the calf. Rachel stopped the cooing talk springing from her lips, when Luke's captivated attention dawned on her.

She stood up quickly and brushed straw from her jeans. Kristina gave one last hug to the baby. The mother cow finished her grain and began to bawl for her calf. Luke reunited them.

Rachel and Kristina waited by the jeep as Luke talked to two farmhands about a sick animal. Rachel noticed the respect the men showed Luke as he ordered a procedure of care.

They passed several other buildings where workers came in from the day's labor on tractors and trucks. Luke threw up a hand at them and they all acknowledged him. Dakota Busby was among one group, but he didn't wave.

"I want to show you our tea curing barn, or factory, as we sometimes call it." Luke turned his eyes from the dirt road to Rachel. "Interested?"

"Oh, yes. I didn't think any tea grew stateside. I thought it all came from China or India."

"We are one of the few places it is grown in the United States." Luke pulled up to another large structure and parked. Kristina ran to play outside with one of the workers' children as Rachel and Luke entered the tea-curing factory.

"This was Uncle Charles dream as a young man. And now Barrett tea has a name among discerning tea consumers and restaurants."

Rachel tried to remember everything Luke told her as he walked her through the tea-making process on sawdust floors. She never dreamed she would view tea leaves cured before her eyes.

"We harvest the tea leaves by hand from an evergreen bush, a relative of the camellia family. Next, it's brought in here and placed on these mesh belts we call withering beds. It sits here for eighteen hours." Bushels of loose leaves moved on the belts.

As they turned to trudge forward, Rachel stumbled and almost fell in the corridor.

Luke caught her. In the moment he held her against his chest, fireworks went off in Rachel's head. The steady beat of his heart against her cheek and his manly scent took her breath away. She quickly regained her footing and pulled away embarrassed.

"You okay?" He actually sounded concerned. But his mouth twitched.

"Yes, thanks. I don't know what happened. A stumble bum I guess."

Luke moved her to the next step in the process. She dared not glance up at him but directed her full attention to the tour and the walkway.

A few minutes later they stood back at the jeep. Luke dropped a bombshell.

"Tell me, Rachel, was a summer babysitting job the only reason you came to Charleston?" His face held no hint of a smile.

The blood drained from Rachel's face. She bent and shook sawdust from her sandals to cover her reaction. So this little tour was an excuse to pump her. She straightened and cleared her throat. "I don't understand why you are asking this again, Mr. Barrett. I think I told you why I came. I didn't relish the idea of the drugstore job and I'd never been to Charleston."

Kristina ran up and climbed into the back seat of the jeep and sprawled out, her face red from hard play. She was full of chatter. Luke turned and opened the door of the vehicle and motioned for Rachel to sit up front. Rachel breathed easier but her shoulders remained tight. How she wished she could tell Luke Barrett the whole story. But that was impossible. She must keep her promise to Ron.

Rachel sat and Luke slid into the seat beside her and they roared off. She glanced at his face, which was noncommittal. Did he believe her? She tried to fix her attention on the passing landscape, the evening breeze over the windshield, and the setting sun as they headed back to Barrett Hall. But she couldn't shake her awareness of his strong hands on the steering wheel and changing the gears, nor the memory of those powerful arms catching her.

In the fading light they passed a family cemetery and, finally, the plantation dock on the river road back to the plantation. Luke never said a word on the way home and neither did she.

Rachel realized Kristina had grown quiet. She glanced in the backseat and found her asleep.

When they arrived at Barrett Hall, the sun cast its orange glow over house and trees, and the drumming of crickets filled the twilight with song. Luke exited the jeep, reached in the back seat, and lifted Kristina into his arms. The child roused and put her arms around his neck. The sight did strange things to Rachel's heart. Luke definitely possessed a father mode.

During the walk from the jeep to Kristina's room Rachel walked ahead opening the doors. At the child's bedroom door, Rachel hung back. The tender affection imprinted on Luke's face as he deposited his daughter on her bed caused a swift intake of Rachel's breath. Was this the real Luke Barrett, the dedicated, gentle father?

Luke glanced up at Rachel as if he'd forgotten she was there. His expression quickly changed. "Will you get her ready for bed?"

"Yes, of course."

Luke strode to the door, and Rachel moved out of his way.

"Thank you for the tour, Mr. Barrett. I particularly enjoyed learning about the tea."

He gazed at her a moment and stepped into the hall. "The name's Luke. And you're welcome... Rachel." He tromped down the hall and stairs.

She turned to the bed and the child, but the memory of Luke's arms catching her, and the way he said her name Rachel so softly, kept skipping through her mind. His suspicious question arose out of a fleecy cloud to taunt her. Why couldn't he accept the reasons she'd given? She shook her head. She hated being secretive. And she still hadn't found a private time to make her phone call. Or did she lack courage—afraid of what she'd learn? Surely, when the public tours began, she would find the best opportunity to call from the upstairs sitting room without having to worry about anyone picking up on the downstairs extensions. But the start date was still three weeks away. She removed Kristina's clothing, sponged her face, hands, and feet, and dressed her for bed.

The next afternoon, after Kristina went down for her nap, Rachel returned to her room and touched up her make-up in the dresser mirror. The golden hue of her arms and shoulders in the sleeveless pink summer top and the freshness of the white peasant skirt she'd made last summer pleased her. Her cheeks, she decided, needed little color. The warm, southern sunshine and fresh air stamped their own healthy glow. She turned to view the thick braid of hair at the back of her head, which took her some minutes to finish earlier. It was still neat.

Kristina insisted her hair be done the same way— Rachel smiled, remembering—but by naptime her plait was unraveling.

Rachel laid down her mirror and headed downstairs.

A woman's rich, husky voice, floated up from the drawing room.

Midway down the staircase, through the open front door, Rachel spotted a silver Porsche gleaming in the driveway. At the bottom of the steps, she glanced into the drawing room and discovered an immaculately dressed blond woman standing next to the fireplace close to Luke.

She started to go back upstairs, but words from a sultry voice arrested her.

"Luke, I can't imagine why you've hired a babysitter all the way from Ohio. And I suppose this is she. Come on in, dear."

Rachel came to stand in the doorway.

"But she's so young," the woman said to Luke, as though Rachel couldn't hear. The voice made the word "young" sound like a fault.

The two of them stood about three feet apart— Luke in his usual work clothes, she in a white linen suit with a deeply cut aqua shell and short skirt. Quite short. Shoulder-length blond hair, straight and silky, framed the woman's tanned face. Rachel guessed her to be in her late twenties or early thirties.

Jessica spoke from the sofa. "Rachel, do come in and meet our guest."

Luke performed the amenities. His gaze flickered over Rachel.

"Morgan, this is Rachel York. Rachel, may I present Morgan Pennington, our nearest neighbor." He glanced at the woman. "I should say Attorney Morgan Pennington. I believe you already met her brother Archer."

"Yes—yes, I did." Rachel remembered mistaking him for a salesman. "How do you do?"

Morgan flashed a bright smile and rows of matched white teeth. The sentiment did not reach past her full red lips. "Archer will never forget being mistaken for a salesman. All of us enjoyed a great laugh about it at the office."

Heat flowed into Rachel cheeks. "I'm—really sorry—I wasn't thinking, I suppose." Morgan's scrutiny passed from Rachel's braided hair, to her peasant dress, and sandals.

"Actually, it was my fault." Jessica motioned Rachel to come sit next to her. "I put the idea in her head by asking her to get rid of any salesmen who might be at the door."

Rachel sat, conscious of both Morgan's and Luke's inspection.

"Luke and I were discussing whatever in the world brought you all the way from Ohio to Charleston for a summer nanny job?" Morgan's eyebrows lifted expectantly.

Rachel folded her hands in her lap. "Charles Barrett made the position sound…interesting and I'd never been south, so I accepted."

Jessica patted her arm. "And we are glad you did, Rachel. Already I believe Kristina is making great progress."

Morgan turned to Luke and said something Rachel did not catch. Both of them laughed. Rachel liked the sound of Luke's deep laughter and the way it made his face boyish. But his and Morgan's familiarity brought a pang to her heart.

"Your degree is in teaching, I believe?" Morgan accented the word "teaching" as a negative.

Rachel nodded.

"Well, I can't for the life of me understand why bright young women still choose to bury themselves in a teaching career. So many careers are open to us gals. Finally." Morgan turned from the mantle and waited for Rachel's response.

Luke stood still, listening. Rachel didn't hesitate. She'd had her answer ready since choosing her career path and having to field similar remarks before from Easton. She peered straight into the mocking green eyes. "I don't consider it burying myself."

Morgan sat down on a Queen Anne chair and crossed tanned, silky bare legs. After flashing a knowing smile at Luke, she turned her full attention to Rachel.

Rachel thought of the children she'd taught during her practice teaching and the joy it gave her to gauge their excitement and progress. She recalled praying earnestly about choosing the right career—her good grades presented many possibilities. "It's a calling, actually," she continued with confidence.

Morgan laughed. "A calling? The few friends I met in college who chose the low-paying teaching field admitted they looked on it as an interim job to becoming housewives—another waste of talents, if you ask me."

Still standing by the mantle, Luke cleared his throat and frowned.

Morgan smiled. "Thank goodness, times are changing."

Rachel thought of her mother who made their home her career until she died, and Ruby's wonderful home-making skills which helped her and Ron grow strong. Moisture threatened to gather in her eyes. She lowered her head.

Dear God, please don't let me make a fool of myself in front of this woman. Please handle this.

She prayed fervently but did not expect the quick answer that came.

Jessica sat up ramrod straight. "I've never had a career other than keeping a family happy and a house or two in order, and it's been a good life, one I thank God for every day." She smiled, and her eyes moved from Morgan to Luke. "And if mothers in this country, who have a choice, are encouraged to disdain homemaking and raising their own children, I can't imagine what we will come to." The tone of her voice broached no argument.

Morgan lowered her glance.

Rachel lifted her chin. Home run for the lady of the house.

"Now," Jessica announced, "I've asked Maggie to bring in something to drink. She has plenty of lemonade and tea and a key lime pie. Do you care for some refreshment, Morgan?"

"Well, I really need to get back to the office, but who can turn down Maggie's lime pie? A small piece, please, and a cup of tea would be wonderful." She stood, removed her linen jacket, and sat down on the loveseat opposite Rachel. Luke came to sit beside her. His work pants contrasted sharply with Morgan's shapely tanned legs exposed by her short skirt. She gazed at Luke with a slight smile and leaned closer.

"Lemonade for me," Rachel said.

"Lemonade for me, too." Luke's glance rested on Rachel before he turned his attention to Morgan.

Rachel diverted her interest to the long windows and the garden landscape beyond them. How soon would she be able to escape this little gathering?

Luke's aunt reentered the room with a tray of frosty glasses with wedges of lemon and saucers of pie. Mrs. Busby came behind with a tea service and placed it on the low table and left.

Jessica poured the tea. "Morgan, I keep reading in the papers about drugs coming into Charleston. Is yours and Archer's law firm involved in defending any drug-related cases?"

"Oh, the usual, Jessica. An occasional street bust, involving marijuana. And I blame the current law for a lot of it. I don't think we'll ever control marijuana. We might as well legalize it, if you ask me. It's not a hard drug."

Rachel's heart banged against her ribs. Legalize marijuana? When this drug led to the substances endeavoring to get a stranglehold on America? She swallowed a sudden lump in her throat. Drugs Ron gave his life to help stop? She didn't trust herself to speak. Instead, she stared at Luke.

Jessica glared at him, too. Her lips tightened into a thin line.

Luke drank half his glass of lemonade and sat the glass down. "That's up for debate, Morgan, and you know it."

Morgan smiled at him, obviously in her element. "Want to dispute it?"

"No," Luke replied, "I've got to get back to work." He stood.

So did Morgan with a little pout on her lips. "Okay, darling." The sulk changed to a sunny smile. She reached for her jacket and turned toward Jessica and Rachel. "Luke has agreed to co-host the museum dedication with me next month. You two will want to come—and bring Kristina, if you like. We will have art on loan from Europe, South America, and Africa. Of course, the museum is already open if you care to visit sooner. Bye now. It's always good to chat with you, Jessica, and glad to meet you, Rachel."

Rachel smiled. "Thank you, same here." *I hope.*

Jessica nodded and reached for the tray.

Luke walked with Morgan to the front door. Their muffled voices and Morgan's husky laugh floated from the hall. A car door slammed and the sound of the Porsche spinning shell gravel faded down the long drive.

Jessica stood. "I am battling a bit of a headache and am going to lie down. Will you catch up with Kristina when she awakens, Rachel?"

"Definitely. Get a nice rest. Hope the pain goes away."

Rachel walked into the hall. The quietness of the house enveloped her. Luke, she assumed, went back out on the plantation after taking leave of Morgan. She glanced at the big hall clock. Kristina would not awaken for another thirty minutes or more.

The earlier conversation about legalizing marijuana bothered Rachel. Up for debate, Luke said.

Obviously, he had mixed thoughts on the subject. What if he agreed with Morgan? A sick wave moved in the pit of her stomach. How many people were so foolish regarding marijuana? Ron never missed an opportunity to down talk legalization.

Rachel walked into the hall and listened. Total quiet. This must be her chance to make the call. She slipped the piece of paper from her pocket, stepped over to the hall phone and dialed.

She held the receiver to her ear as the number rang and rang. She twisted the end of her braid and gritted her teeth. "Please answer!" she whispered and stamped her foot. Finally, she sighed and started to hang up. A slight noise behind her caused her to turn. A few feet away, his face a mask, stood Luke Barrett.

Chapter Eight

The receiver flew out of Rachel's hand. She retrieved it and placed it back in its cradle. "No—no one was there." She hated how contrived her voice sounded.

Luke gave a curt nod and walked past her to the door, but not before a new expression flickered over his countenance. Distrust. She started to call him back, to offer a simple explanation. But it was out of the question. If she tried to explain, she'd need to tell him the whole story about Ron. He would be sure this was the main reason she came to Charleston and believe she'd purposely deceived him. He might even wonder if she hoped to play amateur detective and send her packing. Worse, she realized with a jolt, she would risk blowing the cover of Ron's partner, if he were still in Charleston. All these thoughts flew through Rachel's mind as she stared miserably at Luke's departure down the front walk.

She bit her lower lip. Neither secrets nor deception were her cup of tea. Should she not even be trying to get in touch with Ron's partner? But that thought pierced her like an arrow.

"Rachel?" Kristina's voice at the top of the stairs drew her attention.

As she walked toward the steps, her choice settled in her mind. Ron gave her the number, and she would keep trying to reach his partner as long as she was in Charleston. She owed it to Ron. But what of Luke's distrust?

Lord, help me.

~*~

On Friday Kristina went to spend the weekend with her grandmother, and on Saturday Rachel found a private moment to try the number again in the upstairs sitting room. She still received no answer. Disappointment engulfed her. But she stirred herself to catch up on laundry and write letters to Ruby and to Raven.

Getting ready for dinner, she glanced out her window. Luke walked to the garage dressed in a tuxedo. The sight did strange things to her heart. A blue Italian sports car backed out of the garage. She shrank away from the window.

The sound of Luke's car roaring down the drive settled a blanket of discontent on her shoulders. She had no idea why. Of course, a man like Luke Barrett widowed for three years now, was probably back on the dating scene. Why should she care? Sighing, she forced Luke and his probable date, Morgan Pennington, from her mind and went down to dine in the loggia with Jessica.

"Luke had plans tonight—with Morgan, I believe," Jessica confirmed as Rachel sat down at the table. "So, we'll be dining alone tonight."

"Are—are Luke and Morgan engaged?" Rachel asked as she unfolded her napkin.

"I do wonder at times—but I certainly hope not." Jessica bowed her head to say grace and Rachel did the same. Subject closed.

Sunday morning at breakfast, Jessica invited Rachel to attend services with her. Luke did not make an appearance. She wondered if he took Sundays off or still checked on plantation matters.

Rachel liked the Anglican church with its vibrant minister, and his message stimulated her.

When they emerged from the historic edifice at noon, Jessica suggested the two of them enjoy dinner in Charleston and spend the afternoon at her Charleston house a few blocks from the Battery.

Rachel spent a delightful two hours with Jessica getting all the stories about the house, its owners and guests, and some of the famous houses in the district.

On the way to pick up Kristina from her grandparents, Jessica drove by the Charleston Museum's new building, an imposing piece of architecture.

They drove home to Barrett Hall in the late afternoon with Kristina napping in the back seat. How did Luke spend the day?

About nine-thirty the next morning, after packing a picnic basket, Rachel walked with Kristina down the sandy road to the strip of beach belonging to Barrett Hall. Green tea bushes stretched for acres on their right. To their left, beyond its border of moss-draped oaks and cypress, the river Dakota called "Wacca" wound its way to the Cooper River and the ocean. They passed the old dock, once the busiest place on the plantation in the days of indigo, rice, and cotton, according to Jessica. The goods were loaded on rafts and small boats and floated down the river to English ships waiting in the Charleston channel.

Kristina trudged along at Rachel's side in thick

boots, shorts, and a red top. Rachel wore canvas shoes, Bermuda shorts and a yellow knit top. They both sported straw hats. She'd questioned Kristina about wearing the boots to the beach, but the child explained. "Daddy says I must wear boots like him if I go out on the plantation 'cause of snakes."

Rachel shivered. Surely they'd not need to worry about snakes on a beach. The bright sunlight poured down on the long road. What would Luke be busy doing? Earlier she spotted him and Cade ride out on horseback as the sun peeped over the horizon

The narrow strip of road stretched on and on with no beach in sight. Rachel carried a beach bag on her shoulder and occasionally helped Kristina pull the little wagon holding their picnic container and water. She often wiped perspiration from her face and twice gave in to Kristina's desire to explore a cool side path to the river.

One of these paths ended in a marsh. Rachel steered Kristina back to the road, turning a deaf ear to the child's plea to examine a nest she spotted on a low-hanging branch.

Later, the sound of sea gulls and slapping waves spurred Kristina to action. She dropped the handle of the wagon and ran ahead. She stood atop a sandy knoll and waved at Rachel.

At first, the roar of the tide dragged at Rachel's spirit. Was Ron beneath those waves? But when she passed the copse of yaupon trees and glimpsed the blue Atlantic for the first time, stretching to the horizon, she clasped her hands to her chest and ran toward the surf. How seldom had her heart lightened in recent months since the Drug Enforcement Administration's report of Ron's plane crash over the

Atlantic. She threw up her hands and reveled in the warm sun and foaming tide.

After locating Kristina digging in the sand, Rachel parked their picnic supplies under a tree at the beach edge and held onto her hat in the warm sea breeze. The immensity of the ocean shocked her senses. She could not tell where the water ended and the cloudless sky began. One might become lost in those depths and never be found.

Ron, are you out there in a watery grave? Or are you lost somewhere and trying to get back to us? You could've survived the plane crash. If anyone could, you would be the one.

She squinted southward down the beach. Heat rose in waves. The small beach house Jessica mentioned stood as if propped against a rock wall. But she and Kristina decided to wear their bathing suits under their clothing, so they wouldn't need to change.

Kristina ran up, clutching shells in both hands.

Rachel shook sad thoughts away and joined in Kristina's enthusiasm.

After spreading a blanket in the shade of weather beaten pines at the shoreline, they deposited their clothing and the picnic basket. Rachel slathered suntan lotion on Kristina and herself and they ran to wade in the surf and collect shells for the next two hours.

Finally, Rachel drew Kristina back to their blanket and unpacked the lunch Maggie prepared for them. They feasted on peanut butter and raisin sandwiches, carrot and celery sticks, fresh plums, oatmeal cookies, and lemonade.

Rachel did not need to suggest Kristina try to take a nap after they counted their shells. The child leaned back on the quilt and went to sleep almost immediately. Rachel stretched out and put her arm across her face.

She awoke with her heart in her throat until she spotted Kristina lining her shells up on the edge of the blanket. How long had she been sleeping? It was high time they started home. Rachel left her wristwatch on the nightstand but guessed it to be about four o'clock.

She repacked the basket and shells into the wagon with Kristina's help and trudged over the sandy beach boundary onto the narrow road to the plantation. Kristina ran ahead around a bend pulling her little wagon with the picnic basket.

Endless energy, even in this heat.

Rachel started to call out but decided her charge was probably waiting behind the clump of bushes to jump out and surprise her.

Kristina did not appear past the bend. The wagon came into view the same moment Rachel heard the child's cry ring out from the river beyond the road.

"Ra-chel-l!"

Rachel dropped the beach bag and ran down the path toward the watercourse. To her relief, she spotted Kristina perched in a tree. The limb, on which Kristina sat, spread out over a marshy area dotted with small pools of water. A bird nest sat on one of the branches beyond the child's reach.

"Kristina, come down right now, the same way you went up, but please be careful."

God, keep her safe.

"I can't. I'm afraid-d-d, Rachel." Her voice, strangely low, trembled.

The child did not budge, and Rachel noted with concern the paleness of her face.

"What's wrong Kristina? You can get down. Here I

can almost reach you."

Rachel, a tree climber herself in her younger days, placed her foot in the fork of the tree, swung up and leaned over the branch toward Kristina.

Kristina moaned and pointed to the base of the tree on her side.

Rachel adjusted her handclasp on the rough bark and leaned forward to see.

At the bottom of the tree, beyond a stagnant pool of marsh water, a large, dark snake lay coiled, its head lifted, its white mouth open and its tongue flicking the air.

Rachel stopped breathing. The sharp bark of the tree bit into her hand and moisture popped out on her forehead. With effort, she turned back to the frightened child and kept her voice steady. "Kristina, come on back across the limb. You can do it, just don't look down. In two scoots you'll reach my hand."

Keeping her eye on the snake, Rachel inched her foot further from the side of the tree where the snake lay. All snakes were not poisonous, but she did not know how to identify one from the other. To her a snake was a snake, and it took all her will power to force conjectures from her mind and concentrate on calming the child.

"Come on, Kristina. I'm right here to help you. Besides, the snake would go for me before he'd worry about you," she whispered lightly. "But if we don't make any sudden moves, I don't think he'll go for anybody." *Lord, let this be true.*

Rachel's eyes riveted back down to the snake. A horrible creature, to be sure. It lowered its head and seemed about to slither into the bushes. A shudder passed through her.

She forced her eyes away and smiled encouragingly at Kristina. Finally, Kristina made a movement of one hand clutching the tree limb. A small whimper escaped the child's lips and wrenched Rachel's heart.

She threw caution to the wind and stretched the full length of her body toward the child. As she did so, her foot twisted and slipped and her shoe flew off. She cried out as she plummeted through the air. Mud and stagnant water splashed in all directions as she landed on her back in the marsh below.

When she managed to lift her head from the shallow water and mud, she froze. About two feet from her twisted ankle, the snake reared, licking the air.

Kristina's muffled sobs reached her as though from a well, but Rachel dared not take her eyes off the reptile, even for a moment, to reassure her.

"I'm sure someone cried out." A voice came from the direction of the road. The sound of horses threshing through the underbrush broke upon Rachel's stunned brain.

"For heaven's sake, Miss York, haven't you any better sense than to climb trees like Kristina?" Luke's angry baritone had never sounded so good.

Gabriel gave a sharp, warning bark.

The rest happened so quickly, Rachel scarcely remembered how, later

The sun glinted on metal and a deafening shot rang out. Haidez snorted but didn't budge. The snake fell back, its head severed.

Rachel gasped and tried to withdraw her wooden legs and feet from the proximity of the snake's writhing body. But her limbs refused to obey her in the now much colder water.

"Cade, get Kristina." The little girl's sobs penetrated Rachel's fear.

Heavy boots splashed into the marsh beside her. Luke bent down and slid a strong arm beneath her. As he raised her slightly, she warned him, "I'll—get—you muddy." Her teeth chattered.

"Never mind the mud. Before I move you does anything feel like it's broken?"

"I don't—think—so."

"Now put your arms around my neck—and forget about getting me dirty, Rachel." His voice was firm, but also gentle.

She obeyed, placed her dripping arms about his hard shoulders and clasped her trembling hands behind his thick neck. The tangy smell of his aftershave enveloped her as Luke lifted her from the swamp like a feather.

~*~

Carrying Rachel, trying to ignore the way his heart knocked against his ribs, Luke walked over to check on Kristina held in Cade's arms.

The man consoled her. "And that ole snake never knowed what hit'em. He's gone where bad ole snakes go, and he won't quit jumping until the sun goes down."

The child stopped crying and color blossomed in her cheeks. She turned her head and glanced at her father for confirmation. "Daddy, is it true? Will he keep jumping? And will Rachel be all right? She tried to get me and fell down. I'm glad you came, Daddy." She sniffed and sighed, and laid her head on Cade's shoulder as if the words took her last energy.

Luke turned his attention to Rachel. The stark blueness of her eyes in her white face astounded him. Still in a little shock? "Yep, I guess Rachel will be okay, but I need to get some of this mud off her before I bring her in. Take Kristina on, Cade, and we'll be there shortly. Tell Jessica to draw a warm bath for both these young ladies."

~*~

The conversation passed over Rachel's head. She had trouble focusing her thoughts, especially when Luke gazed down at her.

Cade placed Kristina in the saddle, and mounted behind her. "You bet, Cap'n. Sure was a good shot you got in there. You ain't lost your touch. No sir, not one speck, in case you been wondering."

"What about my wagon?" the child asked as they made their way back to the beach road.

"Now you don't go to worrying about your wagon, little lady. We'll get it later."

Rachel got her mind focused. "I'm sure I'll be able to walk—in a few minutes," she stammered.

Luke sat her feet on the path, and she tried to stand but a sharp pain in her left ankle caused her to fold up on the grass.

Luke bent on one knee beside her. "Let's check the ankle."

"Please don't bother. I was—a little shaky. That's all. I'm sure it's nothing."

"Be quiet and sit still."

His strong hands gently examined her left ankle and foot through the mud covering them. She winced as his probing fingers touched one spot, and she pulled away from his touch.

"Well, if you can do that, the ankle can't be broken, I'll wager. Probably a sprain."

Luke stood up, and his hands being muddy, wiped the sweat beading his upper lip with the edge of his t-shirt. He threw his hat onto a bush.

"What—are you going to do?" she asked suddenly aware of some impending intent in the firm line of his jaw.

"Wash you off in the river so Haidez will let you ride home."

Before he finished speaking, he lifted her in steel-like arms again, her mud-encrusted back and dripping hair pressed against his warmness.

"Please, I can walk, crawl if I have to, you're only going to get yourself grubby." She pleaded to no avail.

"If you don't be quiet, I may dunk you as well. Besides, I am already muddy."

Luke pushed several steps through the brush. His boots splashed into water and its coldness splattered Rachel's back. He had walked right into the river with her. A tremor shot down her body as the water rose around her.

"Don't worry, Rachel, I'm not planning to drown you." His voice had a grin in it. "And don't fret about any more snakes. With all the ruckus we've made, they're long gone."

The water's increasing coldness penetrated Rachel's bones. She clung to his neck as he washed the mud from her back and her hair by making two swings with her through the water. Her plait of hair came loose. She felt herself floating away from Luke and the river. But his strong arms held her.

They emerged from the river trailing water and with Rachel gasping.

Luke placed her on a warm, sunny rock and sat down himself a few feet away to rip off his waterlogged boots. She watched him as if in a daze dump water from his boots before wringing out the cuffs of his Levis, and the bottom of his shirt.

He glanced up.

She turned away, and swung her hair from behind to press it out over her shoulder. But her hands shook and her fingers refused to clasp with any force. She vaguely wondered why the warm sunlight and rock brought no warmness to her limbs. She tried to busy herself squeezing water from her clothing wherever she found a corner but it proved most difficult.

Luke said something as he pulled his wet boots back on.

"What?" she murmured.

"I said, maybe Haidez will put up with us now."

He whistled and the black stallion raised his head from the marsh grass and came toward them, ears pricked and nostrils flaring in a low nicker. He stopped in front of Luke and snorted in Rachel's direction. One hoof lifted and pawed the clay riverbank.

Luke said something in Arabic and the horse immediately quieted. Luke came for Rachel.

"I'm—afraid…" Rachel stammered and a convulsive shudder shook her frame as Luke lifted her into the saddle, and mounted behind her.

Luke called the horse's name one time as their wet legs touched his warm sides and the animal snorted. The Arabian shook his massive neck and obediently turned and carried them out of the clearing to the road.

Rachel tried not to lean on Luke's hard chest

behind her only to have him remark, "What are you fearful of? You can't ride double without leaning, so relax."

She relaxed against him. His strong arms came around her and gripped the reins.

"I was trying to say I was wary of—Haidez," she managed to gasp, amazed that her teeth were clattering so.

"He's fine—are you cold or something?"

"How can I be cold?" Her voice sounded like it came from a well. They were on the narrow sand road and the hot late afternoon sun was still shining on them as the horse moved at a brisk but smooth pace. But she was cold. A chill even convulsed her at that moment. And worse, tears coursed down her cheeks. She found she could not prevent her head from falling back against his chest, or stop her eyelids from closing. She wanted to apologize for her wet tresses flying in his face, for letting Kristina get away from her, for...

Luke leaned over to examine her face. He swore. His arms tightened around her and his boots clamped hard against Haidez' sides. His voice came from a long way off. "Okay, desert horse, let's find out how sure-footed you really are."

He tugged on the reins and the stallion left the road and began galloping across plowed fields and rows of plants. Would his hooves touch ground and jolt them? Lost in the sensation of flying, Rachel's fingers relaxed their grip in the thick black mane.

Chapter Nine

She awoke in her blue-canopied bed, conscious of blankets weighing her down. Late evening bathed the room in shadows.

"Oh, Rachel! I am so glad you are back with us." Jessica came forward from a nearby chair. "How are you?"

"I'm okay. But—my clothes," Rachel murmured, fingering the silky gown she wore.

Jessica perched on the edge of the bed. "In the bathroom, waiting for a good soak in the washing machine."

Rachel sat up. "I don't remember a thing after riding Haidez."

"I'm not surprised. You were going into shock."

"Is Kristina okay?"

"Oh, yes. And the doctor said you'll be fine in a day or two, if your ankle doesn't swell. Does it hurt?"

A doctor came? What did Luke think about the trouble she was causing?

Rachel tried to move her injured ankle, and a pain shot up her leg. "It does a little, but I'm sure I'll be good as new soon, like you said." She blinked at the older woman and confessed, "I feel so foolish."

Jessica patted her arm. "I guess we all do at times, but we do manage to survive. Kristina told me exactly what happened, after she broke our rule about climbing trees. I think you were brave, dear girl, and so does Kristina."

Rachel did not feel brave, and after Jessica left, promising to bring a dinner tray, she mulled over the fact the older woman did not mention what Luke thought. Would he dismiss her for letting Kristina get out of her sight?

She leaned back into the pillow and remembered Luke carrying her in his arms to the river, and the ride back on Haidez until she floated off into a dream world. If he did send her packing, one thing was for sure, she would never forget the surreal journey on the Arabian stallion while leaning against Luke's chest.

"She's still asleep."

Rachel opened her eyes at Kristina's voice. She and Maggie peered around the door at her.

"No, I'm not, come in you two."

The child bounced into the room, carrying Penny. She laid the puppy on the bed, and it scrambled up to lick Rachel's face. Kristina delighted in recounting her tree-climbing experience until Maggie reminded her Rachel needed to rest. Jessica came in with a tray, and the two left, taking Penny with them.

The next morning a brief knock sounded at Rachel's door as she sat in her robe, propped up in a chair with a hairbrush working on her tangled hair. Jessica relaxed nearby, crocheting.

When she called out a welcome, Luke strode in, carrying her ruined canvas shoe. He laid it on the hearth, and came to her bedside.

She tried to still the hammering of her heart, and wished she'd had time to glance in a mirror. Thank you for finding my shoe—and for rescuing us."

"I'm glad you only got a sprain, Rachel." Luke's

gaze lingered on her face, "And a scratch or two. You should stay off your feet for two or three days."

"Oh, I'm sure I'll be up and about faster than that," Rachel murmured and flexed her ankle on the chair cushion. Its tenderness surprised her and she winced.

Luke's expression became stern. "No you won't. A sprained ankle can be tricky."

"Rachel, you might as well relax and enjoy this enforced rest," Jessica added with a smile. Rachel started to insist she really didn't think the injury that bad, but Luke walked to the door.

He turned toward her, his jaw firm. "It's settled. You don't want to end up with ankle trouble the entire summer." He left and his heavy steps echoed down the hall and the stairs.

The summer? At least she was not being dismissed. Luke mentioned a scratch when he stared at her face. She reached her hand to her cheek and found a long scrape at her chin line. It wasn't burning, so it was minor, but she must be a sight.

In late afternoon Morgan Pennington confirmed the thought. She walked into Rachel's bedroom dressed in a sea green silk suit and greeted her and Jessica with a broad smile. She sat down on the edge of the bed and gracefully crossed smooth bare legs. She leaned closer to Rachel and frowned. A strong perfume assaulted Rachel's nose.

"Oh my, Luke told me about the ankle but he didn't say you got a nasty injury on your face."

Rachel stiffened.

Jessica sighed.

"But you were brave. Luke says it was a cottonmouth water moccasin." Morgan raised delicate, arched brows at Rachel. "Do you have any idea how poisonous that snake is?"

"No." Rachel managed. The memory of the coiled viper, its glistening, triangular head, slanted eyes, and open white mouth returned in force. Would she ever forget that horror so close to her foot? She shuddered and squeezed her eyes shut trying to block the image.

Someone entered the room, and her eyes flickered open.

Luke stood at the foot of the bed. He was dressed for dinner in a blue knit shirt and tan trousers.

Morgan gave him a warm greeting. "Hello, Luke, dear. I was telling Rachel how brave she was to attempt Kristina's rescue with such a dangerous serpent at the foot of the tree."

"Good evening, ladies." He nodded at Jessica, but his eyes moved quickly to Rachel. "Yes, she was brave."

He was staring at her scratch again. Rachel turned her face away.

Morgan stood. "Oh, Rachel, don't you worry about that face bummer. I'm sure it won't leave a scar. At least, I hope not. What do you think, Luke?"

A scar? Rachel paled and turned toward Luke.

Luke scowled at Morgan. "I don't see a thing to worry about."

"Said just like a man, wouldn't you say?" Morgan's smile was only for Luke. She glanced back at Rachel. "Men cannot conceive how we women protect our complexions, can they, my dear?"

Jessica stirred in her chair. "I agree with Luke. I'd be surprised if that place doesn't completely clear up before the week is out." She turned to Rachel. "I'll bring you some great cream that works fast on such scrapes."

Morgan shrugged. "Oh, I almost forgot." She rummaged in her handbag, withdrew a small foil-wrapped package, and thrust it into Rachel's hands. "Here's something to express my best wishes for your recovery."

Rachel opened the gift and discovered a delicate bottle of an expensive perfume, if its French label meant anything. "Thank you, so much," she said. But she hoped it wasn't the overpowering scent Morgan was wearing.

"You're welcome, my dear. And we've really got to get going." She turned to Luke. "Rachel will want to be well by the museum dedication and dinner dance on the yacht in June, won't she?"

He turned speculative for a moment. "By all means."

Morgan hooked her arm through Luke's and the two of them walked to the door. Luke's dark head bent toward Morgan as she whispered something to him. Her throaty laugh that followed irritated Rachel as did the realization of how well matched the two appeared.

Jessica came to the bedside and patted Rachel's hand. "I'll go, too, so you can rest a while before dinner. And I will bring your tray, of course, and my magic face cream. Cheers."

Rachel leaned back on the pillow fighting a weight settling on her chest and a renewed memory of her fall.

About thirty minutes later Kristina came in with a book and climbed onto the bed. Rachel read aloud the Bible story, *Joseph and His Coat of Many Colors*.

Mrs. Busby poked her head in the door. "Special Delivery." She set a large bouquet of flowers on the bedside table. Colorful snapdragons, zinnias, roses, and baby's breath filled a crystal vase and brightened the room.

"Wow!" Kristina expressed Rachel's exact thought.

She inhaled the sweet fragrance and reached for the card. Who is the world would send her flowers here? The florist card read simply:

Such terrible things should not happen to so lovely a lady. —Archer Pennington.

As night fell, thunder rumbled over the roof and wind rattled the French doors. Rachel turned out her light and tried to dispel the uneasiness she sensed in the room. It was unexplainable. She should really feel good. Not only was her ankle much better from the bed rest, Maggie came in after dinner and helped her shampoo her hair and bathe. The woman also placed lovely embroidered sheets on the bed and selected one of Rachel's prettiest gowns for her to wear.

"Just to make you look like a new woman 'fore you need to get back in the swing of things," she'd said when Rachel protested all the help.

Now alone, Rachel lay on the pillows with her thick hair tied back with a ribbon and listened as the storm rumbled nearer. She remembered her mother's comforting childhood explanation of thunder. "It's our heavenly Father moving his furniture around upstairs."

The thought made her sleepy.

Thank you, Father, for bringing me through this accident and please heal my ankle fast.

Finally, she slept fitfully with lightning flashing outside the windows.

She moaned lying in the dingy, marsh water. Only inches from her foot, a writhing form with slanted, gleaming eyes stared at her. Slowly the snake's mouth opened, revealing a white interior and long, pointed fangs. Rachel tried to move but her limbs remained frozen. She screamed and sobbed.

A loud sound cut through her dream, and shook her awake. It was her door banging against the wall. Luke Barrett crouched in the light pouring in from the hall, both hands outstretched with a handgun aimed to shoot.

Rachel sat up and wiped tears from her face.

He sprinted into the room in one movement and flipped on the overhead light with his elbow. When he detected her safe in the four-poster, he slowed down and lowered his gun. His hard breathing filled the air. He searched the bath and crossed the room to step out the French doors. He returned, locked them, and pushed the Glock into his waistband. The same kind of firearm Ron used.

Good gravy! Was this the way the Marines landed? The entire action took less than a minute.

Luke strode to her open door and turned to regard her. He lifted an eyebrow. "Are you okay?" His deep voice rolled across the room. "Never heard such screams. Thought we might have our first intruder." He grinned.

Rachel managed to whisper, "I'm sorry. It was a nightmare." The eye patch did not cover his relief. Or was she imagining things? He stood there in a white tee shirt and Levi's, every muscle still taunt. More attractive than any man she'd known and exuding what she could only describe as magnetism pulling at all her senses. Had she been standing, she would've welcomed those brawny arms around her. Was she falling in love? Or stupidity? Something her aunt told another woman describing an infatuated teenager flitted across her mind. *Moonstruck calf.* Thank heaven for the common sense of her aunt.

"What is it, Luke?" Jessica pressed past him into the room. "I heard someone cry out."

Luke turned to the older woman. "Rachel had an old-fashioned nightmare. I went into attack mode, thinking someone had broken into her room."

Jessica reached for Rachel's bed jacket and handed it to her.

Get with it girl. Rachel slipped on the wrap, and drew her knees up to her chin under the coverlet, her face now hot. "Yes. I dreamed a snake writhed at my foot again." Why was she whispering?

Luke grinned. "No snake—see?" He strode to her bedside, swept his hand across the foot of the bed in a searching manner, the corners of his mouth still turned up.

She longed to wipe the silly smirk off his face.

Jessica sat on the edge of the bed. "Rachel, when you get back into your regular schedule. I expect you won't even think of your fall again."

"I am so sorry I awakened you both. Did I disturb Kristina?"

"Nope. She'd be here by now if you had." Luke started to leave but turned back. "Rachel, you need to keep the French doors locked at all times. We have a lot of workers on the place." He gestured toward the flowers on the coffee table. "Who sent the blossoms?"

Jessica noticed the bouquet and raised her brows at Rachel.

Rachel was tempted to tell Luke "a friend" and leave him wondering. Relax. This is no big deal. "Archer Pennington."

Luke left without remarking.

"How nice of Archer. I can stay longer if you need me to. Luke was probably walking to his room when he heard you, so he got here before me. Are you sure you're okay?"

Rachel took a deep breath. "Thank you, I'll be fine." She looked up at Jessica with an afterthought, "Does Luke carry a gun like that all the time?"

"I haven't noticed if he has. Perhaps he mainly wears it outdoors. I guess with all his work around the plantation—and the snake population being what it is." She grimaced at Rachel. "And, you also never know the type work force he brings in seasonally, either." She stood. "Sure you don't want me to stay a little longer?"

"No, no. I only wondered...about the firearm." And how much he reminded her of Ron when he burst in like he did. She lowered her knees and relaxed on the pillow.

Jessica switched the light off and left.

Rachel moved to the side of the bed, tested her ankle, and hopped to the door. She turned the lock. Storm or nightmare, no one was going to pop in her room again tonight.

She awoke early the next morning. Soft light filtered through the windows. The memory of Luke rushing into her room to protect her sent a tingle up her spine. She sat up and shook her head. She would not think about Luke Barrett.

She swung her legs over the side of the bed, slipped her feet into her pink scuffs, and flexed her ankle. Not much pain.

Thank You, Lord.

She donned her pink house robe, opened the French doors, and hobbled out into fresh, crisp air.

Birds twittered softly from tall oaks in sunrise shadow. She drew a deep breath laced with the smell of gardenias and soaked cypress. In the garden below the balcony, a hollyhock, loaded with pink carnation-like blooms, lay trapped beneath a fallen limb.

Whoa! You need help big flower.

She glanced around and listened. The household still slumbered. She made her way over the damp boards of the piazza, favoring her ankle, and down the steps to the hollyhock.

Righting the five-foot-tall flower with its fifteen or more blossoms, proved no easy task. When she removed the limb and stood the plant up, the rain-drenched blossoms weighed it down again. Determined, she pulled the flower upright again and gave it a firm shake. Cool droplets showered her, and she gasped.

Laughter erupted from the balcony above. "I've caught a woodland fairy repairing the night's damage to my garden."

In dismay, Rachel peered up into Luke's grinning visage.

Drats! Two minutes more and she would've been back in her room. Rachel propped the hollyhock against the banister, and, ignoring the wetness on her face and robe, made her way up the steps.

She attempted to pass Luke on the porch with the barest acknowledgement, but he stepped forward. He was probably planning to poke fun at her nightmare last night and the moonstruck expression she must've worn.

When she dared to look in his face, there was no evidence of derision, only a strange tenderness. Her heart started racing.

"You really okay?" His gaze lingered.

She nodded.

He folded his arms and stepped back.

She moved past him as fast as possible.

"I'm sure the hollyhock will survive. In any event, I hope so," he called after her.

Now there was no mistaking the amusement in his voice. She stepped through the French doors and locked them. A sudden thought raced through her like an electric shock.

Had he referred to her surviving, not the hollyhock? Did he think from the way she stared at him last night, she might be falling in love with him? Was he trying to warn her by some obscure means his future was already planned, perhaps with Morgan, and nothing, certainly no moonstruck calf, could change those plans? She thrust out her chin. Fine. She was only here for the summer anyway.

Surprisingly, tears stung the back of her eyes. She forced them away and assured herself they simply attested to the trauma associated with her fall.

~*~

The following Friday afternoon, Rachel descended to the kitchen with Kristina to bake Irish soda bread for an early supper. Maggie was off for the night and Jessica left to spend the weekend with a sister after Rachel assured her it was fine to leave Kristina with her. While the bread baked, Rachel let Kristina peel boiled eggs for a spread. It warmed Rachel's heart to observe the happy child working with her in the kitchen. Soon the finished bread sat on the counter, cooling. Its delicious aroma filled the kitchen. Rachel sliced some of the warm loaf and let Kristina make sandwiches for them both.

Who cared if they dropped about as much egg salad on the counter as they spread on the bread?

They added an apple, a cookie, and a glass of milk, and sat at the table to enjoy their handiwork. Afterwards, they went outside to the swing. A wonderful peace enveloped Rachel as the sunlight softened into early evening.

When they came back in, Luke sat at the kitchen table reading the newspaper. He apparently helped himself to the soda bread, which was almost gone, and the egg container was scraped clean. He munched on an apple.

"Daddy!" Kristina ran to him.

He laid the paper aside, took her in his lap, and hugged her. His glance swept over Rachel in her green cotton dress. "Did you make the bread? What kind is it?"

"Kristina and I did. It's an old family recipe. Irish Soda bread."

"Well, it's mighty good." Luke turned back to Kristina.

"Hey, pup, you want to go see a movie tonight? Black Beauty's playing in Charleston."

"Oh, Daddee! Can we?" Kristina's eyes sparkled with excitement.

"I guess so, if you'll wash your face and hands and change those shorts. And get a sweater."

Kristina jumped out of his lap and started out of the room but ran back and grabbed Rachel's hand.

"Can Rachel go, Daddy? Let's take Rachel."

Luke's glance turned to Rachel. She bent to speak to Kristina. "Oh, no, Kristina, this is a good time for you and your father to spend an evening together."

Luke reached for a toothpick on the counter. "I don't think you'll interrupt our father-daughter time, unless, of course, you've other plans or can't stand the movie."

Rachel swallowed hard. "No—I'm not busy this evening, other than caring for Kristina, and I love horse stories but—"

"Please come, Rachel." Kristina pulled her hand.

"Then what's to stop you?" Luke asked, standing.

Yes, what was preventing her?

"Okay, I'll come along." Rachel smiled and gave in. "But give us girls a little time to get ready."

She and Kristina hurried toward the stairs.

Luke called after them. "I'll meet you two out front in the driveway."

Rachel helped Kristina sponge off and change into clean clothes. She went by her room to check her hair and makeup and collect a sweater. They walked out the door to a waiting luxury German sedan.

Luke slid into the driver's seat after strapping Kristina into her child's safety seat behind him. Rachel sat in the front passenger seat. Kristina chattered all the way. Never had a child's talk been more welcome to Rachel.

As they entered the theater, the wonderful smell of fresh popcorn filled the air.

Kristina walked up to the counter. "Three boxes, please."

Rachel noticed the attention Luke received from other moviegoers and from the girl behind the counter. The young woman couldn't take her eyes off Luke or his patch. He did make quite a figure in a black t-shirt, Levis, shiny cowboy boots, and damp, dark hair.

Luke paid for their snack and for lemonade to go around.

Rachel smiled and accepted the warm box and cold drink when Luke handed them to her. They found comfortable theater seats. Luke stretched out, propped his knees on the seat in front of him, and leaned back. The movie began.

Every time Rachel glanced over Kristina at the hulk of Luke sprawled beyond her, her heart did a strange leap. The child laid her head against her father's shoulder after finishing her popcorn.

Soon Rachel found herself caught up in the story. Tears coursed down her cheeks at the mistreatment of Black Beauty. Embarrassed, she turned aside and hoped Luke did not observe her searching for a Kleenex. "Need this?" Luke held his handkerchief across Kristina to her.

Kristina was sound asleep and oblivious to the movie ending. Luke picked her up and the threesome left the theater.

Rachel opened the car's rear door and Luke strapped the sleeping child in her car seat. He opened the door for Rachel and she moved into the passenger seat. A tingle ran up Rachel's spine as Luke slid in beside her and started the automobile. He maneuvered the car onto the highway in the effortless way he handled a steering wheel. Rachel tried to slow her hammering heart and think of something to say. Nothing came to mind. She turned to stare out the window at the lights of Charleston. They traveled several miles through light traffic without conversation.

"Well, Miss York—Rachel—how are you enjoying your stay at Barrett Hall?"

Luke's deep voice startled Rachel. "Oh! It's fine. I love being with Kristina. She's a wonderful child." She sounded like a stuttering idiot.

He smiled and nodded his head, and floored her with his next statement.

"I'm telling myself someone who cries at a horse movie can't be too bad or, perhaps the word I'm searching for is deceptive. But I still don't believe you've told me the real reason you've come to Charleston."

Chapter Ten

Rachel stiffened. What was he? A plantation owner/detective on the side? Should she share about her brother? Lying was not something she ever wanted to do. She would need to tell him something, at least as much as she could without blowing Ron's partner's cover.

She bit her lower lip and glanced out the window for time to think. The car began to cross the Cooper River Bridge. The view of the Charleston Harbor lights twinkling far below them over the Atlantic thrilled her, and she would've enjoyed it if not for the man sitting beside her, waiting for her answer. She turned to face him. "You're right, there is another cause, but I am not at liberty to share it right now."

"But this has nothing to do with Barrett Hall or anything…illegal?"

Her mouth fell open and her eyes widened. Did he suspect she'd be involved in something criminal? "No. nothing like that," she blurted out. Glancing in the back seat, she lowered her voice and sought his face. "It's personal. I hope you can understand."

His hands tightened on the steering wheel. "Okay, I'm going to believe you, Rachel, until you give me reason not to."

"Thank you," she said, almost in a whisper.

He glanced at her before refocusing on the road.

"If you decide to clue me in, I might be able to help."

She dared to take a quick look at his profile. Be of assistance? She didn't think so. She had a job to do while in Charleston and only God could help her do it.

Kristina stirred in the back seat. "Daddy, are we home yet?"

"Almost, sweet pea."

Saved by Kristina.

~*~

The day of Kristina's birthday party dawned bright and clear. Jessica told Rachel Luke planned a barbecue at six o'clock for family and a few friends, including Morgan and Archer. Some children from church were supposed to come also. Jessica asked Rachel to be in charge of the children's games, which would start at five o'clock.

Rachel, dressed in tan Bermuda shorts and a turquoise pull over, enjoyed the children and the fun as much as they did.

Tables for the adults stretched out under the trees with red and white cloths. Lanterns, to discourage insects and give light as the sun faded, swayed around the perimeter of the patio.

Soon, the tantalizing smell of Luke's barbecue filled the evening air and other guests arrived, including Morgan, Archer, James Sanders, and Kristina's grandparents. Jessica brought the elderly couple over to meet Rachel.

"Rachel, this is Noel and Ruth Owens, Kristina's Grandmother and Papa, as she calls him."

"How do you do?" Rachel liked their gentle expressions. But sadness surfaced in their glances. The house of their deceased daughter probably brought back memories.

Kristina ran up and pulled them by the hand to go see the pile of gifts. After the two walked away, Jessica remarked, "I think I told you Luke's parents died young in an accident, so these are the only grandparents."

She had not forgotten that fact. It was the one common denominator she and Luke shared. The loss of both their parents.

Rachel stood at the edge of the children's game of Red Light, Green Light. Morgan Pennington walked up to Luke at the grill and tapped him on the shoulder. He turned and she greeted him with a kiss on the cheek. She wore white pedal pushers and a red-striped knit shirt that fit snugly on her good figure. A white scarf trimmed in red, held her long, shining blond hair back from her face and red earrings dangled from her ear lobes. The woman gazed around the yard, spied Rachel, and gave her a small wave.

Archer came up behind Rachel and startled her.

"Hey, there, nanny. Didn't mean to scare you. You're the best-looking babysitter I've ever seen."

Rachel smiled in spite of herself. The man was a charmer. His blond hair, brushed away from his forehead magnified his tan and blue eyes. The striped navy shirt and white slacks made him a candidate as a male model for summer clothing.

"Hello," she said. Heat rose in her cheeks as she remembered mistaking Archer for a salesman. And she'd never thanked him for the bouquet. "Thank you so much for the flowers, when I had my little accident."

Archer's eyes danced and he moved closer.

Kristina ran up and Rachel stepped back, glad for the interruption.

"Are we ready to eat yet?" the child asked. "I smell something good."

Rachel checked the patio and Luke lifting hamburgers off the grill. She patted the child's head. "Yes, honey, I believe we are about ready."

"You are most welcome for the flowers." Archer scanned Rachel's feet shod in sandals. "How is your ankle?"

"Oh, it's fine now. It was only a sprain." She smiled. "I guess I'd better go and get the children's plates."

"Sure. I'll help, but I want to ask you something." Archer walked beside her across the lawn.

"Would you care to go to the Museum Dedication with me next week—and the dinner afterward? The banquet's going to be on our little yacht in the harbor."

On a yacht? Sounded interesting, as did Morgan's museum dedication. "Yes, I would. Thank you."

"Great. I'll pick you up next Friday about six, and, of course, it's formal." His eyebrows rose. "Will that be a problem?"

"I don't think so."

"Wonderful." He smiled and hooked his arm through hers as they made their way toward the patio and table laden with boiled corn, potato salad, barbecued ribs, and hamburgers fresh off the grill.

Morgan turned to Rachel and Archer as they came up.

"Brother, your face is glowing like you've just won a case. What's up?"

"None of your beeswax, sister."

Rachel withdrew her arm from Archer's grasp and

greeted Morgan. She met Luke's fleeting glance. A frown creased his brow before he turned to take up the last of the ribs. Morgan held the platter.

How cozy. Like an old, married couple.

Rachel gathered up plates for the children on a tray, and walked across the lawn to dine with them. The adults gathered at a larger table in the center of the patio. Morgan and Luke sat side by side.

Rachel barely finished her food when Luke stood up and beat on his glass with a spoon.

"Hear ye, a certain little girl has a birthday today."

Maggie opened the patio door and Jessica marched out with Kristina's birthday cake and sat it on the children's table in front of Kristina. Luke came to her side to light the candles. The adults gathered around and joined in with the children singing *Happy Birthday*. Kristina blew out the flames, her eyes bright with happiness. The grandparents and Cade snapped photos.

"Can I open my presents now, Daddy?"

"You sure can, sweet pea."

Kristina ran to the patio and tore into the gifts. Cade handed the camera he'd been using to Rachel and walked toward the barn. The children exclaimed over each toy, especially the miniature dollhouse from Morgan. Rachel's crocheted small pink purse she'd created for Kristina received little attention from the other kids, but the child promptly pulled the shoulder strap over her head and gave its creator a hug. When Rachel glanced up, Morgan surveyed the two of them with a smile turned stiff.

Kristina moved close to Luke and squeezed his fingers. "Daddy, where's your surprise?"

"Well, now, I don't rightly know, but I think it's

coming." Luke turned the child around and everyone smiled. Cade came across the lawn, leading a beautiful bay pony with black stockings and mane. Kristina squealed, and with all the children following, ran toward the horse. The little animal stopped, rolled its eyes and snorted, ready to bolt.

Cade held tightly to the halter rope. "Whoa, now. You kids know better than to run up to an animal like that."

They all stopped and let Kristina walk up alone.

She held out her hand. The pony leaned forward to smell it, and the child patted the velvet nose. "Thank you, thank you, Daddy."

Cade invited the other kids to come up, one by one, and pat the Welsh pony.

~*~

"Well, I do believe this has been a good party," Jessica told Luke as the last child left.

"Can I name my pony tomorrow, and ride him?" Kristina asked.

"Sure you can, baby." Luke bent to receive her hug. "Got any ideas yet?"

"Flicka. Rachel read me a story about a horse named Flicka."

"Flicka it will be." Luke tweaked her plait and she turned and ran toward the new toys piled on the patio.

Rachel assisted Maggie and Cade in clearing the tables and lawn. Her heart warmed when she noticed Kristina still wearing her little purse as the child and Jessica carried the new toys into the house.

Almost everyone had left but Dakota and Archer who appeared to be in a serious discussion at the far edge of the lawn. The farm manager folded his arms and frowned as he leaned his head toward Archer.

Luke and Morgan paused in their trek to the side of the house where she'd parked her car. Luke said something to her and strode over to Rachel who had her hands full of trash. "Thanks for helping make this a memorable birthday for Kristina."

She shifted the garbage into a bag. "I enjoyed every minute of it."

Dakota turned and hurried to the barn.

Archer came up to her as Luke left. The easy charm and confidence no longer dominated his tanned face.

"Sure am excited about next Friday night." He gave her a little salute and followed Luke and Morgan, his head bent in thought.

Now what let the air out of his balloon?

Sunday Rachel attended service alone, as Jessica traveled to her Charleston house, and Kristina went home with her grandparents. In the lazy afternoon she sat down and wrote Raven an epistle-length letter and asked a favor of her.

I appreciate your telling me about the breakup of Easton's engagement, I guess you thought I should know. However, please do not let him weasel out of you where I am.

The following week began hot and dry. Rachel kept busy teaching Kristina her letters, phonetic sounds and numbers. She spent her free time reading or crocheting. Easton and his broken engagement with his boss's daughter only floated into her mind once. Why should she care? She did wonder if he'd been turned down for a partnership in the firm as a result of breaking the engagement. It would serve him right. Or maybe he broke the engagement *after* being refused the partnership. That was more his mode of operation.

On Thursday afternoon Rachel put Kristina down to nap and went to her room to plan her apparel for the museum dedication the following evening. The decision about what to wear was easy. She'd brought only two formal outfits—a long, pale blue silk gown with sheer, puffy half sleeves and scooped neckline, and a street length black crepe de chine skirt with a fitted white lace over blouse.

She chose the blue gown and pulled it from the back of the wardrobe. As she did so, a large box fell to the floor.

She laid the gown across the bed and returned to the parcel. When she opened it, the scent of new leather filled the air. Pulling the tissue back, she stared at shiny brown boots. She lifted one and was surprised at its weight and unusual thickness. Expensive. Searching through the tissue, she found a small card.

Hope these will adequately replace the shoes ruined in the marsh. –Luke.

How long had the boots been in her closet? Luke surely didn't place them there. The housemaid probably found the box somewhere in the room—wherever Luke left it after her fall. Since it was not gift wrapped, the girl probably assumed it belonged in the wardrobe.

Rachel could not accept such a costly gift from her employer. No matter how long they'd been in her possession.

That evening Luke did not take dinner with her and Jessica. On her way back upstairs, Rachel heard him come in below, probably headed to his office. She walked to her room and grabbed up the box. At the game room door, she raised her knuckles to knock but stopped as angry voices leaked through the panel. Suddenly, the door flew open and Dakota almost ran into her. He nodded at her, slammed his hat on his head, and rushed out the patio door.

Rachel hesitated. Should she come back later? But Luke might be striding to the door himself or he might have glimpsed her. She took a deep breath, hugged the parcel close, and pushed into the room.

Luke sat at his desk. Anger contorted his brow. Tiredness and dark stubble lined his rigid face and perspiration darkened his army shirt. He glanced up at her.

This wasn't a good moment, but here she was.

"What is it, Rachel?" He leaned back in his chair and stared at her.

"I'm—sorry if I'm disturbing you."

"Well, disturb on. Time is wasting, and I need my dinner."

Rachel stepped forward and laid the box on his desk. "I really can't accept a gift like this."

Luke glared at the box and back at her. "You took your time deciding."

"I think I can explain—"

"I don't want an explanation, Miss York," Luke stood up, walked around the desk and scooped up the box. He put it back into her unwilling arms. "The idea is to keep you safe on this plantation." With his hands on her shoulders, he steered her toward the door. "Okay?"

Too surprised to resist, she moved to the door but turned back before going out.

He picked up a piece of paper from his desk and studied it. "Do whatever you like with the boots,

Rachel, but it will be in your best interest to keep them and wear them anytime you go out to explore the plantation with Kristina."

She strolled back to her room pondering the situation she'd witnessed. What did Luke and Dakota argue about? And why did her resolve crumble in her employer's presence?

Later, she climbed into bed still thinking of Luke. His exhausted, troubled state stirred her sympathy, but she resisted. She'd read somewhere pity was akin to love.

Lord, bless Luke and help him. At least she could pray for him.

~*~

Friday afternoon about five o'clock, Rachel stepped into a warm bubble bath and relished the delightful Gardenia fragrance enveloping her. She shampooed and dried her hair and brushed it until it fell in waves to her shoulders. After plaiting small strands on each side of her face, she gathered them to the back of her head with a tortoise shell comb and applied her makeup and jewelry. She donned the blue dress and the sapphire locket and earrings, her treasured gift from her mother's estate. She stepped into the clear sling heels with blue straps and surveyed herself in the dresser mirror. A young woman with wide blue eyes, full lips, and thick black hair stared back at her. The gown with its modest neckline and sheer puff sleeves fit her perfectly and accentuated her slender waist. She chided her aunt for giving such an extravagant graduation present. The dress came from one of the better shops. Now Rachel was grateful for its good lines.

Archer was to pick her up at six-thirty. At six fifteen, she strolled into Kristina's room as promised earlier.

Kristina clapped both her hands and jumped down from her bed to finger the silky fabric. "You look like a fairy princess. And I want my hair done that way tomorrow. Okay?"

"It will be hot for play but if you insist." Rachel gave the child a hug and made her way downstairs. She was glad Luke had already left.

Archer arrived and gave a low whistle when Rachel met him at the door. He bowed and handed her a cellophane box encasing a flower. His white tuxedo, shining blond hair and manner exuded an easy, moneyed elegance Rachel recognized from slick magazine pictures of the rich and famous.

Rachel touched the snowy blossom with its crimson center. "Thank you for the lovely orchid, Archer."

"I can't believe you're ready—and so beautiful." His bright eyes flickered over her from head to toe. "My sister is never ready on time, but I doubt she'll keep Luke Barrett waiting long."

Jessica's eyes misted as she helped pin the corsage to Rachel's dress. "You two beautiful people have a wonderful evening." She stood at the door as they moved across the porch and down the walk to Archer's red British sports car.

"You look absolutely delicious." Archer's brown eyes swerved to caress her a moment before they pulled out on the highway to Charleston.

Rachel cocked her chin. "Delicious?"

"Yes, and stunning and gorgeous, and I'm not sure

I want to share you with a roomful of hungry stuffed shirts."

"Oh, do they display stuffed shirts at the museum, too?" Rachel asked innocently.

Archer smiled. "You bet they do and Morgan calls them all by name. Poor Luke. He can't escape the boring dedication, but there's no law that says we have to go."

Rachel ventured a glance at Archer. Was he serious? "But—aren't we expected?"

Archer's amber eyes flashed. "We won't be missed, believe me. What do you say?"

Chapter Eleven

"But where will we go? And what about the dinner on the boat?" Rachel asked. A pang of disappointment pierced her at the thought of missing it. And Luke. Would he miss her?

"Oh, we'll be at the blast on the yacht. We don't want to skip that. All I am asking you to do is forget the dedication and do a little sightseeing instead, and I don't mean walking in those cute high heels."

Rachel breathed a sigh of relief. They wouldn't miss the banquet. *Or Luke.*

They ended up in a two-seater carriage harnessed to a beautiful white horse with a driver the next hour and a half. Archer gave Rachel a quick history review of famous landmarks and some infamous.

"Here in this block is where forty-nine pirates were once executed in a single year by the colonial council."

"Wasn't Luke's ancestor a pirate?"

"Yep. Barrett Hall plantation started with a reformed pirate who managed to capture the fancy of an English rice planter's daughter, I believe. Think of it, if original old Barrett hadn't reformed, he might've been hanged right here." The driver paused the buggy at the curb.

Rachel shuddered, and fixed her attention on the current structure occupying the area. A sign above the storefront announced,

Redemption Hope Church,
Sunday Services 10:30 A.M.

"How interesting that a house of worship should be located on the same spot proclaiming redemption instead of penalty."

Archer turned to stare at her. "Wh-at?"

"You do understand about redemption versus penalty?"

He grimaced. "Hey, come on, you're not going to start preaching religious stuff on a night like this, are you?"

Rachel didn't respond. A memory of a similar fruitless conversation she'd once had with Easton floated across her mind. She would check out this little church in the heart of the old city.

Rachel glanced at her wristwatch and gasped. Eight-thirty. She held up her arm to Archer and pointed at the time.

"Hey, kid, don't worry. The night is young and the dedication folks Morgan has invited to the dinner, will just be arriving at the yacht. Besides, we're not far from the dock now."

The buggy dropped them back at their car. Archer tipped the driver handsomely, if the profuse thanks meant anything.

In two minutes, they were off in the car.

At the busy City Marina, Archer led her down a walkway past many docked vessels rocking gently with the tide, to a huge gleaming white yacht with the name, *Summer Dream,* painted in blue on its hull. He assisted her aboard the brightly lit craft. Romantic music filled the air and drifted across the glassy Atlantic now bathed in golden and pink hues.

Archer ushered her to the open door of the main deck area. A haze of cigarette smoke clustered around fuchsia lanterns hanging on golden chains from the ceiling. The first person she recognized was Luke. He stood leaning against the bar, dressed in a black tuxedo, his tanned face and black hair accented by a crisp, white, wing-tipped collar and red silk tie. His eye patch was toward the wall. Their glances met and her heart bounced against her ribs. Luke's face expressed surprise and something else. Worry? His gaze traveled over her, and she stumbled over the door molding.

Good gravy! *Lord, please don't let me fall.*

Archer steadied her with his hand on her elbow as smoothly as if nothing had happened, and led her across the floor toward Luke.

Rachel took a breath, ignored all the eyes upon them, and smiled a thank you to Archer.

"It's about time you showed, little brother." Morgan sidled up to Luke.

Her sleek black gown fitted her like a glove. Diamonds winked at her throat and from the one ear lobe not covered by draped blond hair touching her bare shoulders. Perfectly manicured, pearl-tipped nails curved around a cocktail glass. She sported a little pout on her lips as she fixed her eyes on Archer. She acknowledged Rachel as if a second thought. "Welcome to our home away from home, Rachel."

This belonged to the Pennington's?

Rachel didn't miss Morgan's quick inspection of her outfit and she resisted an urge to check the combs holding her hair since the stumble. "Good evening." She managed to include Luke in her greeting. He nodded, but cast a reproachful look at Archer.

Archer grinned, balled his fist and pressed Luke

on the shoulder. "Boy, am I thirsty after our carriage ride through history. What are you drinking, old man?"

"A Devil's Triangle," Luke answered, swirling his glass and staring straight at Archer. "Minus the devil."

Rachel observed Luke and Morgan. They were the most striking couple in the room. Something about Morgan leaning close to him annoyed her.

"Luke's still walking his teetotaler plank," Archer's voice brought Rachel back to face him, "But I'm going to order a Wild Affair, what would you like, most beautiful lady in the room?"

Rachel had never heard of the drinks mentioned but assumed they included alcohol. "Coke—or ginger ale, please."

"Oh, no, another teetotaler in the house." Morgan bemoaned with a grimace on her perfect features.

Luke turned to Rachel. He motioned toward the black bartender. "This guy's been trained on Barbados, and he's famous for his fruit and berry concoctions. You don't want to settle for a soda, not here, Rachel. At least try my drink—you can get it minus the alcohol."

So that's what Luke meant. "Okay, I'll take a Devil's Triangle—minus the devil." The bartender handed Rachel a tall glass. She took a sip and delighted in the rich strawberry-lemon fruit drink with a touch of mint.

Later, Rachel walked over to the abundant buffet with Archer.

During dinner, James Sanders and several other people joined their table with Morgan and Luke. Morgan talked about the museum until boredom threatened to make Rachel sleepy. Luke said little.

Was he tired or bored too?

The band in the corner started playing. Archer stood up and touched Rachel's hand. They danced two sets. The loud music and stuffy air made Rachel dream of relief as she sat down.

"I'm going over to the band and ask for some other music. Want to go? Or just rest awhile?"

"Oh, you go ahead. I think I'll go on deck for some fresh air. Do you mind?"

"Absolutely not. Enjoy yourself." Archer strolled away and a young woman jumped up and followed him. He turned, smiled, and put his arm around her waist.

Outside, Rachel took a deep breath of the cool sea breeze, glad to be out of the cigarette smoke. She noticed a narrow flight of stairs up to another level of the boat. The view from the top must be something.

She climbed up, holding on to the guardrail with one hand while lifting her gown with the other.

The sight, as she stepped out on the upper deck, caused her breath to catch. The sun, like the final sliver of an orange ball, hung at the western horizon. A full moon rose, casting silvery strands across the Atlantic. She walked to the nearest balustrade and stared down at the gentle waves lapping the boat.

"Get tired of the smoke too?"

Rachel whirled. Luke appeared coming up the stairwell. He stopped to lean on the railing some feet beyond her. He had discarded his tuxedo jacket and opened the collar of his shirt. The red tip of his tie peeped from his breast pocket. Romantic music wafting up from below made the deck suddenly too small and private. Her heart started racing, and for a moment, she thought about turning and going back down to the lower level.

But he came to stand beside her, with his good eye toward her.

"The last time on this behemoth of a boat, I was with my wife."

"Your wife?"

"Georgina. She loved parties like this, but I came to be with her."

"I am so sorry about Georgina. This must have brought back memories."

Luke turned to stare at her. Pain crossed his face for a moment but it disappeared as quickly as it had come. "Have you enjoyed your evening with Pennington, Miss York?"

"Oh, it's been pleasant. He talked me into playing hooky from the dedication to take a carriage drive through the Historic District. It was interesting."

"So that's where you were while I was mixing with the stuffed shirts."

Did Morgan have any idea what her brother and Luke thought of the civic responsibilities she pressed on them?

Suddenly, Luke moved closer to her. His manly scent laced with spice enveloped her. She found it hard to breathe but managed to whisper. "We should get back. Archer and Morgan will wonder—"

"Why don't we forget them?" He laid a broad hand over hers gripping the railing.

She battled a kaleidoscope of emotions from euphoria to foreboding. The strains of the classic romantic song *Fascination* rose from below. She closed her eyes but still saw the stars and harbor lights and heard the surging of the waves against the ship. Was she dreaming? Or drowning?

Luke lifted her hand from the railing and kissed

her palm.

Her eyes shot open and a tremor shook her body. Close on its heels came resolve born of desperation. She discerned a precipice one short step ahead—a drop off from which there could be no return in her relationship with her employer. Besides, his mind was clearly on his lost wife. She tried to pull her hand from his, but he held on. "Luke, please let me go." Her firm voice surprised even her.

He did.

She turned and reached for the railing, thankful for the firm support it offered her trembling fingers. As soon as she could walk, down those steps she must go.

Luke leaned on the balustrade beside her. "What is it about you that's so different? With any other woman, I wouldn't believe she wished to be released." He grinned at her. "And I would not have done so."

How many other women were there?

He waited for an answer. Rachel had no idea what to say. "I—I think we'd better get back."

"Not until you've answered my question."

"I'm not aware I am so different, as you put it."

"Every man here tonight noticed you."

"Me?" Surely, he was mistaken. Morgan Pennington had drawn all the eyes.

"Yes, you. There's something unique about you, besides those sapphire eyes." Luke touched her hair. "And this raven mane."

She moved away from him, forcing her weak knees to remain stable. She gazed out over the gently swirling Atlantic, and her mind seized on a reply, an answer she was unsure about sharing. But Luke waited beside her. His gaze burned into her being.

Suddenly she knew it was the right time, the exact

moment, to draw the lines, to set things straight — before moonlight and romantic music drove resolve, sanity, and vows from her heart.

"If there is anything different about me," she began, "it's probably because I am a believer, one who tries to take the Bible and its truths seriously." With the uttering of the words, a new confidence came, and she turned her eyes straight to his handsome face.

He met her gaze, frowned, and stared out over the ocean. "How about, 'He'll give his angels charge over you.' You take that seriously?"

"Yes, yes I do. Don't you believe the Bible?"

"I did once."

Oh, she was in deep water now — the loss of his wife, his eye. How could she forget? She couldn't think of a thing to respond that wouldn't sound flippant.

He walked back to the steps and waited for her to precede him, his face hidden in shadows. The beautiful music finished the last notes. Silence fell like a wall between them.

She descended the narrow, metal stairs, disturbed. At least, now she understood where he was spiritually. Maybe.

Father, if You ever give me this opportunity again, please send the right words.

At the bottom, Luke gave her a slight bow and strode away. She headed back to the banquet room.

"Hey, I got to missing you, little lady." Archer pulled her toward a table set with drinks, snacks, and fruit.

The crowd was thinner, but Morgan still stood across the room with several admirers gathered around. Her cool stare chilled Rachel as much as the conversation above deck.

Rachel accepted a fruit drink and sank into a nearby chair. Luke entered from another door and walked toward Morgan's group. He now wore his jacket and the tie was looped loosely around his collar.

Archer sat beside her. "Hey, why so glum? The evening's still mighty young."

She noted his bright eyes. Did the man ever wind down? "Oh, I guess I'm a little tired."

"Wanna go?"

Rachel checked her watch. Eleven-thirty—would be after twelve when they arrived at Barrett Hall. "Yes, I think so."

Archer bounced up, astounding Rachel with his energy. He called out goodbyes to several people and waved at Morgan and Luke.

Luke came toward them as they made their way to the door.

"Leaving?" He directed his question at Rachel, and glanced at Archer.

"Yes, Rachel's tired."

"Well, be sure you take the tired little lady home —if you're capable of driving, that is."

Rachel gasped and her eyes flew from one man to the other. Luke appeared dead serious, but to her surprise, a soft look spread across Archer's features. "Sure, man. I wouldn't drive if I wasn't okay." He took Rachel's arm and guided her out the door. Luke's stare heated her back. What was *that* all about?

They were in the car driving through Charleston before Archer spoke. "You've heard his wife was killed in a car wreck, right?"

"Yes, Jessica told me."

"Well, she'd been drinking."

Oh, no.

"And the funny thing is, she wasn't a drinker. Not at all, as far as most of us knew. But it seems she was with friends while Luke was away and, I guess, someone pressed her to take a drink or two. Not being used to it, it took a strong effect. And it was raining cats and dogs. She ran off the road, hit a tree, not three miles from the entrance to Barrett Hall."

Archer turned to glance at her. "Bet you didn't hear that part of the story."

"No, I didn't. So sad. I can understand why Luke doesn't drink."

'Oh, no. He was already a teetotaler. And I don't have that epistle. But enough of sad stuff. How about playing tennis with me some Sunday afternoon? You play?"

"Yes, in college, but I'm probably a little rusty now."

"No problem, we'll deal with the rust. I'll give you a call."

When they pulled up to Barrett Hall, Archer jumped out and came around to get Rachel's door. He escorted her up the walk and onto the porch.

She turned to face him. "Thank you for a nice evening, Archer."

He leaned on the wall beside her. "Tell me, Rachel. Why did a smart and lovely girl like you take a summer job babysitting?"

Rachel, caught off guard, cast about for something to say, and gave her pat answer. "I had never been south, and I love children, and it seemed an exciting adventure."

He searched her face as if weighing her words. "If it's excitement you crave." He moved closer and pulled her into his arms.

Rachel stiffened and drew back.

He backed off and put up both hands. "Okay. No kiss on the first date. Right?"

She smiled. The man did have a way about him.

Later, she tossed and turned in bed, remembering the time with Luke on the upper deck when he kissed her palm, touched her hair. But cold water splashed upon her heart. He admitted he no longer believed the Bible.

Would a man like Luke Barrett ever find his faith again? She could find no answer and, finally, sleep pulled her into forgetfulness.

The drone of a plane awoke her.

Chapter Twelve

Rachel arose quietly, slipped into her house robe and scuffs and opened the French doors. Stepping out onto the dark balcony, she listened again. Only silence greeted her beyond the drumming of crickets. Had the drone of an airplane awakened her or was she dreaming? She stood for a moment in the dimness as her eyes adjusted to moonlight filtering between clouds.

Muffled sounds came from the direction of the barn. Startled, she drew back in the porch shadows and tiptoed around the balcony until she viewed the barn's outline. A man stepped out of the barn's interior into the moonlight on the road, leading a horse.

Luke and Haidez.

Luke mounted and urged the horse into a canter down the soft sides of the beach road under cover of the trees. The stories Ron shared about drug drop offs on secluded beaches flooded her mind. She slumped against the wall. Was Luke involved in criminal activity? There was only one way to find out. She hurried to her room, pulled on jeans, a dark tee and started to slip on her tennis shoes, but reached for the boots Luke gave her. No snake episodes tonight, she prayed.

Penny, who now slept in a carrier at the foot of the bed, roused and began to whimper.

"Sh-h-h, little girl," Rachel whispered as she picked up the small Dachshund and gave her a hug. "I can't let you wake the house so I guess you get to go."

She grabbed the dog's tiny collar and lead and slipped out the French doors and down the steps. She listened for the sound of hoof beats and heard none. Luke had surely reached the shore and the convenient silence of the sand. She collared the puppy and put her down to walk.

Rachel followed in Luke's path, under the cover of trees. A brisk, humid wind lifted her loose hair and fanned it out behind her. Why didn't she think of putting it into a ponytail or something?

Before emerging onto the seashore, she picked up Penny and slipped behind a thicket of barrier trees and bushes. Now she was thankful for the boots.

She found a breakthrough path that led to the shore. Keeping to the shadows, she trudged up the sandy incline and stooped. A gap in the thick bushes revealed the beach, white in the moonlight. The roaring of the tide filled the night. She scanned up the coast as best she could without coming out into the open. Nothing. She examined the coastline to her left and froze. Out in the water a small plane bobbed and a boat rowed its silent way to shore.

She dropped onto the sandy dune, clutching the puppy in her arms. Her breath caught in her throat. Was this a drug drop off? Were these criminals the same ones Ron investigated and lost his life trying to capture? She squeezed back tears and forced herself to edge around the cover to take a wider scan down the beach. No sign of Luke or Haidez—unless Luke was the lone oarsman in the small craft.

What, if anything, could she do?

The service revolver Ron gave her lay hidden in the zippered compartment of her suitcase in her room. She sat for long minutes, helplessness overpowering her.

The sound of the plane taking off jolted her. She crawled up and peered down the beach. The boat had disappeared and the twin-engine craft lifted in the moonlight and flew out to sea. Again under cover, she sat on the warm sand as more questions bombarded her mind. Was Luke involved in drug smuggling? Or, was she jumping to conclusions? Maybe he heard the plane, too, and came to investigate.

She stood, brushed the sand from her jeans, listened for any movement and hearing none, made her way to the house, keeping to the shadows as much as possible. Penny fell asleep in her arms. Tomorrow she'd try to call Ron's partner again. If she received no answer, should she call someone else, like the Solicitor James Sanders?

The fact Luke might be involved in drug smuggling left her cold. Granted, she had not actually caught him on the beach. But where else could he have gone?

As she came near the barn, a figure stepped out from its shadows.

"Oh!" She almost dropped the puppy.

"Rachel, what *are* you doing out here this time of night?" Luke's voice, though lowered almost to a whisper, cut the air like cold steel. He stood before her in the moonlight, his face a stiff, glowering mask. "And don't tell me walking the dog."

Should she ask him the same question? Rachel sat the now squirming Dachshund down and it ran toward Luke wagging its tail. He ignored the little dog.

Rachel drew Penny away, reached down, and picked her up.

Rubbing Penny's ears, she stared at the master of Barrett Hall and decided to test him with the truth. "I thought I heard a low-flying plane and remembered what someone once said about drug drop offs on beaches—and I decided to check it out." Her voice sounded calm. Only the puppy knew how her hands shook.

"Decided to investigate it?" He uttered an oath. "Do you realize how much danger you are inviting pulling something like this?" He wasn't whispering anymore. He shook his head for a moment, as if too angry to speak. He sucked in a breath.

Would he fire her on the spot? She gripped Penny so tightly, the puppy whimpered.

"I am only going to say this one time, Rachel. If you ever do anything half as foolish as this again, I will send you packing immediately." He spat the words out.

He hadn't even asked what she'd discovered.

"Do you hear me?"

"Yes." Sir. Captain. Boss. Maybe drug smuggler.

He moved for her to pass, and she hurried toward the house and to her room without glancing back.

Rachel placed Penny in her basket and the puppy curled up to sleep. Climbing into the four-poster, Rachel tried to assimilate the apparent drug drop off she'd witnessed and her confrontation with Luke. Was Luke involved in drug smuggling? Or was he checking things out? Did he think her reason valid for going to the beach? Had she lost his trust? The clock on her nightstand flipped to three, and she fluffed her pillow. Tomorrow she would figure out what, if anything, she should do.

However, her mind refused to rest. Several times she'd questioned Luke's odd night hours, his leaving to go out on the plantation after telling Kristina goodnight, even his not wanting her to walk in the garden after dark. Another disturbing fact clunked down in her mind. He also didn't profess to be a strong Christian anymore—but could he be involved in drug smuggling? The man didn't even drink alcoholic beverages. That thought brought some relief. The next moment, though, a single, bothersome word popped into her mind. *Money.* Ron said the real backers and financiers of smuggling operations were seldom users. Money was their addiction.

Did Luke need money? How could he be in financial straits— with the handsome salary he paid her, the cars he drove, and the plantation busy producing tea, beef cattle and pecans? If Luke received money smuggling drugs, why would he break his back with honest labor? Perhaps he'd been out helping a cow to calve instead of meeting planes the other times he'd ridden off in the night, but tonight a plane landed near Barrett Hall's beach. Was Luke somehow involved?

She finally slept but dreamed of pirates, one with an eye patch and a tanned, granite jaw, burying a plastic sack of white powder in warm sand.

~*~

Luke watched Rachel until she closed the French doors. He tried to block from his mind how attractive she was in the moonlight, in jeans and a baggy tee and her thick, curly hair loose and fanning her shoulders.

And she wore the boots he'd given her. Brain, one—common sense, zero.

He shook his head. Had he made a mistake hiring her? Was she really who she said she was? But what schoolteacher would pull a stunt like she did tonight? He should go back over all the information he first gathered about her. Something was surely missing in the picture. From the warning signals in his gut, he should've sent her packing. Why didn't he?

He mulled over these thoughts as he walked back to the house to record notes to share with James Sanders about tonight's episode. It was a drop off, but it was not quite on Barrett Hall's property—but below it. Pennington property. What would the solicitor make of it?

~*~

The next day, a Saturday, Barrett Hall opened its gates to summer tourists. Rachel couldn't hide a strange sense of anticipation from the moment she awoke. Was it a premonition her planned call to Ron's partner would be answered? After breakfast, she assisted Jessica, Maggie and Mrs. Busby preparing the downstairs for tourists. They roped off the stairs to the upper levels and the kitchen entrance.

After lunch, a woman from the historical society came in a hooped skirt and bonnet. She took her post at the front door to handle the talking tour of the first floor. Cade stood sentry on the porch to send in groups of fifteen at thirty-minute intervals. Dakota and some other farm workers gathered at the entrance of the barns posted with signs that read, *Look but Don't Touch the Animals*

Luke drove away from the plantation in his jeep. Was he stationed at the tea factory? Or was he escaping? A more important question, was he waiting after the tour to question her again?

Jessica left for her Charleston house. She took Kristina to drop off at her grandparents for the weekend. Mrs. Busby and Maggie stayed on the first floor to monitor the visitors as they toured the rooms. So far Barrett Hall had not lost small historic objects that could fit in purses and pockets.

At two o'clock two buses, followed by several cars, rolled up the graveled drive and avenue of oaks. Rachel observed from the upstairs sitting room window ensconced with a book, her crochet, and an apple. She patted the paper in her pocket. Today would be a great day to make her phone call while everyone was busy or away.

Families with children and strollers piled out of the cars and strolled across the lawn to the garden and the row of old slave cabins.

When the tours began downstairs, she dialed the number Ron gave her. *Dear God, please let someone answer.*

On the seventh ring, someone picked up the receiver but didn't speak. A noise in the background clued her in she had a connection.

"Hello? Hello? Please don't hang up. Please." Her voice almost broke. This might be her only chance to contact Ron's partner. They would change the number.

"I'm Rachel York—Ron York's sister. Ron gave me permission to call before he was…lost. And I've tried it several times."

"I have no idea what you're talking about lady— must of got the wrong number." A man's disinterested

135

voice spoke to her.

"Wait, please! I've come so far! I'm here in Charleston—at Barrett Hall." Her voice broke.

"You're where?" The tone of the man changed.

"At Barrett Hall," Rachel repeated with relief. What triggered the interest?

"Hold on."

She heard muffled voices, then the same man spoke again.

"Miss York—if you are Miss York—what are you doing at Barrett Hall?"

"I'm teaching Luke Barrett's daughter for the summer. It's a long story—but I'll be glad to share it with Ron's former partner. Were you Ron's partner?" Hope rose in her heart.

"Don't know a Ron."

"You people have passwords or something, but Ron only gave me this number. Can't you ask me something—to verify who I am?"

"Why should I?"

"To make sure I'm Ron's sister—and because I want to meet Ron's last partner so much."

Silence.

"Please!" Rachel held her breath. If the man were going to hang up, he'd do so now. Tears of disappointment formed in her eyes.

Father, don't let my trip and all my prayers come to nothing.

Muffled voices again. The man spoke, this time without hesitation.

"Tell me Ron's middle name—and spell it."

Rachel smiled and flicked away a tear. "Flanoie, F-l-a-n-o-i-e." Ron hated the name. Refused to write it out even for records. He was Ron F. York to everyone but family.

Silence.

"Hello?" Rachel's fingers tightened around the receiver.

"What was your final high school grade point average, Miss York."

Now tears dropped like rain. Ron had always been proud of her grades, but she never dreamed he would brag about them to anyone. She swallowed the huge lump in her throat. "97.7."

"Okay, Miss York," the voice said more softly, "what can I do for you?"

"It's asking a lot—but could we meet—just for a few minutes somewhere?"

"There's nothing else I can tell you about Ron. They would've told you and your stepfather all there was."

"I understand, but—I would love to meet the last person who shared a part of Ron's life. It would mean so much."

A small silence.

"Sunday afternoon at three o'clock at the new Charleston Museum."

Rachel's heart danced. "How will I know you?"

"I'll recognize you."

Chapter Thirteen

Sunday morning Rachel rose early and dressed for church. She decided to visit Redemption Hope Church and have lunch somewhere nearby before her appointment at the Charleston Museum. She chose a khaki skirt, pink shell and beige pumps. She sped on her way into Charleston at nine-thirty in the car Luke put at her disposal.

From Highway 17 South, she took the King Street exit. A couple of blocks further, the church appeared on the right. She pulled into the side parking lot early, and a momentary qualm gripped her. Was it safe to leave Luke's car parked there? Few other cars were evident. Soon, a young man with a yellow Parking Attendant band across his shoulder came up to her window. She lowered the glass.

"Hello, ma'am. Nice wheels. We sure are glad you're visiting our service. Don't worry about your car. Redemption has an attendant out here the whole time. I'm it today."

She walked in the front door of the storefront church. A middle-aged couple greeted her warmly and gave her a bulletin. "Help yourself to coffee and rolls if you're interested." The woman gestured to a coffee urn and a counter piled high with baked goods

"Thank you, but I'm fine."

Rachel sat near the back of the small auditorium

and glanced around. A Plexiglas lectern stood in the middle of the pulpit area and a keyboard, drums, and other instruments flanked the left side. The church began to fill with couples, singles, young people, and families. A familiar figure came toward her with a big grin and outstretched hand. Cade Gant attended this church?

"Well, hello there, Miss York."

Rachel shook hands and smiled. "Oh, hello, Cade, and please call me Rachel. Is this your church?" The big man stood out in a gray suit, white shirt, and yellow tie.

"I'm happy to say it is. Found it right after it started and been coming ever since. We are pleased you came to visit, Miss Rachel."

"Thank you, Cade." He moved to stand at the back door, his hands crossed in front of him.

The musicians took their places and a tall man with runaway brown hair and Levis strode to the lectern.

"Hello to all of you and welcome to our service. I'm Gordon Cushwell, the pastor, the last time I checked." Several people chuckled. "We appreciate your coming this morning. If this is your first visit, please do make yourself at home. We don't stand on formality here." He glanced Rachel's way before he led in the opening prayer.

The music began and the strong voices singing with confidence delighted Rachel. She soon joined in.

As the pastor stood to begin his message, a pretty, young pregnant woman, out of breath, entered and sat beside Rachel. She boasted a smooth blond ponytail tied with a ribbon matching the maternity top. Rachel gave her a warm smile.

The minister preached a stirring sermon on the power of prayer. Pastor Cushwell concluded his sermon with an invitation for anyone needing prayer to come to the altar. The girl beside Rachel went forward and later returned to her seat, wiping her eyes with the back of her hand. Something about her wrenched Rachel's heart.

Am I sensing a real need here, Lord?

"Is this your first visit?" the young woman asked Rachel after the benediction.

"Yes."

"Well, I'm Ava Jenkins, and I love this church."

"Rachel York, and I'm in Charleston for the summer."

They both stood and moved toward the door.

"I hate I was late, but the lady I usually ride with was out of town and I forgot to call the church office, so I had to walk. But I guess exercise is good for me and the baby." She patted her large stomach.

At the front door, Rachel stopped to meet and shake the pastor's hand. He was as tall as Luke.

"We were delighted to have you visit, Miss York. Hope you'll be back." His amber eyes exuded warmth. He turned to the woman beside Rachel. "And I see you've met our Ava."

"Thank you, and yes. I hope I've made a new friend."

The two walked out to the front sidewalk.

"Did you really mean that—about being friends?" Ava cocked her head at Rachel and widened her large green eyes.

"Of course." Rachel smiled encouragement.

"Well, I sure need a friend, believe me. But you probably don't have time to hear about it, and I've got a long walk back to the apartment." She squinted at the noonday sun and turned to go. A bus pulled out of the parking lot. Cade sat in the driver's seat, and he waved at them.

"Wait." Rachel checked her wristwatch. She had three hours to get to the museum. "Can I give you a lift? I'm not sure about my way around Charleston, but the car has a global positioning system."

"I'd love a ride. I really don't relish walking, hot as it is now, and I can't bare the crowd on Cade's bus now I'm past seven months."

Rachel led Ava to the parking lot. The young woman gasped when they stopped beside Luke's luxury automobile.

Rachel laughed. "Don't even go there. It belongs to my employer." Rachel opened the door and Ava got in on the passenger side.

As soon as they snapped their seatbelts, Ava turned wide eyes on Rachel. "What kind of work do you do?"

"It's kind of a glorified babysitting and teaching job for the summer."

"Oh, I get it. You're nanny for some rich folks."

"Something like that."

"I live about four blocks away." The girl pointed down the street. "My baby's daddy is wealthy."

Rachel turned to glance at the attractive face of her passenger. "Really?"

"Yeah, he said he owned a plantation somewhere, but he broke up with me when I wouldn't agree to an abortion. But I can say this about him. He does send money real regular, and he says he'll pay for the hospital and stuff."

Sensing the great heartbreak shared with her,

Rachel searched for something kind to say.

"Ava, would you like to have a sandwich somewhere? I won't need to be at an appointment until three o'clock. So there's time."

"Sure. Sounds great. I love Wendy's and there's one right up this next street."

The joy in the young woman's voice blessed Rachel but also twisted her heartstrings.

Lord, help me never forget how easy it is to bring a little happiness into someone's life.

"This is on me," Rachel told Ava, as they stood in line. "Get anything you want."

They both ordered chili and a salad. Ava added a hamburger and baked potato and grinned. "Eating for two, you understand."

Over lunch Ava shared how she'd met her baby's father while waitressing at an upscale restaurant, her first job after high school. He swept her off her feet and swamped her with expensive gifts and exciting dates. Until she got pregnant.

Later, in the car, she confessed, "I can't imagine what I'd done if I'd never found Redemption Church. The people wrapped their arms around me and my baby. They reached out to me on one of their Saturday ministries. I came to church the next day, gave my heart to the Lord Jesus Christ and here I am." She patted her thick waist. "Here *we* are, I should say. Pastor Cushwell said God loves me and my baby, and everybody's happy I wouldn't go for that abortion."

Questions loomed in Rachel's mind. What about her family? Her parents?

Ava gazed out the window. "My place is in the next block." She soon pointed to an apartment building. "That's where I live."

Rachel pulled over to the curb. "Ava, I'm happy we met. I plan to visit Redemption again, probably next Sunday and I'm going to save a seat for you if I get there early."

"Gee, that's great and thanks so much for everything today." She started to heave herself out of the car, but hesitated. Sadness shadowed her face." You work for rich folks, you said. So you probably get to meet other rich folks sometimes who come to visit. If you ever meet a guy..." Ava's voice cracked and she blinked. "He's a little bit older than me—by the name of Daniel Barrett, tell him..." Her voice broke. "Oh, never mind. Tell him nothing." She ducked her head, left the car, and trudged up the walk. At the apartment door, she turned and waved.

Rachel pulled back into the road and drove three blocks before she realized she had no idea where she was going.

Did Luke have a cousin named Daniel? Or was there another Barrett family who owned a plantation?

Rachel shook her head to clear alarm bells ringing in her ears and pulled into the nearest side street. Forcing her mind on the map, she found her route and prayed before heading in the right direction.

Lord, please bless Ava and her baby. You meant for me to get to know her, become her friend, but what she has shared has really set my mind in a whirlwind. Help me get settled and ready to meet Ron's partner.

Rachel arrived at the museum twenty minutes early. She lingered at the entrance and stared up at the mammoth skeleton of an Atlantic Right Whale. The huge rib cage brought reality to the story of Jonah.

"This animal is perfectly capable of swallowing a wisp of a thing like you whole."

Rachel gasped. A tough, middle-aged man with shaggy hair and large sunglasses stood beside her. She recognized the voice on the phone, but was surprised to see a DEA agent dressed in faded denims, a motorcycle tee and sandals. He took her elbow and continued to talk as if they'd been carrying on a conversation.

"But come, Miss York, I want to show you the amazing Research room. There are all sorts of documents available to researchers."

They walked down the hall into large room filled with shelves. He grabbed a thick leather-bound book at random and led her to a corner table.

Rachel smiled. He played like a character in a mystery drama and she determined to act out her part.

"You can call me Joseph. But it's not my real name. And you mustn't share this meeting with anyone. Understood?" He opened the tome and pretended to read something.

"Yes."

In a low voice he began to talk about Ron, to repeat what she already knew—Ron's assignment somewhere in South America, his flight home to Charleston and his plane sabotaged and exploding over the Atlantic.

She studied Joseph as he talked and tried to arouse a kinship with him, a last connection, somehow with Ron, but she failed to get past his wharf bum disguise. Had Ron dressed the same?

She'd expected too much.

"Tell me about Barrett Hall. You say you're a nanny at the plantation for the summer?"

"Yes, and there's been some strange stuff happening."

The man perked up. "Tell me the sort of things, Miss York."

"A time or two I've been awakened by what I think is the sound of an airplane flying low over the plantation or the beach area." Why didn't she tell him about the previous evening and actually spying a plane in the water? Was she protecting Luke? "Of course, some of this might be my imagination or a dream." Except last night.

He leaned toward her. "Miss York, there's imagination and bad dreams, and there's also role-playing pushers and fat-cat pirates dressed up like lawyers and businessmen as real as daylight—or moonlight—on almost any continent today. And the drug pirates have found big drug sources, and enlarged their spheres of trafficking and all its attendant crimes and horrors until the whale skeleton out yonder—if it represented them ten years ago—wouldn't be no more than a flea compared to their size today. And lots of folks, even some unexpected ones, are getting swallowed up in the mess and promise of big money."

Rachel's eyes widened at the strange exchange. Did he think she was holding something back?

"The trick, of course," he continued, "is learning how to tell the difference between reality and imagination." He smiled at her. "I am trained to do this, by the way, so pretty things like you can go on with their lives as unhampered as possible—and not go begging for trouble."

A warning?

"Ron was trained to do this?"

"Yes, and he did it well, believe me." Joseph stood and glanced at the door. "I've got to go." He reached into his pocket. "But here's something you might like to keep. It was a little gift from Ron's, a keepsake, he gave me once."

He handed Rachel a two-inch scripture plaque.

"Oh, thank you, but we received so many of Ron's things. You may keep this, if you like."

"Na-ah, never actually understood what it meant. Ron kept it on his nightstand. He gave it to me before his...last assignment."

Rachel turned the small piece around. It read: I am the resurrection and the life; he that believeth in me, though he were dead, yet shall he live (John 11:25).

Tears blurred Rachel's eyes. Suddenly, she understood why she couldn't connect Joseph with Ron and why the man couldn't comprehend the text. Joseph probably was not a Christian.

Well, she would share the good news with him, like Ron surely tried to do. Would Joseph listen? She reached for a Kleenex in her handbag, dabbed at her eyes and nose, and looked up.

Joseph had disappeared.

"I am almost sure I saw Rachel head into the Research Room." Morgan Pennington appeared in the doorway, followed by Luke.

Chapter Fourteen

"Well, Rachel, how nice to have you visiting our museum." Morgan looked stunning in a blue and white outfit. But Rachel's attention riveted to Luke and the frown frozen on his face. He turned and stared down the corridor. Had they seen Joseph?

Somehow, Rachel managed to make the appropriate small talk with them as she slipped the plaque into her purse and replaced the volume on the shelf. When she left the Research Room and headed toward the front entrance, her head was splitting and her shoulders tight.

She drove back to Barrett Hall swallowing lumps of disappointment over her meeting with Ron's partner. The image of Luke and Morgan together in the museum interjected into her thoughts. She recalled his terse "forget them" a few nights earlier on the ship's upper deck. Empty words.

After dinner that evening with Jessica, Rachel went to her room early. She pulled Ron's plaque from her pocket and laid it on the nightstand.

Sitting up in the four-poster, she read the plaque again. Why did it bring her little peace? How could she talk to Joseph or to anyone about God when she still had a question heavy on her heart relating to Ron's death?

Finally, she laid the miniature piece down, and got

up and walked to the wardrobe. From the top shelf, she took down her Bible. With shame, she realized how seldom she'd opened it since her first night at Barrett Hall.

She turned to John 11. She read the familiar story of the two sisters, Mary and Martha, whose brother Lazarus became deathly ill. For the first time she experienced the agony of the siblings waiting for their friend Jesus to arrive. Why didn't he come when they sent for him?

Suddenly, the sisters' loss became Rachel's. She wept. Martha's words escaped out of Rachel's lips. "Sir, if you had been here, my brother wouldn't have died."

Rachel realized she'd wanted to speak this, or something similar, for two months. Words she dared not say, because they carried with them accusation. But now, as she studied them from Martha's lips, she thought she understood what Jesus must have gleaned, what God must always see in the grief-stricken "Why God?" pleas of his children. An expression of faith in who He is.

Why God? I have to ask You why because I know who You are and that You could have prevented this, had You so chosen. That's why I've come with my question which sounds like an accusation. I believe You did not want Ron to die, any more than You wanted Lazarus to die. I know You are working some good out of whatever happened to Ron. I choose to trust Your heart.

A load lifted from Rachel's mind. She pored across the passage once more to read Jesus' response to Martha's accusation. The promise reverberated through her spirit as never before.

I am the resurrection and the life; he that believeth in me, though he were dead, yet shall he live.

She fell into a deep, peaceful sleep.

The following week flew by with Rachel teaching Kristina her letters and numbers each morning. The child made excellent progress and now counted and wrote to one hundred, and printed all but a few letters of the alphabet well. She also read beginner books with limited vocabulary and comprehended what she read.

On Thursday afternoon after Kristina's nap, Rachel made good her promise to the child of a horseback ride with her birthday pony. Dakota saddled a horse for Rachel.

The two of them ended up on a narrow path to a shack across the river Kristina insisted on visiting. "This is where Granny Eller lives. She has good-smelling flowers."

The elderly black woman, who wore sachets pinned to her skirt, stood and smiled broadly when she saw them approach her porch. She invited them to her garden and helped Kristina quickly make up a bouquet. She called out the names of the blossoms and stems. "Ambrosia, lavender, borage, ginseng, curled mint, chamomile, and gray horehound." She rattled off some herb uses—chamomile for tea, mint for flavoring, horehound for cough medicine, ginseng for long life, and lavender for sachets.

"Pinch off a leaf right here, rub, and smell." The wizened hand pointed toward a large stem with purple flowers. "And when you get back, tell my daughter Maggie I need a few groceries."

Maggie was her daughter? Rachel squeezed the leaf between her fingers and the crisp fragrance of sage tickled her nose. She thought of turkey dressing Ruby flavored with the herb.

Rachel and Kristina mounted and began the trip back toward Barrett Hall as dark clouds and thunder rolled above them. They made it into the house before the sky split in a downpour.

Later, they found Maggie in the kitchen with Cade having a cup of coffee. Rachel relayed Granny's message. She did not miss the eye contact that passed between the cook and Luke's sidekick.

She helped the child arrange the herbs in a vase. "Where would you like to place this wonderful arrangement, Kristina?"

"I'll show you."

Rachel followed the child to the game room.

"Put them here, so Daddy'll be in a good mood when he comes home tired tonight."

They placed the bouquet on the corner of Luke's desk.

Luke did not appear for dinner. Rachel sat in the small alcove off the drawing room, reading, after tucking Kristina in bed. The patio door slammed about nine o'clock and she recognized Luke's heavy tread toward the game room. She closed her book and prepared to go upstairs to her room.

Suddenly, Luke passed her door carrying the vase of herbs. He backed up and stood in the entrance staring at her. Dirt lined his frowning face and his shirt clung to his body with damp stains.

"Do you have any idea where this came from?" His voice grated from between tight lips.

"From Kristina. We visited Granny Eller's today on our horseback ride, and Kristina begged a bouquet." Rachel's brow rose.

"I don't want this, and I never need anything

from that woman's yard. Her place is off limits for my daughter."

Rachel's hand flew to her lips.

"You had no way of knowing this, Rachel." His voice came down a notch. "Some things have gone down in the past I don't care to discuss. Surely, you realized she's practicing root doctoring, and I ask you to keep Kristina away from her place in the future."

"All right."

He strode out the front door. He returned with the vase, minus the herbs, and without a glance in Rachel's direction, headed toward the Game Room. His heavy steps echoed in the quiet house.

What was that about? Rachel went up to her room, determined to find out.

Chapter Fifteen

The next afternoon, after Kristina went for her nap, Rachel asked Jessica about Granny Eller.

Jessica lifted her brows. "So you've met Granny Eller?"

"Kristina and I dropped by her house yesterday while horseback riding. And I wondered about her since she said she was Maggie's mother."

The older woman took a deep breath. "I don't have the whole story but Charles and Luke ordered her off the place after she kept practicing her root doctoring. I understand she had a stream of folks coming and going neither of them approved of. They warned her and gave her ample time to change her ways, but she wouldn't give it up."

"So she's on the Pennington's property now?"

"I believe she is. Not far across the river that separates the two plantations. And, actually, I'm glad she's close enough for Maggie to keep an eye on her. But Granny can be one stubborn little woman, I understand."

Later, Rachel walked to the barn to give a carrot to "her" mare. She ran into Cade unsaddling the buckskin he usually rode. His tan work shirt clung to his thick torso with perspiration. He smiled, pushed his hat back, and mopped his brow with a red and yellow bandana. "Hello, Miss York." His deep voice reminded her of a baritone in the choir at home.

"Please, call me Rachel."

"Okay."

"I am really enjoying my summer at Barrett Hall." She hesitated, wanting to bring up the subject of Granny Eller.

"I'm glad to hear it." He finished untying the girth, lifted the saddle, and placed it on its stand.

"Cade, can you tell me what you know of Granny Eller? Is she really practicing some bad stuff or is it bad blood between her and...Luke?"

Cade studied her before replying. "I'm thinking it's a little of both. She's probably been a bad influence on some of the folk, undermined their faith. And Captain Luke— that's a whole *nuther* story and I only have part of it. It happened before I came. But I understand when he was home on leave, he and Mr. Charles gave her an ultimatum to give up the root doctoring or move off the plantation. She threatened to put curses on both of them." He removed the saddle blanket from the horse's back and began to wipe him down. "I don't believe in her pronouncements, but there are a few folks who do. That's why Luke doesn't like to hear anything about Granny."

"I think I understand. Thank you for sharing, Cade."

He started to lead the horse to its stall, but stopped and turned. "Oh, Miss York, Rachel, can I tell you it's good to have you here?"

"Why, thank you, Cade."

She walked back to the house. How long ago were these curses spoken? Did Luke connect them to his war wound or to his wife's death? She shuddered.

~*~

Friday, after Kristina's grandparents picked her up for the weekend and Jessica went upstairs, Rachel sat in the kitchen alone, with a cup of tea and a plate of fresh scones. She split and buttered one and spread some of Maggie's blueberry jam on it.

As she polished off her second one, Luke strode in from the farm. He pulled off his cowboy hat and hung it on the back of a chair. "I thought I smelled something mighty good in here. Mind if I join you?"

Why did her nerves suddenly sizzle and her heart start pounding? She did her best to sound nonchalant. "Not at all."

Luke headed to the washing alcove off the kitchen.

Rachel took down another cup, saucer, and small plate while Luke washed up. Was this going to be more talk related to Granny Eller or another warning to keep her nose out of whatever criminal activity was taking place on the beach? Luke had never said anything else after the night he confronted her. That, in itself, was strange.

Luke took a seat at the table, reached for a scone, and added apple butter before he wolfed it down in two bites.

Rachel eased back into her chair and studied him as more scones disappeared. She and her aunt had enjoyed seeing Ron eat hearty the same way.

With his freshly washed face, he didn't appear as tired as he often did in the evenings. He had apparently splashed water on his head and his short black hair glistened. The short sleeves of his army shirt, with their additional roll up, displayed tanned biceps.

After making quick work of the rest of the scones,

and two cups of tea, he swiped his mouth with a napkin and regarded her. "You got any plans for the next hour or so?" He adjusted the eye patch while he spoke.

Rachel's heart did a flip-flop. She stood and moved her cup and plate to the sink, averting her face. "No, I can't say I do."

"I want to show you something."

She glanced down at her Bermuda shorts and tennis shoes and fingered the thick braid at the back of her neck. "Do I need to change or get a scarf?"

His glance flickered over her, making her forget to breathe. "Nope, you'll do fine."

Soon they were in the jeep and heading out of the plantation the route she and Kristina traveled on horseback. Luke turned south onto a dirt road Rachel had not noticed before. The sun was still bright but low in the sky as they drove past fields, pecan orchards and, finally, open areas and marshes. Rachel stole a glance at the man beside her handling the steering wheel with one hand, his other on the gear stick between them. A thick dust cloud followed in their wake, but the air over the windshield smelled clean and refreshing. Luke drove silently and a little fast. Once, he glanced over at her and smiled. Was this the happy Luke she'd never met?

Rachel's mood lifted and warmed her. Perhaps, she told herself, this is the real man minus his masks. To hide her bubbly insides, she turned to gaze at the isolated landscape flying by her open window. Seven hundred acres would take a long time to comprehend, but she was getting an idea. Once or twice, over a rise, she caught a glimpse of the Atlantic to their left.

Luke turned on a narrow, sandy road. The tires

screeched and dust billowed behind them. Soon the jeep braked to a standstill at a seawall of sand and small shrubs. He jumped out and bounced around to open her door.

"Here we are, almost. We need to hike a little."

His fast walk and smiles cast back at her betrayed his enthusiasm. She followed as best she could over the thick grasses and dunes. Why had he brought her to this deserted beach? The sound of the surf assured her they were close to the water. Luke headed toward the incline. He stopped so abruptly at the top she almost collided with him. He turned up a narrow path.

Luke stood in an open corridor and stared out to sea. She came beside him and followed his gaze. A rock formation jutted out from the land, forming a peninsula. A wide white sand beach stretched before them to the swelling ocean beyond. The beautiful scene took her breath away.

Luke continued to stare without speaking.

"Why are we here?" she finally asked, hoping to get a clue of what was on his mind.

"I'm thinking of all the coast lines I've visited but this one is still my favorite."

She inspected the incoming tide, churning its silver froth against the rock formation. "It is striking."

He turned to her. Meeting his glance did strange things to her heart, and she searched for something to say. "Do you think pirates ever visited here and buried treasure? It's secluded enough."

"It's possible," Luke replied. He stooped down and scooped up a fistful of white sand. "But this is probably the only real gold here." His face shone as he let it sift through his strong fingers with a boyish grin.

"What do you mean?"

He stood up, still smiling, brushed away the crystal grains, and held out his hand. "Come with me."

She placed her hand in his and a tremor traveled up her arm. What was he so enthusiastic about? She much preferred this new outlook to his former brooding one.

He led her through protruding rocks and bushes to the edge of the sea. "Take a good look at this beach."

A soft breeze loosened strands around Rachel's face. She brushed them aside and gazed at the postcard seascape, and, for a moment, it all seemed like a dream. A wide shoreline with a rock formation at one side stretched before them. The sun slipping toward the horizon, painted the seashore in pink and gold. "It is so special, it makes me understand what a loving God we have."

He let go of her hand and walked away. He bent and picked up a small piece of driftwood. He examined it and stuck it in his pocket, reminding her of his woodcarving hobby. Was this an opportunity for another kind of whittling? "You don't think He's a loving God, Luke?"

He turned to gaze directly at her. "You insist on having this conversation?" When she didn't reply, he turned back toward the sea. "Sure, God so loved the world, learned it in Sunday school, but He has a little trouble taking care of His children. I would think that might have occurred to you at one time or another." He glanced back at her.

"You're referring to the loss of my parents and...my brother. I can't say I never thought it. But, with some help from a pastor friend I began to see it differently."

"How different?"

"Well, for one thing, I learned I wasn't the only one who ever lost a loved one. The world is full of people, good people, suffering as much as I was and many a whole lot more."

"Translate—I should be glad I kept one eye, didn't die like my wife died, and I still have our child?"

She stared at him, and realized she'd not noticed his eye patch the whole afternoon. She thought of a high school friend who come back from the Middle East totally blind and absent an arm, but who brought light into every room he entered.

Are you ready for this, Luke Barrett?

"That's a good starting place. But what I am getting at is we live in a sick, fouled up world and evil and wicked people are real. All we need to do is read the newspaper to believe it. And being a Christian doesn't make us exempt. Christians are still martyred for their faith all over the world. The question is, 'Why *shouldn't* bad things happen to me?' not 'Why should they?' They come to most everyone."

Luke interrupted, his voice laced with anger. "But why should they hit anyone? If God is so powerful and loving, why does he allow evil to succeed? Why doesn't he stop it instead of sitting on his throne while the terrible things happen?"

Rachel stamped her foot in the sand. "Whoa, we can't blame God for the shape we've gotten our world into by doing our own thing. We're the ones who've made the mess. He created everything so perfect, we're still uncovering the treasures—like this." She waved her hand over the beach bathed in all the colors of sunset.

"I didn't bring you out here to preach."

Oops. End of opportunity. "I'm sorry. Why did

you show me this place?"

Luke moved up the path, and shook his head as if to clear his mind. He gestured toward the shoreline. "I think a well-planned beach resort in the middle of this 'treasure' could be a gold mine." He turned back to her, a strange vulnerability in his face. "What do you think?"

Was this why he brought her here? To share a dream? Pleasure rose so fast inside, she felt giddy. "Wouldn't it cost a lot of money to build?"

"Yep, more than I've got hanging loose right now, but, there are ways and means, and I've thought about it—even come up with a name, "Kingdom by the Sea." His voice had regained its boyish excitement, and he waited for her response. He bent to pick up a shell.

It was many and many a year ago, in a kingdom by the sea. Poe's poem in his wife's diary.

"You don't believe it's a good idea?" He turned to face her. "I don't understand why I'm sharing this with you. I guess it's because I drive by this place all the time and want an honest opinion from a visitor." The defenseless look about him, so different from the strong Marine image he usually exuded, did something to Rachel's emotions.

His whole demeanor vibrated along her sensitive nerves. He'd shared a dream with her, even asked her opinion. And he'd at least listened to her "preaching." The precipice with Luke she had seen clearly on the ship's deck, no longer looked frightening. Instead, romantic involvement with him appeared safe and attracted her entire being.

"You haven't answered my question." He pushed the turkey wing shell into his pocket beside the salvaged driftwood.

Question? What question? Surely the words of love bubbling into her mind were not the answer. She forced them away, shocked.

"Do you think this might be a great place for a resort to attract customers year after year, especially those who don't often have a view of the ocean?"

She broke away from his gaze and scanned again the breath-taking area with its rugged backdrop and snowy beach. Seagulls danced and squawked in the blue-green surf. "For whatever my Yankee-who-does-not-often-see-the-ocean opinion is worth, yes, I think it would be." And he could fulfill a dream he had with Georgina.

"One other question, Rachel." Luke folded his arms across his chest. His brusque, military manner settled back on him like armor. "Who was the beach bum, or the guy trying to be one, you met at the museum yesterday?"

Chapter Sixteen

Disappointment filled Rachel's mouth like cotton. His bringing her to this lovely spot, the sharing of his dream resort, and probably even listening to her talk of faith—all had been part of his plan to find out about Joseph. Tears of frustration formed at the back of her eyes, and she turned to walk away. He whipped around and stood in her path.

"Rachel, I've got to know who you're meeting— and why. You're no good at playing games. You're transparent as water. Tell me, please."

She hung onto the pleading note in his voice. Did she dare hope the entire afternoon had not been a pretense?

"I'm not meeting anyone—for any wrong purpose."

"Are you denying you met a guy at the museum yesterday?" The biting words and angry contortion of his face trashed her hopes.

Rachel lowered her head. "I did," she murmured, "but I can't tell you why, other than it was because of—an old friendship."

Luke stared at her, clenched his jaw and stalked back to the jeep. She scrambled to follow.

So much for bubbly, deceiving feelings, boyish smiles, and marvelous ocean views. *Foolish girl*.

When she reached the jeep, he stood holding her

door, his face granite. He did not speak on the way back to the plantation, and she was glad. An electric mixer continued scrambling her insides.

At the plantation, he let her out without killing the motor. She watched the jeep roar down the drive and turn right toward the river. Or the Pennington's?

An hour later, staring in her mirror, Rachel realized what a luxury yacht, harbor lights and romantic music had not been able to accomplish, white sand and boyish grins had almost achieved. Was she falling in love with Luke Barrett?

Well, she would fall right back out, she decided, getting ready for bed. She recognized that thought as one springing from Ruby's common sense approach to life, and she was thankful. After all, it had gotten her through the disappointment with Easton.

When she laid her head on the pillow, the face of Easton Watkins, III, floated into her consciousness. That simple romance and the problems she thought so large at the time, appeared insignificant compared to the war now in her heart. How fast things had changed.

When Rachel finally slept, reality fled, and she dreamed of those long moments with a different Luke on the lovely, rugged beach. She awoke with tears on her face. Before going back to sleep, a chunk of truth flashed into her troubled mind. Luke did need money. Lots of it to build his dream resort. Was drug smuggling part of his 'ways and means?'

The next day, Saturday, brought the tourists. Rachel spent the morning in the upstairs sitting room bay window reading and glancing at the visitors arriving below. Disquieting thoughts bombarded her mind. Could Luke be involved in drug trafficking for extra funds? This would explain his suspicions about her. Did he imagine she might be a secret agent, perhaps for the DEA? Or, was he clean and suspected *she* might be involved in illegal activity? Was she or was he the deceived one?

One reflection pervaded her mind—the different Luke she witnessed as he shared his dream. That side of him did something to her heart.

The next morning, after church service, Rachel shook Pastor Gordon's hand and told him how much she appreciated the message. He thanked her and surprised her with a question.

"Do I understand correctly you are living at Barrett Hall Plantation?"

"Yes, I am, for the summer. I help care for a child there."

"I once knew your neighbor, Morgan Pennington. We went to the same high school." His eyes twinkled. "But she probably doesn't remember me. We didn't run in quite the same crowd."

"O-o-kay." Rachel doubted Morgan had attended the same high school with the tall, good-looking man and never noticed him. Besides, with his height he probably played basketball. Everyone learned the players. Rachel smiled to herself. Had the single pastor been interested in Morgan at one time but found her unattainable? According to Jessica, Morgan married after law school but divorced and took back her maiden name.

The following week passed at a snails' creep for Rachel. She spent the mornings teaching Kristina to read and the afternoons entertaining her after her nap. Sometimes they hiked with Penny and Judge. She had no trouble avoiding Luke. He scarcely appeared for a meal with them. Jessica said he was busy with the summer harvest in full swing.

Whatever kept him away from the house was fine with Rachel. The tension of thinking he might confront her again about Joseph left her fatigued by the end of the week. She also fought a quickening of her pulse every time she remembered the different Luke she'd encountered at the beach.

On Friday morning she turned down Jessica's invitation to drive into Charleston with her and Kristina.

Instead, after breakfast, she chose a quiet corner of the drawing room and curled up in a roomy armchair with Jane Austen's *Persuasion*. Given half a chance, the interesting story would relax and settle her mind. The only sounds came from the basement kitchen where Maggie and Mrs. Busby were beginning lunch preparations for the workers.

She'd been reading for about an hour when someone entered through the patio door and started up the steps to the upper floors. Her heart leaped into her throat. Luke never returned in the middle of the morning, but the heavy tread going up the stairs surely belonged to him.

She lowered her head and concentrated on her book. Hopefully, when he came downstairs he would not glance into the drawing room.

Dakota Busby's voice startled her from the doorway. "Well, hello there. I figured you'd be gone into town with Jessica and Kristina." Dressed in his usual Levis and boots, he stood with his cowboy hat in his hand and grinned at her.

Rachel lowered her book and glanced up at him. "I decided to enjoy a quiet day."

Dakota came into the room. His eyes flickered over her. "You look mighty cozy, curled up in that chair."

Why hadn't she'd donned jeans instead of shorts? She laid her open book across her knees.

Dakota stepped closer and the odor of alcohol assailed her nose. "Why don't you have a quiet evening with me? I have just the place in mind."

"I—don't think so, Dakota, but thanks for asking."

He twirled his hat, still gaping at her. "If you don't like a quiet evening, we can manage any kind you like at the best night spots in Charleston. Bet you haven't even tasted the real Charleston yet."

Rachel squirmed. "Dakota, I'm sorry, but I really can't go."

"Why not?"

Give it up, knucklehead. "I—just can't. I'm sorry."

He shrugged, gave a mock bow, and placed his hat back on his head. "My lady says no but she means maybe later." He grinned and swaggered out the door.

This lady means *never.*

What was it with this man? What did it take to convince him she had no interest in him? In fact, he made her skin crawl. She closed her book and stood, her morning marred.

On Sunday morning, Rachel awoke with a headache and depression as well. She called Ava and told her she wouldn't be at church, but would definitely meet her the following Sabbath.

The plantation, seeped in its weekend quietness, gave her an idea. She took an aspirin with a glass of water, read her Bible, and went to search among her clothing.

She pulled out her yellow two-piece swimsuit, sighing. The summer was almost half-over and she still had no definite teaching offer for September. But at least she'd return to Ohio with a tan.

She avoided sunbathing most days, since so many workers came and went around the plantation, but Sunday was different. The house and surrounding gardens appeared quiet. Jessica and Kristina were in Charleston, and apparently Luke, too. His fancy Italian sports car roared down the drive earlier. Maggie and Mrs. Busby usually retired to their cottages after serving Sabbath breakfast.

Rachel's spirits lifted as she slipped into the bright swimsuit, beach robe, and sunglasses. She met no one as she walked to the patio with a blanket, a bottle of lotion, and a straw hat with Penny following beside her on a leash. She did not allow the young dog to run free outside. Too many things attracted her attention, including two peacocks which roamed the grounds.

For privacy, she avoided the patio and chose a grassy area in the gardens, sunny and secluded with its circle of hedges. As she spread her blanket, Judge trotted up, found a shady spot near Penny, and slumped down. How was that for *two* guard dogs?

She covered her legs and arms with oil, and lay back with her face and neck shaded under the straw hat. The sun warmed her limbs and tension oozed away from her body.

She awoke with a start and the sun hat fell away from her face. A well-worn boot came into focus at the edge of the blanket.

"Gal, you make me think of a ripe daisy waiting for a lucky someone to pluck."

She sat up, disturbed by Dakota Busby's drunken

voice.

He threw his cowboy hat on a bush and plopped down beside her on the blanket. From her shady bed, Penny growled her puppy growl. Judge whined.

Rachel froze but she forced her voice to remain calm. "Dakota, I really need to be getting back to the house, if you don't mind." She reached for her robe and started to get up.

"I do mind, beautiful lady." He slipped his arm around her waist and pulled her toward him.

Chapter Seventeen

"Dakota, let me go." Rachel ground out the words and pushed him away, nauseated by his alcohol-reeking breath.

"You can be a little spitfire when you wanna be, can't you?" He drew his arms tight around her. His foul scent made her stomach roil. Panic rose in her throat.

Father, help me!

Judge began to bark and Penny jumped out of her basket and started dancing around the blanket growling and baring her little teeth. Dakota laughed and swiped at the puppy like she was a gnat.

Rachel managed to free one arm. She slapped him across the face so hard her hand stung. It didn't budge him. His weight now pushed her backward.

Dear God.

Suddenly, she remembered something Ron taught her. She twisted and brought her knee up fast into his groin. He groaned and fell to the side. She scrambled to get up but he recovered and grabbed her around the waist.

"Now you've done it." His voice had a nasty ring to it. He threw his arm across her neck and pressed her back down on the blanket. His disgusting mouth loomed over her face.

"No! You've done it, Busby!"

Luke broke through the hedge, grabbed the surprised farm manager by the collar, and pulled him up to face him. The next second Luke's fist crashed into Dakota's jaw. The man fell sideswiping a shrub and onto the ground. Air swooshed out of his lungs.

"Get out, Busby. You're fired." Luke's breath came in short blasts, his face contorted with rage like Rachel had never witnessed.

Dakota sat up, shaking and gasping for air. He grappled around for his hat, pushed it on his head and stood. He confronted Luke with pure hatred lining his face and shuffled away, cursing.

Luke's thunderous glare turned on Rachel. She trembled like a leaf and fought an urge to burst into tears. Somehow, she managed to reach for her robe and pull it around her shoulders. Penny jumped into her arms. Grateful, Rachel hugged the puppy close.

"Do you have any idea how lucky you are I happened to come home when I did?" Luke spoke through clenched teeth.

She nodded and ducked her head as tears pushed from beneath her lids.

His voice softened. "My God, Rachel, don't ever take risks like this, coming out here on this plantation—in a bathing suit. Look at me. There's always someone around on these grounds."

Rachel turned her face up to him, brushing away a tear.

He came closer. "I don't want anything to happen to you while you're here, do you understand?"

His demeanor was serious, yet so tender, for one crazy second she thought he might reach down and pull her up into his arms.

"But you seem bent on flirting with danger." As

quickly as flipping a coin, his face hardened and his voice turned harsh.

Flirting with Dakota? She gritted her teeth. "I came out her to enjoy a simple, private sunbath," she replied between tight lips.

Luke's only response was to cast a sarcastic glance at her. He turned and crashed through the hedge. Judge followed at his heels.

Rachel took a deep breath, released Penny, and gathered up her things. She stumbled into the house, praying she would not meet any one.

In her room, after she settled the dog down with a chew bone, and changed into Bermuda shorts and a pullover, she stood in front of her mirror and placed cool hands on her hot cheeks, remembering Luke's scornful insinuation.

And Dakota? He was drunk, and she hated even the sound of his name right now. But the thought of Luke firing him on her account made her shoulders slump. The man had been employed at Barrett Hall for no telling how many years. And his mother was the housekeeper.

Later, a soft knock sounded at Rachel's door. She opened it and Jessica came in carrying a lunch tray. A delicious aroma filled the room, but Rachel couldn't imagine eating anything. She told the older woman what had happened and shared how she regretted Dakota losing his job because of her.

"Not to worry, Luke mentioned to me he'd fired Dakota." Jessica clicked her tongue. "I've expected this might come to pass for some time. I think Mrs. Busby may have also. You are not responsible, Rachel. Dakota knew not to bother you, not to mention, his continued drinking on the plantation. And there's been additional things, too."

"But surely Luke needs Dakota right now during all the harvesting. Doesn't he?"

"Yes, he probably does, but don't worry. Luke has plenty of other help and can probably get more if he needs it.

"Now, I'm going to rest and get out of these Sunday clothes. You enjoy your lunch and think nothing more about this." Jessica patted Rachel's hand and slipped out the door.

Feeling some better, Rachel took a few bites of broccoli-stuffed chicken and brown rice. But the thought lingered in the back of her mind. If she had not been out sun bathing, Dakota would still be employed.

The next morning Rachel awoke continuing to think about the firing. If she had taken an aspirin and gone to church, the situation never would have happened. Should she try to talk to Luke about Dakota?

At breakfast, Mrs. Busby's reddened eyes did little to relieve Rachel's thoughts. Even a letter from her aunt informing her of a teaching position offer in the fall did nothing to lift her spirits.

All day, as she worked with Kristina and went about her other activities, gnawing little thoughts attacked her. The plantation had been Dakota's home most of his life. No one would want to be involved in severing that kind of relationship. Certainly, he gave her quite a fright, and she preferred never laying eyes on him again. But didn't Luke need him at the height of the harvest season? Her mind went around in circles.

After putting Kristina down for the evening, Rachel descended to the drawing room. The patio screen door slammed and Luke's heavy tread crossed to the game room. Rachel hurried across the loggia and knocked on the door.

"Come in."

Luke sat behind his desk, as tired and dusty as she'd ever seen him. He held the phone in his hand. Placing it back in its cradle, he motioned for her to sit.

She sat on the edge of the leather chair and took a deep breath. "I've been thinking all day about Dakota losing his job."

Luke's eye flashed, his voice turned hard. "Well quit mulling over it. He got what he deserved along with three month's severance pay he didn't deserve."

Severance pay. Did Luke share second thoughts about the firing, too? "But isn't there a lot of work to do on the plantation right now?"

Luke's lip curled. "Dakota has been shirking his work for some time, and, for your information, he had gotten to the point he took a drink on the job almost daily."

"Oh."

Luke frowned at her. "If you think I fired him only because of yesterday, forget it."

Was that comfort or mockery in his voice? Heat rose in Rachel's cheeks. She stood and walked to the door. His voice stopped her.

"Miss York—Rachel, my young'un's going to need some school clothes. It's almost too much for Jessica to make it around the shops with her now. Would you like to take her shopping and help choose her wardrobe?"

Rachel's mouth curved into a smile. "Yes, of course. We could go tomorrow, in fact." Who wouldn't love a shopping spree of any kind in Charleston?

"Good. Jessica will tell you the shops we use, and I'll give them a call to place your selections on our account." He studied her for a long moment. "You may even take the sports car, if you're interested."

Excitement flowed through Rachel. How she'd love to drive that baby, but could she handle the car? "I—I'm not sure I know how to drive it."

"Nothing to it. I'll show you."

Rachel walked to her room, amazed at the change in Luke. He'd been angry with her the day before and at the beach earlier when she refused to tell him why she'd met Joseph at the museum. Had he accepted her explanation of an old friendship? And did he really not blame her for the situation with Dakota?

The biggest marvel, though, was Luke asking her to select Kristina's clothing and offering his personal car. She fell asleep thinking about the clothes and supplies a child needed to begin school and wondered if she would be able to drive the beautiful blue automobile.

The following morning, she and Kristina stood in the drive as Luke backed the sleek car out of the garage. Rachel's throat went dry. Luke got out and held the door for her to sit in the driver's position. The smell of leather, the gearshift in the floor and the many controls on the shiny dash overloaded her senses. Was she really going to drive this vehicle? Thank God, she knew how to change gears. Ron had taught her the year before.

Kristina bounced like a ball into her car seat behind Rachel. Luke leaned in close and explained the panel of knobs and gave other instructions for the car. Rachel forced herself to ignore the tangy scent of his aftershave and her racing heart and listen. Finally, he shut the door.

Rachel drove slowly down the driveway, trying to remember all his instructions.

Luke stood a moment gazing after them, and walked toward the barn.

To Rachel's surprise, the Italian sports car handled easily and not so differently from Ron's American sports car still sitting in their garage at home.

On the freeway into Charleston Kristina pointed out a restaurant ad on a billboard.

"Let's buy our lunch there, Rachel."

"If I can locate the place," she told the excited child.

She enjoyed shopping with Kristina, and by lunchtime was as ready as the little girl to find the restaurant. She piled their packages in the back of the vehicle and, after referring to her map, struck out in search of Queen's Restaurant. She guessed it to be near the Rainbow Market Jessica recommended she visit one day for fun and flavor.

She finally found the restaurant and a good parking space.

The cool interior of the historic dining house welcomed them. Rachel chose a lovely patio area in which to be seated. They sat in wicker chairs at a round marble-topped table surrounded by potted green plants and placed their order. The Charleston She-Crab Soup was to die for. Kristina ate all her shrimp and grits to Rachel's surprise.

"Can we go to the Rainbow Market, please, just for a little while?" Kristina asked as she finally dug into her dessert.

Rachel turned to the young waitress refilling their glasses with tea. "Is the Rainbow Market nearby?"

"Oh, yes, ma'am. It's only a short walk back down Meeting Street to the Confederate Museum."

Rachel paid for their lunch, and they walked a couple of blocks to the famous rows of shops and vendors filling the area behind the museum. Slaves were once bought and sold on the site, a sign informed. The heat, coupled with the glare of the sun, affected Rachel. She drew Kristina into the shady corridor. Other visitors made the same move.

They joined the throng of shoppers. Feeling a strange lethargy, Rachel stopped at one shop and gazed at the display, scarcely noting Kristina's exclamations over the stuffed animals behind the glass.

Rachel caught a reflection in the window. Shock riveted down her spine. Whirling around, she scanned the crowd up and down the corridor. But the reflected image had vanished. She blinked and shook her head. The face, though bearded, bore a stunning resemblance to her brother Ron.

Kristina tugged at her hand. "Why did you turn around so fast?"

She peered down at the child, smiled, and forced her voice to sound normal. "Oh, I thought I saw someone I knew. Do you want to go in and find a stuffed animal to add to your collection?"

The little girl's face lit up like a sunrise, and she pulled Rachel through the entrance.

Kristina flew from one bin to the next one examining fluffy animals. Observing her, Rachel tried to regain her equilibrium, shaken from the reflection she'd seen. How could her mind play such tricks?

"Wonder if there's a whale," a male voice whispered at her side.

She turned quickly. "Oh! Joseph!"

He smiled at her exclamation. His eyes searched her face a moment before pretending to scan the nearest bin. "Is everything okay at Barrett Hall?"

"Yes, I guess so." She wanted to blurt out she'd just imagined seeing Ron's reflection in the store window, but Kristina made her choice and headed toward them.

"I'm glad everything's okay. Stay calm, and don't go searching for trouble. She's a cute kid. Bye, now." Joseph turned and walked out the door.

Kristina thrust a soft brown horse into Rachel's arms. "This one. It's like Flicka."

"It's a fine choice. And it does resemble your pony."

Walking to the register, Rachel glanced out the window. Joseph disappeared in the crowd of shoppers in the corridor.

Before they left, Kristina drew Rachel to an ice cream shop across the street.

In its outdoor patio, a potter sat in the shade with an earthen pot on his wheel. The two of them stopped to observe the skillful hands forming a beautiful bowl whirling before him.

Lord, why do I feel like I am twirling faster and faster on Your potter's wheel?

On the way back to Barrett Hall, Kristina fell asleep, leaving Rachel to her thoughts. Whose reflection had she viewed in the window? What made her think it was Ron? He'd never worn a beard.

When they arrived home, Mrs. Busby gave Rachel a message to call Archer. An excited Kristina pulled Jessica upstairs to examine their purchases. Rachel went to the sitting room and returned Archer's call. He invited her to go sailing and dining afterwards on

Saturday afternoon. He assured her there was a beach house where they could change for dinner.

She only had a few weeks left in Charleston. Why not enjoy them? She accepted his invitation, but regretted it the moment she hung up. What was the matter with her?

Jessica met her in the hall, and ordered tea served in the drawing room. Rachel spirits rose. She could get used to this tea thing, she decided, as she surveyed miniature chicken salad sandwiches, apple slices, and chocolate pound cake slices on the small table. The wonderful smell of tea brewing tickled her nose.

Jessica poured. "You've done a beautiful job with Kristina's school clothes, Rachel. I don't know how Luke and I can thank you enough." She handed the platter of goodies to Rachel.

"Oh, I enjoyed shopping with her."

Jessica's eyes glowed. "We are going to miss you when you return home to Ohio."

Munching on an apple wedge, Rachel regarded the older woman. Jessica appeared about to say more but changed her mind.

~*~

Late that evening, Luke came in the kitchen door, removed his hat and eye patch, washed his face and hands in the large pantry sink, and dried off. He slipped the patch back on and smiled. The tea harvest was going right on schedule. Even without Dakota Busby. He started whistling as he entered the kitchen but stopped when he found Jessica sitting at the table with his supper laid out.

"Hey, Jess, you still up?" Luke recognized the firm

set of her lips and her ramrod back. What was on her mind?

She smiled and her face softened. "Thought I'd join you for a few minutes."

He pulled out a chair, said a quick blessing, and dug into the sliced roast beef and dressing with its carrots, potatoes, and green beans on the side.

He was acutely aware of Jessica, still smiling, watching him devour the cooked food, interspersed with chunks of fresh tomato and cantaloupe. "I want to talk to you about Rachel," she finally said.

Luke stopped chewing for two seconds and glanced at her. "She didn't do a good job with Kristina's clothes?"

"Oh, no. She did a beautiful job. Perfect."

Luke reached for a slice of pecan pie and polished it off.

Jessica moved back from the table and crossed her arms. "I want to talk to you about her personally. She's really a nice girl, Luke. Even special."

He wiped his mouth with a napkin. "So?" He took a deep drink of tea and pushed the empty plate away. "Want to come on and say what's on your mind, Jess?" As if he didn't have an idea where she was headed.

"You know exactly what I am getting at." Jessica's blue eyes flashed. "Why are you so bull-headed? Surely, if you have a choice, you don't want to live the rest of your life alone. It may come, like it has for me, but fight it, shove it out as far as you can."

"She's too young for me, Aunt Jess." Among other things.

"Oh, fiddle-de-de. At the age you two are, it doesn't matter a hill of beans. And I discern Archer Pennington certainly isn't letting it hinder him, and he's only a few years younger than you."

"Frankly, I would really hate to see her and Pennington—." Nope, won't go there. "Jess, appreciate you thinking about me, but it's my life, and no one will ever replace what I had before." Luke started to get up, but Jessica's eyes held him, with her jaw set. Like a pit bull.

"Luke, have you really given up?"

She'd not sounded as serious in a long time. He brushed crumbs from the tablecloth, leaned back in his chair and stared at her. Here we go. "On what?"

"On getting married again to a nice girl, and realizing God still has a plan for your life. Perhaps He brought Rachel here this summer. Has that crossed your mind?"

Rachel's conversation at the beach tumbled back into his head.

Jessica's face brightened. "You're remembering something."

"She can almost preach, I found that out."

"Has Rachel spoken to you on spiritual matters, Luke?" Excitement rose in her voice and Luke scowled. This conversation needed to end.

"Yeah, she worked me over about God being a loving God, and I told her, He may be, but He's got a real problem taking care of His children."

Tenderness filled Jessica's face. "Luke, did anything she say sound familiar? Like what I've told you, or the pastor at our little church you used to attend shared with you, and I'm sure what you've discerned in your own heart several times over the last three years?"

Luke drummed his fingers on the table. Things he didn't want to receive.

Jessica got up, came around the table, and laid her hand on his shoulder. He turned and glanced up into the kind face, the one in place of a mother's for many years. Tears gathered in the mature eyes, and something broke loose inside of him as she spoke the words he didn't want to hear again. Only now, somehow, they appeared to carry more authority and liberating power.

"You must forgive God, yourself and everyone else for what's come your way, Luke. The war and your eye, and what happened to Georgina."

Luke swallowed. "That's a big load, Jessica, to throw aside as if none of it ever took place."

"It's exactly why you must cast it away, Luke. It did happen, and you may never understand the whys and ifs, but you mustn't keep carrying it. The bitterness, the anger, will crush you and sabotage all God's plans for a happy future."

Wasn't it trampled already? Luke had to break the seriousness of the moment before it choked him. He cocked his chin. "You're pretty good at preaching yourself. In your old age."

She laughed and pulled a handkerchief from her sleeve and dabbed under her glasses. "Well, remember, the invitation is always there, Luke, when you're ready." She patted his shoulder and left.

Luke found he couldn't stand or move a muscle. Something hovered in the kitchen, a benevolent presence he hadn't discerned since his first stint in the Middle East. It was a wooing, gentle prodding he recognized. But he wasn't ready to yield. He stood and gently lifted his chair back into place, as if sound would dishonor that stillness. He walked away, thinking about Rachel.

~*~

The following evening after dinner, Rachel sat in a rocker on the front porch. The song of crickets filled the air. She gazed out over the garden encased in rosy shadows—a long southern sunset in progress. Soon she would be leaving for Ohio and home. How different and far away that now seemed. A terrible sadness seized her. She leaned her head back in the chair and closed her eyes.

Ron, I've grown to love your southern city. I'm not sure I want to go home.

"A penny, a dime, a quarter, for your thoughts."

Rachel jerked her head up and opened her eyes. Luke, his brows raised, stood at the bottom of the steps.

He took them two at a time and sat down in a rocker next to her. Her heart began silly cartwheels. She noted the fresh blue shirt and clean shine of his face and hair. And his manly scent that seemed so right. Where had he been at dinner? She and Jessica ate alone.

"You're still not worrying about Busby, I hope."

Rachel shook her head and forced a happier expression on her face. How long had he observed her?

"I want to thank you for taking the load off Jessica with Kristina's shopping. Jess said you did a fine job. I owe you for a lunch and one stuffed pony."

"No, you don't. I enjoyed every minute with Kristina." The unsettling reflection she'd glanced in the store window flashed back across her mind. Well, almost each moment.

Luke regarded her for a second. "Whether I do or

not, would you have dinner with me and catch a play at the Dock Street Theater?"

Rachel's eyes flew to his face. No charade there, only his steady gaze, stopping her heart in her throat. She must decline. "I—

"No one should come to Charleston without dining at the Old Colony and enjoying a drama at historic Dock Street."

Why not? He simply sought a way to thank her. It would not be like a real date. He was, after all, heavily involved with, if not on the verge of becoming engaged to, Morgan Pennington.

"All right. I'd love to go."

"Friday, 5:30?"

"Yes. I'll be ready."

Luke grinned and made a big deal swatting his arms. "Are you getting eaten up by mosquitoes? Or do they prefer southerners?"

The corners of her mouth quirked up. "Possibly, they're not bothering me."

He threw up his hands in mock surrender, stood, and strode away.

Chapter Eighteen

When Friday evening arrived, Rachel pulled her black crepe de chine skirt with its fitted white lace over blouse out of the closet and laid the garments across the bed.

After a warm bath and shampoo, she brushed her hair up into a simple chignon and secured it with a pearl comb. She applied her makeup, donned the skirt and lace top, and fastened her pearl earrings. At five-thirty she slipped into black satin heels and started down the stairs.

Her heart lurched when she caught a glimpse of Luke at the bottom of the steps. He lifted his head toward her. His tanned face burst into a smile. In a white dinner jacket and black silk trousers, and more handsome than ever, he appeared ready to say something, but shook his head instead and gave a low whistle. Still grinning, he took her elbow and steered her down the hall toward the drawing room.

"And hello to you too." she said softly, letting him guide her.

Jessica gasped as they came toward her. "My goodness, you two appear like models stepping off the page of a magazine ad—matched. Rachel, that hairdo makes you quite sophisticated."

Rachel flashed the elderly woman a smile.

Luke walked to the cocktail table, picked up a

square florist box, and handed it to Rachel.

Through the cellophane cover Rachel glimpsed a corsage of white rosebuds and violets. She lifted it out and smelled the sweet fragrance. "Oh, thank you. It's lovely."

Jessica came forward. "Want help pinning it on?"

"Yes, definitely, thank you."

Jessica finished attaching the flower to Rachel's shoulder and stepped back. She inspected both of them. "You two are so beautiful I may cry." She turned her face away and pulled her handkerchief from her sleeve. "Have a good time," she called after them as they walked toward the door.

Sorry, Jessica, but we are not a twosome.

Going down the drive in the sports car, Luke glanced at Rachel. "Jessica's right. You're beautiful, Rachel. Is this the real you? The Yankee girl at her Yankee best?"

Heat brushed her cheeks. Morgan's sophisticated, designer clothes flashed through her mind. "I was not aware northern girls look much different from southern girls dressed up," she finally responded.

"I wasn't either, until tonight."

She slipped a glance at Luke, but the driving drew his attention.

The Colony Restaurant proved to be everything Luke's invitation promised. The designers of the restored waterfront warehouse successfully blended the old and the new. The lower floor boasted models of pirate schooners flying the skull and cross bone flags which once sailed along the Charleston coast. Luke led her upstairs to an English garden under the stars. An orchestra filled a small stage in one corner.

"Your table, Mr. Barrett." The headwaiter in a

crisp white shirt seated them with an excellent view of the waterfront. He placed menus in front of them.

Luke opened his and began scanning the choices.

Rachel stared out at the ships docked in the harbor and listened, enthralled, to the romantic music floating across the tables.

"Would you be comfortable with my ordering for you?"

She turned her attention to Luke and smiled, wondering what surprise dishes he wanted her to try. "I'm game as long as you don't pull escargot on me."

Sternness stiffened Luke's face and voice. "Do you think I'd touch a snail with a ten-foot pole—except to make sure it's slimy life ends before it gets to my plants?"

Perhaps there was hope for him after all. Anyone who agreed with her about snails ought to be called a friend. Rachel grinned at her private thought and exclaimed over each delicious dish brought to their table—broccoli cream soup, crepes Florentine, stuffed flounder with crabmeat and shrimp dressing— Barbados Salad, and Charleston Red Rice. For dessert, Luke suggested she try Chocolate Almond Torte, a Low Country specialty. She should decline, she was getting too full, but who could turn down chocolate anything? She managed to eat half of it.

"It's almost curtain time. We'll go, unless you're thinking of some other dish you would like to try," Luke said with a wry smile.

"I am full to the gills, sir." Rachel touched her napkin to her lips. "Thank you for this unforgettable treat."

Luke paid for their dinner and tipped the waiter who gave him a warm smile as he pocketed the cash.

As they left, Luke reached for her hand. She almost jumped at the shock of his touch.

For the first time she found herself comfortable with him, but in the car he hardly spoke to her. She glanced at him once and was surprised his brows were knit together as if in deep thought.

"Here we are." Luke turned the car off the narrow street and pulled into a lone space that was too small for larger cars in a corner of the parking lot.

"Thank You, Lord." Rachel remarked. She'd have hated walking much distance after their heavy dining and in her high satin heels.

"What?"

"I was…thanking God for the parking space."

He turned toward her a moment and raised his brows before exiting the car and coming around to her door.

Walking toward the front of the Dock Street Theater, Rachel admired its ancient stucco and wrought-iron façade.

"It opened in 1736," Luke told her as they came to the entrance, "and it was the first playhouse built in the United States." He handed her a program and excitement flew through her. *Madame Butterfly,* an opera she had never seen performed live, was the night's offering.

"Like my selection?"

"Oh, yes."

With his black eye patch and white tuxedo, Luke drew a lot of attention when they entered. The people certainly wouldn't be staring at her.

Inside, Rachel drew in her breath and marveled at the old world charm of the sculptured architecture, lighting, and curtains. Luke led her to a reserved box on the upper level. He seated her, and made himself comfortable beside her. He leaned back, propped a knee on the wall of the box and rested his chin on his broad fist. His short black hair glistened, and he retreated into thought, almost frowning.

Was he tired? Or still thinking about something? Or someone?

The next moment the house lights dimmed and the production of the early twentieth century love story between an American service man, U.S. Navy Lieutenant B.F. Pinkerton, and a Japanese girl he marries "for a season" began.

Rachel, too conscious, at first, of Luke's large frame so close to her in the balcony box, soon lost herself in the production and its wonderful music. In the last act when Cio-cio-san, Madame Butterfly, agreed to give up her little son to Pinkerton's new American wife, Kate, and then committed suicide, a small sob escaped Rachel's lips. To her surprise, tears coursed down her cheeks.

Embarrassed as the lights came on, she tried blinking away the wetness and fumbled in her handbag.

Luke's broad hand, proffering a handkerchief, appeared before her swimming eyes. She took his offering and murmured her thanks. Later, he waited for her in the corridor to visit the powder room and repair her face.

He smiled and reached out his hand to her as she emerged. "Not much for sad operas?"

"Oh, no. I enjoyed the production." She accepted his warm handclasp, conscious of envious eyes following them as they passed from the elegant foyer of the theater.

The moment Luke moved into the car beside her and closed the door, a strange, delicious, languor enveloped her. She sighed and blamed emotional burnout and the late hour. She tried to shake the drowsiness to no avail. The soft romantic music flowing from the sound system fed it, as did Luke's silence as he maneuvered the sports car through the narrow Charleston streets and finally back on the freeway toward Barrett Hall.

She glanced at him. He appeared to be absorbed with driving or the music. Or his thoughts. Did he wish someone else sat beside him?

She reminded herself he'd only taken her out to express his gratitude for the shopping. Was he thinking about Morgan Pennington?

She leaned her head back on the headrest and surrendered to the lassitude pressing against her eyelids as they crossed the Cooper River Bridge.

~*~

Luke kept stealing glances at the young woman asleep on the seat beside him. Tender emotions he'd not experienced in a long time battled with his realistic determination not to become involved. *Get a hold on, Captain.*

At dinner, he'd gotten more out of observing her tasting the various dishes than enjoying the well-prepared food himself. She watched the play like a child totally engrossed with him blocked out entirely at times. That was new. Few women had ever appeared to forget he was beside them. *There's nothing false or pretentious about her.*

He remembered her tears. Like a rainstorm,

similar to Kristina's outbursts.

She was still a child in a lot of ways. Definitely too young to—. He shook his head, determined not to carry the thought further, and succeeded for the next few miles.

But when he pulled the car into the garage and cut the motor, and she still didn't awaken, he found himself entranced, watching her gentle breathing, the way her lashes lay on her cheeks, the contrast of dark hair and creamy complexion shining in the moonlight, the sweet fragrance of her perfume. Gardenia? He needed to get out of the car and as far away as possible, but he couldn't move.

~*~

Rachel became aware the car no longer moved. She lifted her head and viewed with amazement the outlines of the garage's interior. She turned to glance at Luke. He sat staring at her, his head tilted against the window, his shirt open and his tie slung across the steering wheel.

"Oh, my, I'm sorry—I don't know what possessed me. I've never fallen asleep—like this." Her voice sounded hoarse and she cleared her throat. She was thankful the shadows covered her burning cheeks.

Luke exited the car and approached her side. He opened her door, still without a word.

She got out, glanced up at him in the moonlight flooding the garage entrance, and found her heart pounding out of her chest. An irresistible force drew her toward him. She fought it with every ounce of her strength, turned and took two shaky steps away.

"Rachel."

In one stride he was beside her. His hands touched her shoulders and wheeled her around.

Facing him, she trembled and every resolve she'd had all the past weeks drained out her toes.

He whispered her name again, lifted her chin and gazed into her eyes. "You exclaimed over each dish at the restaurant. You wept over Madame Butterfly and forgot I was even there. You slept in my car —and I know you're still keeping a secret of some kind—but," his voice grew husky, "I give up, I'm mesmerized." He gently drew her to him and kissed her lips, softly at first, then again, and this time the kiss was more startling and telling. When at last it ended, he pulled back and regarded her intensely.

The surprised, tender, protective attitude on his face baptized Rachel with awe and joy. Rainbows danced around her. Every fiber in her being recognized and responded to the look of love imprinted on his countenance.

"What have you done to me, Rachel York?" he whispered, leaning back on the car still holding her. He released her for a moment and her knees buckled. He chuckled and pulled her close again.

His heart beat fast against her cheek pressed to his chest. "I could ask you the same thing," she murmured dreamily and wondered what her earlier worries about him had been.

Luke lifted her chin and kissed her once more. His lips lingered gently on hers for infinite sweet moments.

"I think I discerned you were a threat the first evening you walked into the game room." He spoke this against her hair.

She pulled back. "A threat?"

"I never wanted to feel this way again, or thought

I didn't."

Was he referring to Georgina or to Morgan?

"What about—?"

"Morgan?"

"Yes, aren't you two…?

"In love? No." .

"But—"

Luke touched her lips with his finger. "Oh, I have a date with Morgan tomorrow night, which I will keep, and I understand you've one with Archer. That one you'll break, please."

Rachel laughed and feigned indignation. "How fair is that?

"Nothing is fair in love and war. But, on second thought, you can keep your appointment with Pennington—as long as it's the last one."

Rachel smiled.

Luke lifted his head for a moment and scrunched up his face. "In fact, I guess, to be as fair as possible and give folks time to accept the inevitable, we should keep our beautiful discovery tonight secret until after the Harvest Festival and Costume Ball. I suppose I do owe Morgan something. We are co-hosting."

Rachel could scarcely breathe. "And after that?"

"Afterwards, before, and meanwhile, Miss York, I am at your mercy."

Luke drew her to him and started to kiss her again, but stopped. He held her out from him. "You're too beautiful and precious for me to remain out in this moonlight with you another second. Go to the house, young lady." He turned her around and dropped his hands.

"Good night." Rachel gathered her strength and forced her legs to walk to the patio entrance. At the door, she glanced back. He was propped against the car watching her. He gave her a cute salute.

In the house she floated up the stairs not daring to let go of the railing. Was she dreaming or what?

A smile was permanently imprinted on her lips, still warm from his kisses. As she prepared for bed, she shook her head to no avail. She climbed between the cool sheets and something like a chuckle escaped her lips.

Lying on her pillow, she floated in the moonlight pouring through the top of the windows. Everything she'd ever read about falling in love she now acknowledged as true. Giddy, euphoric, happiness so real she could almost touch it with her fingers. Surely, love of this sort must be a wonderful gift from God. She closed her eyes and a sharp pain struck her heart like an arrow. Doubts threatened to engulf her. *"Dear God, please let this be okay. I love Luke. I love him. And he loves me. Please work it all out."*

She opened her eyes. Luke Barrett most assuredly loved her, even though he didn't say it. How wonderful to finally experience love given and returned. She dwelt on this warm thought and the memory of his tender expression and kisses for a long time before falling asleep.

Once during the night, she awoke gasping, her throat dry, her palms sweaty. Then Luke's love flowed over her like balm and banished the anxiety. She laid her head back on her pillow and fell into a sweet sleep.

Sunlight dancing over her pillow awoke her. She stretched, closed her eyes and hugged her wonderful new knowledge of love to herself. The room vibrated and glowed with it.

It overflowed into the hall later, when she

emerged. The colors in the Oriental runner gleamed brighter. Potted plants arching toward the sunbeams at the window stretched with much more life and vibrant color. Her feet weighed less than a feather as she started down the steps. She wondered how she would keep from smiling all through breakfast with Jessica and Kristina.

The child provided the solution. She was ecstatic over a note her father left on her door earlier. He promised her a surprise after lunch. Rachel smiled often in anticipation with the child, hopefully not risking Jessica's suspicions.

Since there were no lessons on Saturday, Kristina went on a romp outside after breakfast, and Rachel and Jessica sat in the loggia.

The older woman's eyes rested on Rachel, and a smile creased the porcelain cheeks. "Well, dear, I must admit something down south has agreed with you. You are positively radiant this morning in your yellow sundress."

Rachel averted her warm face and wondered if she and Luke would ever be able to keep their secret from this precious lady until after the Costume Ball.

"What do you suppose Kristina's surprise is?" she asked, eager to change the subject.

"I suspect it's a kitten. She's wanted a pet to keep in her room—she got the idea since you've been keeping Penny in yours and Judge is not an inside dog."

"Well, I hope she does get her kitten."

"Luke is a good father." Jessica took a deep breath. "I'm proud of him as a father and for other things. He's such a hard worker. I truly think there is hope for the plantation staying in the black." She paused and something like sadness flitted across her face. "I only wish…" Jessica peered into Rachel's face. "I was going to say I wish Luke was as strong in spiritual matters as he is with Kristina and this plantation. I believe you're a Christian, Rachel, am I right?"

Rachel's heart plummeted at her words. Was this a warning or a plea? Apprehensions she'd suppressed the night before burst painfully over her. She wished she'd gone back to her room, her room full of love, after breakfast. But she hadn't, and now she must respond to this wise woman beside her.

Rachel nodded and cleared her throat. "Was—did Luke ever show deep interest in spiritual things?"

"Oh, yes, before he left for service. I believe he possessed a strong faith. He went to church with us every Sunday. But, a lot happened in the war, and Georgina's sudden death. I've tried to talk to him about giving it all up, letting the past go." Jessica clicked her tongue. "But, he can be stubborn, when he wants to be."

Rachel had witnessed the obstinate streak, but she'd also glimpsed something else, thank God.

Kristina burst in from the patio, out of breath, Sadie and Penny at her heels.

"Is it time for lunch yet, Aunt Jess?"

"No. It's not. Play a little longer, dear. I'll call you."

A few moments later, Rachel picked up Penny, excused herself, and went up to her room. Alone, she was able to push the nagging conversation with Jessica from her mind. Her resolve and mental battle along the same lines over the previous weeks seemed like a bad dream, as she allowed thoughts of Luke, his attitude of love, the tender moments of the previous evening, flood back into her day. She picked up the toy dachshund and hugged her, talking to her as if she were a friend. "He's wonderful. He's gentle and good. And he was once interested in Christianity and he will be again."

Penny licked her mistress's hand and stared up at her with soft brown eyes.

I'm glad you agree, girl.

~*~

Luke stepped into his room an hour before lunch. He'd fought distraction, a happy, whistling kind, all morning. Cade listening, flashed him a broad smile twice while they prepared for the afternoon tourists. Luke picked up the framed photo of Georgina he'd kept on his nightstand for the past three years. He walked back into the hall and up the stairs to the attic.

He found the olive trunk and laid the picture on an old chair beside it. Opening the storage box, the ruffled skirt of a white antebellum dress with green bows, popped out. He recognized it as the one Georgina wore to her last Harvest Ball. He remembered his first thought when he saw her coming down the stairs that night long ago. A blond Scarlet O'Hara. His beautiful wife.

He reached into the side of the box and pulled out a scrapbook, and sank down in the discarded wing back chair. His wife had painstakingly cataloged their years together with photos and occasional handwritten notes.

Our wedding.
Our honeymoon cruise.
We arrive home.

Luke's beautiful gift horse.
Our beloved baby girl.

Kristina, a butterball at nine pounds, with her mother's lips and his black hair, filled their hearts with joy. He managed some time home from the Middle East right after her birth. He sat for several minutes flipping through more pages. Georgina in jeans and boots, astride her white mare, rejoicing over the first colt's birth. Kristina growing so fast. Georgina sitting in a rocker on the front porch in the early evening, leaning back, a sleepy smile on her face. A good stopping place.

I've come to say goodbye, my love, but I don't know how to do it.

Luke slowly replaced the album in the bottom of the trunk and laid the framed photo on top of it. He pushed the ruffles of the dress back inside and closed the lid.

To have loved and been so loved. How could one imagine having another chance at that kind of love?

Thoughts of Rachel flooded his mind. From their first kiss, his shattered world started coming back into order. Remembering brought light and comfort, even thankfulness. He scanned the disarray in the attic and gave in to the urge to straighten up. He bent and moved a few boxes, pausing to study the almost life-size painting of a pirate ancestor and namesake. He wiped the dust off the bronze plate. *Captain Lucas Bloodstone Barrett, 1730.*

Probably his last painting in his pirate garb before becoming a gentleman landowner. Should he resurrect the old fellow for the Harvest Ball?

~*~

In her room, almost directly under the attic space, Rachel noticed the rumbling and moving of boxes and the heavy walking. Curious, when steps descended the stairs, she cracked open her door. Luke, in his work clothes, strode down the hall.

Joy flowed over her. She closed the door, tidied her hair and hurried down for the mid-day meal.

At lunch, the glance Luke turned on her as she sat down, warmed her as if he had touched her.

After that first gaze, Luke put on his usual demeanor and banter with Kristina, and Rachel found it easy to follow.

"Well, we might as well eat fast," he said, "or Kristina will fall asleep on us. She's ready for a nap, I'm sure"

"No, Daddy, I'm not so. I'm waiting for my surprise."

Jessica smiled. "I'm expecting a clean plate, Kristina."

Kristina proceeded to finish her lunch in record time.

Rachel tried not to stare at Luke, but he appeared so happy and different, she kept stealing glances at him.

Finally, when they all moved out to the patio, Luke sat Kristina on a bench and told her to shut her eyes. Cade walked up with a fluffy, white kitten, and Luke placed it on her lap.

Kristina's eyes shot open. "Oh, thank you, Daddy." She pulled the kitty close to her face and put her cheek on the soft fur. The kitten mewed softly. Kristina's joy over the bundle brought smiles from everyone, including Mrs. Busby and Maggie who slipped up from the kitchen. "I'm naming her Angel." Kristina announced and ran to hug her father. "Do you think Nana will let me bring her to her house today?"

"Oh, I expect so. Who would be able to pry her loose from your pudgy little hands?" Luke swatted her on the bottom.

Jessica and Kristina left to pack the child's overnight bag to go to her grandparents who were due to pick her up momentarily.

Cade sidled up near Rachel. He leaned toward her to whisper, "Do you have any idea what's come over the Captain? He sho seems different today. Distracted might be a better word and I don't think it's the kitty. You know anything about this, Miss Rachel?"

Rachel shook her head but warmth spread over her cheeks. She excused herself to go write some letters before getting ready for her afternoon and evening date with Archer.

Luke followed her into the house. "Miss York, may I see you in the game room?" His business-like voice halted her when she started up the steps.

Rachel glanced at his face, which gave no clue of the previous evening's emotion, and followed him to the game room.

As soon as he closed the door behind her, he swept her into his arms.

"Luke," she gasped, the breath rushing from her lungs.

He kissed her deeply and released her. He opened the door and said matter-of-factly, a smile playing at his lips, "I believe that's all, Miss York—and don't be out late tonight."

Rachel walked to her room on a cloud. She hardly noticed the tour buses arriving.

At three o'clock Rachel's happiness diminished as she dressed to go sailing and packed a change of clothing for dinner. While she was with Archer, Luke would be with Morgan. Why did it trouble her? She was being ridiculous. His warmth, his kisses reassured her. He also had assured her he did not love Morgan Pennington. Still, the woman was beautiful. And rich. And seductive. She cast these thoughts aside as she pulled her hair into a ponytail and plaited it.

Ready a few minutes early, she went to Jessica's room and sat down to chat a few moments, glad the elderly woman had not gone to her Charleston house yet. Something bubbled up on the edge of Rachel's mind. Suddenly, she remembered what she'd been meaning to ask Jessica for several days. Who was Dan Barrett whom Ava claimed was the father of her child? "I've met someone at the church who mentioned a Dan Barrett to me. Do you know of such a person in the family?"

Jessica gazed at her quizzically. "That's strange. Luke's middle name is Daniel, but he never goes by it. Who did you say mentioned it to you?"

Rachel's heart plummeted to her feet. She turned her shocked face away. "Oh, someone in passing. I probably misunderstood."

Mrs. Busby appeared in the doorway. "Mr. Pennington is at the patio door awaiting Miss York."

Rachel gathered her beach bag and purse and stumbled into the hall and down the steps toward the back entrance to avoid the tour groups.

So this is how it feels to have a grenade blow up in your face, Mr. Luke Daniel Barrett.

Chapter Nineteen

"Hey, there, beautiful." Archer's eyes flickered over her red top and white Bermuda shorts and came back to her face, concerned. "Whoa, you okay?"

Rachel nodded and managed a little smile as they walked to his sports car. She willed a different expression on her features as he opened the door for her. "Sorry, I looked so...whatever when I came out of the house. But I wasn't sure I really wanted to try sailing. You've got a greenhorn on your hands." Simple words for a normal conversation.

"Wait a minute, you're with the best sailing instructor this side of the Cooper River." He laughed. "At least I don't think Luke has time to sail anymore."

Of course he wouldn't. Rachel leaned her aching head on the back of the seat.

"You can take a little catnap, if you like," Archer told her, as they pulled onto the main highway. "We're sailing on a special beach at one of the islands and it'll take a bit of a drive, but it will be worth it." He turned on a tape of classical music. Rachel glanced out the window.

Thank God she wouldn't need to make conversation.

Slowly, as each additional mile stretched behind them and the strains of Strauss, Liszt, and Wagner filled the sports car, Rachel's seesaw emotions leveled off.

There could be another explanation for Ava's Dan Barrett.

That thought lifted Rachel's spirit as they parked near a white sandy beach and sparkling water. She worked hard to make it through Archer's sailing instructions when they set out on the tide. But questions continued to plague her.

"Whoa! Go to your other right." Archer's voice brought Rachel back to full attention as the sailboat almost capsized. She swung her weight in the opposite direction.

After some fast maneuvering, Archer righted the boat, but Rachel was done. She convinced Archer he'd be safer with another sailing partner. He dropped her off on the beach and an attractive blond ran up and boarded. They both waved at Rachel as she dropped onto her beach towel.

Luke's earlier kiss came back to warm her more than the late afternoon sun. What would it be like to give completely into passion as his wife? She shook her head, shocked at where her thoughts were taking her. Luke, after all, did not mention marriage and, at the present moment, he was probably dressing for his date with Morgan.

She scanned the waves for Archer's sail and wished the afternoon would end quickly.

He returned about thirty minutes later. His sailing partner jumped out into the surf, waved at Rachel and walked away. Rachel helped Archer pull the boat back to its space and waited while he tied up.

He grinned up at her. "You miss me?"

Can't say I did.

"Not one bit on this lovely beach, but at least your

life was saved without me in the boat."

He laughed and grabbed her hand as they walked to the car. They picked up the bags with their change of clothing and headed across the parking lot toward a group of elegant, driftwood-colored buildings. Rachel was expecting a small bathhouse like Archer mentioned and began to wonder as they stepped onto a slatted, wooden walkway and proceeded up two levels in the building complex. Where was Archer taking her?

He stopped at a door and selected a key from his ring.

"Archer, what is this place? You said there was a beach house to change in for dinner, and this is hardly that."

He smiled and drew her around the corner of the building. An entrance way boasted an elegant sign stating in bold letters "Beach House." In smaller letters, Rachel read "Private Condominiums."

"Beach House." he said with a big smile. "Did I tell you wrong?"

He turned back to the door, and she followed him, indignation rising in her heart.

You are a weasel.

He unlocked the door and pushed it open. Rachel didn't move. A muscle twitched in her jaw. "Archer, I was under the impression you were talking about some sort of public facility at the beach, not a private condominium. I am not in the habit of—"

"Hey-y," he whispered, as a couple came around the corner, "let's at least go in to discuss this."

Against her better judgment, Rachel stepped into a luxurious foyer onto mosaic tiles reminiscent of a Persian rug. The pleasant scent of a large bouquet of scarlet roses on a carved side table tantalized her nose.

Archer closed the door and walked ahead of her. He pulled aside red and brown striped satin drapes on the far wall to reveal a balcony with a beautiful view of the ocean. He flipped on soft music on his way to the kitchen. "Boy, am I thirsty. Want a soda?"

Rachel, still standing at the door with her beach bag, glanced around. The condo with its grass paper on the walls, the furniture and appointments, including carved animals on a glass-topped table—all in shades of oyster, brown, and red—as well as the large portrait of a lion over the leather sofa, definitely made a male statement.

"Archer," she said in a calm voice, "I'm sorry, but I'm not in the habit of visiting men's condos. I prefer not to change here."

He came toward her and offered a chilled can of Coke. She shook her head, and he placed her drink on the counter and popped the top of his. After taking a long swallow, he crossed his arms and gazed at her thoughtfully. The corners of his mouth turned up and a dimple stood out on his tanned chin. "Okay."

Startled by his fast capitulation, Rachel stared at him.

He swung around the counter, pulled a set of keys from a hook on the kitchen wall, and thumbed through them. "Here it is—the key to Morgan's condo—one flight up, three doors down." He removed the key from the ring and hesitated. "On second thought, what you really mean is you cannot stay in my place with me, so I'll go to Morgan's and change." He swiped up his clothing laying across a chair and headed to the door but turned back. "Unless you'd rather use Morgan's condo? I don't think she'd be there this early." He glanced at his wristwatch and studied her face before adding, "If she and Luke follow their usual plans, I imagine it'll be quite a bit later."

His words fell like a sword on Rachel's heart. Her lower lip trembled. So Luke *usually* visited Morgan's condo? She turned quickly and walked woodenly to the glass sliding door, as if to check the view.

Archer followed. "Whoops, I slipped up, didn't I? Does it surprise you your hardworking employer is just a man after all? Bet you idolized him, huh, the war hero and all?"

Rachel finally turned to face him. When she spoke, the calmness of her voice surprised her. "No, I certainly didn't. Nothing about Luke Barrett would surprise me."

Suddenly, she wanted to cry. With her back to him again, she locked her gaze on the ocean beyond the balcony where white caps and mammoth waves now tossed and twisted two small sailboats as their occupants stretched and strained to keep from capsizing. She understood how the sailors felt.

"Well, I'm real glad to hear it, if it means a fellow like me might have a bit of chance." Archer touched her shoulder and fingered her plait of hair.

She moved away.

"Okay," she said, wishing to be alone with her turbulent thoughts. "I—I'll change here if you'll go to Morgan's place."

She couldn't bear to step foot in that condo.

"That's my girl." Archer walked to the door. "Can you be ready in about an hour?"

"Yes. That'll be fine."

Rachel locked the door behind him, and fell against it. Tears burned her eyes.

Luke said he was not in love with Morgan. *But was he carrying on an affair with her?* And what about Ava? Did morality mean anything to a man like him?

Probably not.

She stumbled to the bathroom and blotted her face with a cool, damp washcloth. Then she showered, not a bit surprised to find a number of feminine toilet articles available.

Later, she stood before the mirror and applied her makeup with mechanical hands. One part of her mind kept saying, *So what? Luke loves me now. The past is the past.*

Another side of her responded with, "Rachel York, you are fooling yourself big time. You would never want to fit into the carefree, immoral lifestyle apparently led by Archer and Morgan Pennington and at least *shared* by Luke when it suits him."

Could Archer be lying, or exaggerating?

Somehow, Rachel managed to present a placid countenance to Archer after he returned. But the battle continued in her heart. She longed for the evening to end. However, if she asked Archer to take her home before dinner, he would know for sure how his revelation affected her.

He took her to a cozy, ocean side restaurant several miles down the beach road. She chose the broiled flounder and managed to eat a few bites while trying to keep up a running conversation with Archer. Her mind kept returning to Barrett Hall. Would Luke be there when she returned? Or at the condo?

On the drive home, Archer's car began making a knocking sound.

Archer cursed and quickly apologized. He pulled over at the next gas station, hopped out of the British import and raised the hood. He slammed it back down with his mouth set in a hard line. He leaned in the window and spoke to Rachel. "I need to call my mechanic. But it shouldn't take long to fix this. Would you prefer I hire you a taxi, Rachel? Or can you wait with me at that little café?" He indicated the restaurant two doors down. "I'm sorry this has happened." He whipped out his cell phone.

Rachel glanced at the time. Eleven-thirty. "I think I can wait with you, Archer, if it's not going to be long." She worked hard to keep disappointment out of her voice.

"Good girl."

Soon a mechanic drove up and began work on the car and they settled in a booth in the café with chocolate sundaes. To Archer's chagrin and repeated trips out to the sports car, it took over an hour and a half to correct the problem. And the drive home never seemed longer.

He walked Rachel onto the dark porch at Barrett Hall at quarter till two. She was too exhausted to resist when he took her into his arms. But she broke away from his attempted kiss without apology. She breathed a prayer of thanks the front door was not locked and entered. Groping for the hall switch, she gasped as a hand closed over hers and light flooded the hall.

"Where in tarnation have you been?" Luke's voice sounded like it ground over gravel.

She blinked at him, standing before her in his black tuxedo, tie discarded, angry lines contorting his face. Before she had time to answer, his voice, even though a whisper, cut the silent hall again like a rapier.

"I almost opened this door to give Pennington something he could really remember about this evening."

"I can explain why I am so late. But do you want to awaken the whole house?" Rachel bit her lower lip and sat her beach bag on the rug.

His response was to take her wrist and pull her to the game room. He shut the door behind them, without any effort to be quiet and flipped on the light. He released her, went behind his desk, and stared at her, his face blazing. "I asked where you've been."

Although Luke hadn't hurt her, Rachel rubbed her wrist for lack of anything better to do. His angry demeanor and impatience disappointed her. How different he was from twenty-four hours earlier. "I might ask you the same thing." Sadness edged her soft answer.

He hesitated. "I've been waiting for you way over two hours, Rachel."

The pleading note in his tone wrenched her heart. She lowered her eyes and thought—hoped—Archer had lied about Luke's visits to Morgan's condo, and Luke was not Ava's Dan Barrett.

"We had car trouble."

"Car trouble?"

She nodded. Relief and remorse rose in his face, but a terrible ache began in her throat as well as a burning behind her eyes. She needed to know if he were carrying on an affair with whoever. And was it the real reason he wanted to keep their relationship secret for now?

Luke rushed from behind the desk, swept her into his arms, and gazed into her eyes as she blinked back tears.

"Rachel," he whispered against her hair, "I'm sorry I flew off the handle. I was so worried about you." He reached for her wrist and brought it to his lips. "And, I'm sorry if I hurt you propelling you in here. Can you forgive me?"

"You didn't injure me."

He lifted her chin and gently touched her lips with his. He held her at arm's length and searched her face. "There's something else isn't there?" His voice was low, harder and he released her. "What did Pennington pull, besides his car trouble routine?"

She turned toward the fireplace as if she might draw strength from its hard rock mass.

"Well, he tricked me into going to his condo," she said in a voice hardly sounding like hers.

Luke stiffened. "The slick bum. I warned you."

"Don't worry. He discovered soon enough what I thought about it—and I found out how he thought about—a few things." Rachel forced her voice to normalcy before continuing. "He told me there was a beach house where we could shower and change for dinner after sailing. I had no idea he owned a condominium by that name." She turned and faced Luke. His steady gaze gave her courage, hope. "Nor did I know Morgan had one there, too. Archer used hers to change clothes, since I refused to stay with him alone in his condo."

Luke stood so still, he hardly seemed to breathe. His gaze did not flicker, but something hardened in his face.

Suddenly, she wanted to stop, to rush into his arms, to forget what Archer said but she inhaled deeply and rushed on. "Archer is, evidently like you intimated, a liberated playboy."

Luke took a long ragged breath and regarded her. "I'm glad you found out."

She peered into his face. Her words came out like a dam had broken, and she couldn't keep her voice from rising in pitch. "I don't care what Archer is, but what are you, Luke? Are you also a liberated playboy when the notion strikes you?"

Luke turned and walked back to his desk, but not before a fleeting sadness clouded his countenance. When he faced her again, however, a cynical smile creased his thin lips.

Hope oozed out of her like drops of blood.

"I didn't imagine falling in love with you was going to call for a high school confession session."

"Luke, it hasn't."

"Because if it has," his face turned hard, "you've got a little explaining to do yourself, like why you really came here and who the guy was in the museum, the one you also spoke to at the market."

Had Luke followed her? Rachel blinked back tears. Was it possible she could share the truth of her own situation? Would it be okay to tell him about Ron, at least set that much straight? However, when she glanced at Luke, his bitter expression shocked her speechless.

He turned his back and walked to the fireplace, as if to put space between them.

Sorrow for him engulfed her, but disappointment filled her mouth like sand. How could they, one day earlier, have clung to each other in joy, and thought they'd discovered something precious? She simply needed to discover if he still shared Morgan's and Archer's carefree lifestyle—if, indeed, he planned to ask her to be a part of it.

Minutes passed in thick silence.

"Rachel."

He spoke her name so softly she barely realized it. She walked to the fireplace and stood near him. When he turned toward her, genuine sadness filled his face. His voice and next words rolled over her like a spring shower.

"You are the best thing that's happened to me in a long time. Something I've been searching for these last few years. But at times I confront a force of some kind holding us apart. It happened on the ship." He touched her hair. "And again now when I realized you'd been listening to Archer's gossip, and it makes me furious. But I shouldn't have become so angry."

He took her shoulders in his hands. "And I'm not interested much in why you came here, I'm just glad you did."

She went into his arms, tears overflowing her eyes. He held her gently for long moments.

"I'm not proud of everything in my past," he said finally. "But who is?"

Was Ava Jenkins and her child part of it?

Rachel lifted her head from his shoulder. "Luke, I really don't care about what's already happened. It's what you plan to do in the future that interests me."

He moved her out from their embrace to study her face. "I hope you're not going to tell me I have to be a goody-two-shoes to appeal to you."

"You know how you attract me." She pressed her cheek against his strong hand on her shoulder. She took another deep breath. "But I've got to tell you, I believe a relationship between a man and woman is— is incomplete unless both are committed Christians."

"I don't think so at all. Love is the strongest link. Can you deny how we care about each other?" Luke pulled her close until his lips were an inch away from hers and her heart pounded against her ribs and her knees trembled. He smiled. "What's your answer?"

"No, Luke, I cannot deny it."

"Then why are we discussing this? I'm not a heathen," he whispered against her hair. "I know there's a God, but not like you and Jessica believe. God helps those who help themselves. I learned that much in the military."

His words stung her and rolled around the room like bowling balls, cracking, splitting everything in their path, including her heart. Stepping back from him, she gazed up into his face. "I'm sorry you feel that way, Luke, but I'm glad you've been honest."

His expression hardened into disbelief. "You're sorry, and you're pleased I've told the truth, but you can't accept it or me?"

A jackhammer drilled its way through her insides and moisture flooded her eyes. "I'm afraid I can't, Luke."

Silence filled the room as her words settled between them like lead.

~*~

Luke stared at Rachel. She was the most beautiful, desirable woman he knew. She stood only two feet from him, yet the same presence he'd confronted in the kitchen after Jessica's talk separated them like a brick wall. He recognized it, and knew it should make him fall to his knees. Instead, it made him determined. Brick walls were for demolishing.

He reached out and grasped her shoulders. "Do you love me, Rachel?"

"Yes, Luke," she whispered and a tear escaped.

"Marry me. If it's a matter of going to church, I'll go with you." His hoarse voice wrung her heart.

She caressed his tight jaw. "It's more than attending services, Luke. It takes a real commitment to Jesus Christ. Without it, you'd grow to hate me, and I'd be torn between submission to you and to…God."

What hogwash was this? He released his hold on her and stepped back. "It appears I'm not good enough for you, Miss York."

Rachel opened her mouth to respond, but he continued, "I thought being honest and hardworking made a man worthy. But I guess, by your lofty standards, it doesn't."

Tears rushed down her cheeks.

He wanted to hit the wall with his fist. Instead, he turned and strode to the door.

"What of Ava and her baby?" Rachel whispered.

He hesitated, without glancing back. "I have no idea what you're talking about."

~*~

After the door closed, Rachel stood as though everything living stopped breathing until the sound of the jeep gunning down the drive jolted her back to reality. She stumbled out of the room, retrieved her beach things, and trudged up the steps, dragging her grief behind her like a sack of rocks.

The hall clock struck three as she sat on the edge of her bed trancelike. Her eyes fell on Ron's plaque, and she sank to her knees and burst into fresh tears.

"Twice, Father," she prayed, "in this same year, I've had to give up men I loved." She buried her face in the crook of her arm and wept. Soon, relief and peace came. Tomorrow, she would check out the teaching position, her aunt described in her last letter. It might work, even if it was five hours from home. She wouldn't mind relocating.

At least she wouldn't have to worry about running into Easton Watkins, III. Or Luke.

She wept again.

Chapter Twenty

August descended, stifling and hot. Mosquitoes came in droves from the river. Rachel helped Mrs. Busby check windows and lock down those without tightly woven screens.

Rachel's room faced the setting sun, and often felt stuffy until the night breezes came through her French doors. Sometimes, she retreated to the balcony to await the cool relief and easier slumber. But the insects would attack—and agonizing thoughts of Luke.

Jessica asked her one day if she were sleeping well.

"Yes, I am for the most part." Rachel said with a little smile.

The woman's kind eyes rested on her for a moment. "This heat is enough to give any one a turn."

Rachel changed the subject to the coming Harvest Festival at the end of the month. The house fluttered with anticipation. Everyone would be involved in some way. Maggie and Mrs. Busby readied bright jars of pickled watermelon rind and pepper jelly, green beans, and vegetable soup for the market booths in town. Rachel enjoyed assisting them. It reminded her of helping Ruby can summer vegetables from their garden at home.

She tried to appear interested as Jessica told her details of the weeklong festivities, but she found it difficult to express enthusiasm—even for the final event, the Costume Ball at Pennington Plantation Morgan and Luke would be hosting. She wished she hadn't promised to attend. Somehow she'd make it through the ball, because she would be leaving the next day.

After their painful confrontation, Rachel did not run into Luke for three days and then, only to pass in the hall. His burning gaze rested on her face for the briefest moment, causing her whole body to tense. He nodded, greeted her as "Miss York" and passed without another word. Now she was simply an employee.

These thoughts flowed through Rachel's mind one afternoon while making sugar cookies with Kristina. Rachel stood at the kitchen counter with flour splattered almost to her elbows. Kristina leaned over from a stool, biting her lower lip as she pressed a pink cookie cutter into the soft yellow dough.

"Good job, Kristina! Now lift the cutter slowly."

Kristina lifted the press, safely separating the cookie, and looked up. "Daddy!"

Rachel gasped. Luke stood in the doorway in his Levi's and faded army tee. He acknowledged her with a small salute. Warmth rushed to her cheeks as his glance passed over her and rested briefly on Mrs. Busby's apron around her waist.

With a half-smile he turned to Kristina and her outstretched arms and bent to hug her. "I don't guess the flour on you is going to make much difference when it mixes with the all the dust on me."

The child pointed to the horse cut in the dough. Her face beamed. "I'm naming this one Haidez for you."

"I wouldn't mind tasting my fine horse, but he appears raw." Luke's mouth quirked up.

Kristina giggled, slipped off the stool and pulled him by the hand to the table where the finished cookies lay cooling—ponies with fluffy manes, elephants with curving trunks and giraffes with long, fragile necks.

Rachel wiped the flour from her shaking hands

Luke sat down. "Let's think. I believe I'll start with this fat elephant, next a couple of your ponies." He ate several cookies, exclaiming over each one to Kristina's delight.

Observing him demolish the cookies with obvious relish and good humor, released some of Rachel's stress at his nearness. She turned away to fix him a glass of tea.

When she placed it before him, he glanced at her. "Thanks. I don't think I've eaten cookies like these since Jessica made them for me years ago."

"I'm glad you're enjoying them." She worked hard to make her voice sound casual.

Their glance held briefly as he tilted the glass and drained it. Rachel turned to the counter.

Luke stood and left the kitchen.

"We'll make plenty more cookies for you, Daddy, when you get your work done," the child called after him.

Rachel's eyes prickled. She swiped at them with the back of her fingers and busied herself rolling out the last batch.

~*~

Sunday at Redemption Hope, Rachel sat with Ava and tried to follow her conversation before service. Her ears perked up when Ava shared how her "Dan" called and wanted to get together.

Smooth operator. Break up with the current girl, go for the earlier one.

She forced her mind from that thought and listened as Ava whispered a quick message before the service started. "I told him my life was totally changed now. I'm not the same person." She blinked away a tear. "He hung up on me."

"Don't you worry, Ava, I'm sure the Lord is going to provide for you and your baby." Rachel's lips tightened. Even if it meant taking a drastic step to make certain before she left Charleston.

During the next two weeks, Rachel decided Luke cared little about his effect on the household. He seldom presented himself at meals and appeared completely occupied with the tasks of running the plantation. Kristina missed her father, but Rachel tried to console her with special projects and more books.

Twice, Morgan came by about teatime to plan details of the costume ball. Luke drove in from the fields, and the two of them withdrew to the game room, Morgan chattering and Luke scowling. On these occasions, Jessica raised her eyebrows after them, and excused herself to Rachel and went to her room.

Once she whispered to Rachel. "Morgan hopes she's going to get Luke to the altar through all this involvement. She's not fooling me."

Would Luke and Morgan announce an engagement at the Ball? She wished she'd never committed herself to attend. She even toyed with the idea of leaving Charleston early, especially after she received a positive reply about the teaching position. For several days she tried to make up her mind to leave before the ball.

Archer called on Saturday, two weeks before the gathering, and asked for a date. She turned him down flat.

"Well, at least I can expect to see you at the Harvest Ball. And, of course, I'll be glad to pick you up."

"I—don't think so, Archer."

"What do you mean? You haven't changed your mind about coming, have you?"

"I may leave a day or two early."

"Put that bad idea right out of your head, Rachel Ann York. You really must come. You'll be sorry if you miss this. There'll be period costumes in a plantation setting you may never have a chance to see again. And, of course, there's me."

Yes, you. And possibly Luke and Morgan's engagement announcement.

"Hey," he continued. "Be here. Drive yourself in one of Luke's cars and only stay an hour, if you don't like it. But come. Got to run."

"Archer," she began, but he'd hung up.

Later, before the bus tour people filled the house and grounds, Jessica talked Rachel into going into Charleston to check out the booth and table displays being set up in the Rainbow Market for the festival. Kristina left with her grandparents earlier.

Wearing her white sundress with its crocheted trim and her hair in a cool upsweep, Rachel found herself enjoying the busy throng and heavily laden tables of trinkets, grass baskets, seashells, t-shirts and the musty smell of leather goods mingled with scents of fresh flowers standing in buckets of water.

She gazed at the multitude of brilliant flowers. "I'll

take these," she finally told the seller. She breathed in the pungent fragrance of the fluffy zinnias before handing them to the vendor. He wrapped the stems in a damp paper towel and white foil, tied them with a ribbon, and handed them to her. The bold scarlet, yellow, and orange blossoms lifted her spirits.

When Jessica stopped to talk to friends, Rachel walked down the passageway to a booth and observed two women making grass baskets.

A voice at her side startled her. "You will only find this kind of weaving in Charleston."

"Joseph!"

When he smiled, the tired lines creasing his face relaxed. "You look like a bride standing here dressed in white with that bouquet in your hand."

She gave him a bittersweet smile and gently touched the velvet petals of a yellow blossom. "Definitely not."

"How long will you be remaining in Charleston?"

"I guess until after the Costume Ball at Pennington. Why?" She searched his brown eyes, but he averted his face.

"I was wondering. That'll probably be long enough."

She opened her mouth to ask, "For what?" But Dakota Busby, with his cowboy hat bobbing in the throng, advanced toward her. Joseph followed her gaze and, as if on cue, turned and disappeared into the crowd.

"Well, well, so it's our own Miss York and still as fresh as the proverbial daisy in this southern heat." He took off his hat and wiped his forehead with a red bandana.

Rachel ignored the wolfish inspection he gave her.

He appeared prosperous in designer jeans, a blue embroidered cowboy shirt and shiny leather boots. Had he found a new job? Females in the crowd flowing past flashed him admiring glances.

"Hello, Dakota."

He twirled his hat in his hand a moment. "I guess I owe you an apology."

If he meant it.

She glanced up the corridor to give him a cue she was not planning a long chat, but she did desire to find how he fared. "What are you doing these days?"

"A little of this, and a little of that," he said with a shrug. "Nothing I don't want to do. But next week I'm going to be at the ball. I wanna do that."

This surprised her.

"Guess you're wondering how I got invited, huh?"

"Not really."

"Put it this way. Archer and Morgan and me been friends longer than Luke and me been, let's say, a little less friendly."

When Rachel failed to reply, he strolled away, but called back over his shoulder, "Save a dance for me."

Not a chance.

Jessica joined Rachel. "Was that Dakota?"

"Yes."

"He certainly looked well, rather like the cat's whisker, I must say."

Rachel smiled at Jessica's description.

Later in the afternoon, the two of them walked by the potter near the ice cream shop. He took his eyes off his creation long enough to smile at Rachel, as if he remembered her.

"I've never understood how these potters can tell what they are forming with their wheel going so fast,"

Jessica remarked. "Want an ice cream?"

"Why not?" Might as well enjoy her last few days in Charleston, ice cream and all.

They walked in the door and into the cool air conditioning.

"Hello to you two." A familiar female voice floated across the room.

Rachel's heart dropped to her shoes. Morgan sat with Luke at a corner table and she motioned them over.

Rachel followed Jessica toward them, aware of Morgan's eyes sweeping over her like a north wind. Luke's glance flickered over her as warm breath. Dressed in a green knit shirt and khaki slacks, with a large shake in his hand, he looked as if all was well with his world.

His and Morgan's world.

He nodded at the two of them, set his cup on the table, and pulled up chairs for them. When he leaned to assist Rachel with her chair, his closeness and scent of spicy aftershave caused her heart to dance against her ribs. The small table had no space for the bouquet so she laid it in her lap. When she glanced up, their eyes locked. She trembled and broke the moment by turning toward the bulletin board menu.

Morgan sat her sundae glass down on the table with a bang. "Dear Aunt Jessie, how in the world are you making it in this heat?"

Jessica smiled. "Oh, I'm certain I don't keep as cool and fresh as Rachel does, but it will take a lot more than a little August heat to trim my sails."

Rachel told the server she wanted a chocolate sundae.

Jessica ordered mint lemonade.

Morgan turned to Rachel. "Well, how have you enjoyed your visit south?" Her voice was too bright.

"I will never forget my time here," Rachel said, steeling herself as she met the chilly green eyes.

Luke stopped drinking his shake.

"And what do you plan to do this fall, if I might ask?" The woman's silky voice held a note of sarcasm.

No, you may not ask.

Luke and Jessica waited for her answer as well as Morgan.

"Teach, I expect."

"You don't have a contract yet?" Morgan probed with a thin brow raised.

"I mean—I *will* be teaching. I've accepted a position in a private school in Ohio." Her voice sounded wooden, distant.

Luke's eyes were still on her, but Rachel turned to the sundae the waitress placed before her. Its sweet, chocolate flavor soothed the sadness trying to rise in her throat.

"So teaching it is." Morgan said with a shrug. "You have my sympathy."

Rachel ignored the comment, but out of the corner of her eye, she saw Luke frown.

Jessica pushed her shoulders back. "Have you two pretty well wrapped up plans for the costume ball?" She addressed her question more to Luke.

"Let's just say, I've done all I'm going to do." Luke's deep voice rolled over Rachel like a refreshing tide. Until now she hadn't realized how much she'd missed his voice. She fought the pleasure it stirred in her.

Lord, help me be able to eat this ice cream and get out of here.

"Oh, we've got it under control. Right, darling?" Morgan hooked her arm through Luke's free one as he finished his shake. "Luke is coming as one of the pirates who used to plunder our coast. I'm keeping my costume a secret." She turned to Rachel. "What are you going to wear?"

"I—haven't thought about it." Rachel pushed her fluted glass away.

"You are still coming, aren't you? We really want you to come, don't we, Luke and Aunt Jessie?"

Luke leaned forward. "We certainly do, Rachel."

She dared not look into Luke's face.

Jessica took a deep breath. "You definitely don't want to miss the ball, Rachel."

Kissing goodbye the thought of escaping the ball, Rachel forced a smile. "I'm sure I'll think of something to wear."

Luke spoke up. "If you need help with a costume, there's a trunk of them in the attic. I ran across it a while back." Still looking at Rachel, he continued. "Do you remember it, Jessica?"

"Yes, I do. It's up there." She patted Rachel's hand. "We will most certainly find something for you."

The shop door swung open and Pastor Cushwell entered. Rachel waved at him and he walked over, cool and neat, all six feet, four inches of him, in a yellow T-shirt with a Christian emblem, cotton slacks and leather sandals. His thick brown hair, closely cropped, resembled Luke's military style.

"Well, hello there, Rachel and friends." He smiled at the gathering, his countenance exuding good cheer. His eyes lingered on Morgan.

Rachel introduced the group. "Pastor Gordon I would like for you to meet Jessica Buckner, Luke

Barrett, and Morgan Pennington."

"I know Morgan, but she probably doesn't remember me." He reached out a hand to her, after Jessica and Luke.

"This is Pastor Gordon Cushwell from Redemption Hope church where I've been attending this summer."

The minister continued to gaze at Morgan and red spots rose in his cheeks.

She stared back, then released her breath dramatically and pointed a red-tipped finger at him. "The basketball guy at Mt. Pleasant High."

His face crinkled with pleasure. "You've got it right. One of them."

"So, you went into the ministry? I thought you won a scholarship in basketball or something." Now Morgan cast a long glance under her thick lashes at the lean man.

"I did, but when God calls, it's kind of like you must answer. Of course, He got my attention in one of the Middle East hotspots while I was fighting for Uncle Sam." He threw up a hand which could wrap around a basketball and grinned. "But don't worry. I'm not going to preach, since it's not Sunday."

Luke leaned forward at the mention of the minister's military service in the Middle East, new respect etched across his face. The pastor turned penetrating brown eyes on him.

"Thank you, Luke, for having Rachel in Charleston this summer. She's been a great visitor, and we'll miss her when she leaves, especially Ava who counts her a good friend."

Luke's hands tightened on the table edge.

The man turned back to Rachel. "By the way, how

much longer will you be with us, Rachel?"

"Two more weeks."

"I'm sorry to hear it. Well, I must be on my way. Got a gang of boys waiting in the church bus for ice cream." His face lit up in a comical grimace. "You can be glad I didn't let'em loose in here." He spoke to Jessica and Luke. "It was my pleasure meeting you two, and seeing you again, Morgan. Bye, Rachel." He moved to the take-out window.

Jessica tilted her chin. "What a nice young man. Does he have a family, Rachel? Is this the Ava?"

"No. He's never been married. And after visiting the church, I can probably tell you why. He's busy with all sorts of ministry in Charleston helping the needy. It's an inner city church that reaches out to hurting people." She dared not glance at Luke. "Ava is one of them."

"Where exactly is his church?" Morgan surprised Rachel by asking.

Rachel told her. Luke glanced her way as if listening, reached for his wallet and pulled out cash.

Luke and Morgan stood. He deposited a generous tip for the waitress and ambled over and paid for all the ice cream and returned. His glance swept over Rachel, warming her. " Bye, you two." He and Morgan threaded their way through the tables to the exit.

Rachel blinked moisture away. She glanced out the window. Luke and Morgan stopped to watch the potter a moment before disappearing down the street.

Jessica propped her elbows up and leaned on her folded hands. "We are going to miss you, Rachel. I admit I hoped things would turn out differently—that perhaps Luke had found someone who would—but there I go meddling again, like an old lady who hasn't enough to do. Ready?"

Unable to speak, Rachel turned and flicked away a tear that escaped and nodded. She lifted the bouquet from her lap and trekked out into the sunny cobbled stone street with Jessica. How much had the older woman discerned about her and Luke? Probably everything.

Chapter Twenty-One

The next night, after a battle with a strange fire he and his men barely caught in time in the tea barn, Luke entered through the kitchen door. They'd lost most of the summer harvest but not the barn. For that he was thankful. In the alcove he stripped off his damp shirt and washed off most of the smoke and grime, and walked to the game room. Moonlight from the window illuminated the room as he sat down behind his desk. A white envelope lying on top caught his attention. He picked it up and read the simple typed address, *Luke Barrett.* He turned on his lamp and tore it open. A single sheet fell out. Letters cut from a newspaper, spelled out the words, *The next time, it won't be the tea barn.*

He cursed and threw the paper back on the desk.

So the drug sharks discovered he was on the lookout for them. And they knew he would find them. Every stinking scum ball one of them.

He reached for the phone and glanced at the time. One o'clock. A new day. He'd call the solicitor tomorrow or drop by. Bone weary, he replaced the receiver, turned out the light, and headed to his room. Thanks to the letter, he now knew for sure it was someone close. The thought brought no pleasure.

Finding his bedroom warm and oppressive, he stepped out onto the balcony. A sound caused his body to stiffen. Someone else occupied the porch beyond. He slipped back inside the room, pushed his Glock into his waist band and went to investigate, walking soundlessly like he'd learned in his reconnaissance training.

~*~

Rachel lingered for a few moments, enjoying the cool breeze on the balcony. The air had freshened and no longer smelled of smoke. She pulled her robe closer and turned to go back to her room. Someone stepped around the corner in a crouch. Moonlight glanced off the gun in his hand. She gasped and froze.

Luke lowered the Glock. "I didn't think anyone belonging here would still be up."

His deep voice vibrated along Rachel's nerves.

She let out her breath and relaxed. Luke was shirtless. Probably had to scrub off soot. Did he also suffer burns? His dark hair gleamed with wetness. She cleared her throat. "My room was filled with—"

"The smell of burned tea." He finished for her. He pushed the pistol in the back of his waistband, leaned on the railing, and stared out over the plantation. Weariness etched every line of his body.

Compassion and sympathy flowed over Rachel. She fought the urge to go to him, put her arms around him, and weep. But deep down, she realized he would not want her kindness. Not after her rejection. She tore her eyes from his broad, muscular back and folded her arms. *Girl, get to your room.* "Luke, I am so sorry about the fire. So it was the tea factory?"

"Yep, but we saved the building."

"Do you have any idea how it happened?"

He turned to stare at her now. "I don't see why you should be concerned."

The coldness in his voice caused her lip to tremble. "You're right. I only want to say I'm sorry this has happened. Good night." She started toward the French doors.

But he moved to stand in her path. She lifted her eyes to his face and the damp curliness of his hair. Her breath caught in her throat. He reached out and drew her to him. His manly scent edged with smoke and tea enveloped her and his close bare torso spread tingles to her toes. She took a ragged breath. "Please, let me go, Luke."

"You've got the same scared-doe look again." Luke held her so near his warm breath feathered across her forehead. "Why are you afraid of me? Can't your lofty standards save you?"

Rachel fought weakness and a crazy desire to give into the warmth of his embrace. Panic rose in her throat. She tried to push away from him. Her balled fists met springy hair on his chest. Resolve flowed into her spine. "I am not afraid of you, Luke Barrett, but you are acting like Dakota Busby."

He dropped his arms so fast, she staggered.

"I'm sorry." Luke stepped away. He looked at her for a long moment, his face like granite, his lips a thin line. "Miss York, it's probably going to be better if you don't come back out on this balcony the rest of your stay." He ducked his head and left.

Cold water washed over her as she remembered how fast he released her. He acted as if she'd shot him.

Lord, I'm going to need Your help big time to make it through the days I have left here.

She stood for a moment listening to his heavy

steps retreating over the wooden boards. They seemed to be withdrawing across the corridors of her life—forever. A load of bricks settled on her shoulders, and dark shadows seeped into her heart. She stumbled into her room and fell on the bed. Burying her face in a pillow, Rachel moaned. *Dear God, I do love him. I can't deny it. Please help me do whatever I must. And help Luke find You and faith again.*

Her aunt's favorite scripture from the book of Romans flowed into her troubled mind. "And we know that all things work together for good to those who love God, to those who are the called according to His purpose."

Could her love for Luke ever work good? She didn't understand how, but comfort came. She got up, washed her face, returned to bed, and slept.

~*~

Luke walked to his room and dropped into a leather armchair. She compared him to Dakota Busby. He slammed his fist down on the armrest, and dropped his head into his hands.

Finally, he got up and fell across the bed, every muscle in his body stiff now from fighting the fire. Even in his stupor, he confronted the same presence in the room he'd felt before in the kitchen. A gentleness, a soft wooing fanning the air in the room like butterfly wings. But he refused to yield. He fought it until heavy sleep claimed him.

His gear pressed against his back like a ton of lead after two days of slipping and sliding on the mucky path. He adjusted a strap, and gripped his automatic rifle in ready position, scouring the bushes and grass for any movement.

Sweat poured down his back and soaked his shirt. Cade and two other special ops followed in his tracks. Out of nowhere came the whistling sound of a grenade, and all four hit the mud, cursing. Fire exploded around them. The screams of a dying man filled Luke's ears, and everything went black. The next thing he became aware of was Cade carrying him and dragging another. Something warm ran down his face and across his mouth. He tasted it. Salty. Blood. He blinked his eyes. Harder. Blackness.

Luke awoke, stifling a bloodcurdling bellow rising in his throat. Sweat poured down his body. Thank God, he'd awakened in time. He got up and went to the bathroom and threw water on his face, head, and shoulders. He slumped down in a chair and clenched his fists. This one was worse than the last. A new thought trickled into his mind. The Cushwell guy said he'd served in the Middle East. Did he ever battle what the docs called post-traumatic stress disorder? Maybe the minister knew how to beat it. Perhaps he'd drop in to visit him, and while there he would ask about the Ava person Rachel mentioned.

Chapter Twenty-two

Rachel woke late the following morning. Birds sang in the trees outside and sunlight poured through the windows. The desolate cloud of the night before faded in the streaming light. She arose and drew the French doors open and took several long, deep breaths before she remembered Luke's caution. Okay, I'm not actually out on the balcony, sir.

The smell of the fire, less discernible now, did not dampen the tiny flag of cheer in her heart. With only a little time left in Charleston, she determined to make it a good day. At least, it might be nice for some, she decided, as the past night's pain threatened to wash over her. Luke would hardly think it a fine morning after losing his tea harvest.

She closed the doors and with effort, pressed thoughts of Luke from her mind. After showering, she pulled on green slacks and a matching shell, and plaited her hair.

Downstairs, the household help, as well as Jessica and even Kristina, held subdued conversations about the fire. The topic pre-empted discussion of Rachel's soon leaving. She breathed a prayer of thanks.

According to Jessica, no one knew if arsonists were responsible or whether it'd been caused by an internal problem. Mrs. Busby appeared tight-lipped and with dark circles around her eyes as she helped bring food from the kitchen. Did the woman worry Dakota might've had something to do with it?

Jessica poured Rachel and herself another cup of tea as they finished breakfast. "Luke drove into town this morning. I'm sure to report what's happened."

"Can I read to you?" Kristina asked Rachel later in the drawing room for the morning's lesson. Rachel smiled and sat down as Kristina pulled a small book from the shelf, full of pictures and a beginning vocabulary. She read well.

"I am so proud of you, Kristina." The child's happy face with its sprinkle of freckles drew a pain across Rachel's heart. She would miss this little one, but she consoled herself that her employer's daughter had made excellent progress.

~*~

Luke dropped by James Sanders' office and learned he'd already heard what happened. The solicitor, dressed in a navy suit, white shirt and red tie was spotless and professional as he always appeared. He offered Luke a cup of coffee and a chair.

"Hated to get the news about your fire from one of our operatives. Glad you saved the building. Do you have any idea what might've caused it?"

Luke pulled the note from his pocket and slid it across the desk. Sanders set his cup down and read it. A frown crossed his smoothly shaven face. He walked to the window waving the paper.

"Luke, this is dead serious stuff. We are dealing with some bad-to-the bone folks and some of them even live in fine, big houses. People you'd think would never stoop to drug smuggling and certainly not to arson."

Luke's brows rose.

James came back to his desk. "I need to show this to Deeson. This shines a different light on things. It puts a rush on, in fact. Something has to be coming down the pike. If we can figure out what pike in time. Do you mind if I keep this? And we don't report it to the sheriff's office right now? We'll all be working together soon, I think. But we don't want the media involved."

"Fine with me." Luke leaned back in his chair.

The solicitor opened his desk drawer and placed the note inside. "You told anyone else about this note?"

"Not a soul."

"Well, don't. Until we decide what to do. I'm sure we'll be back in touch over the next few days. You still plan to be at the Harvest Ball next weekend?" Sanders smiled. "But, of course. You and Archer's sister are hosting it, right?"

"Oh, yeah. Nothing short of our nation declaring war could get me off the hook." Luke stood.

"Well, I will be there, too, at least for a little while. It might be an important night. I think this thing is going to explode soon. Stay vigilant." Sanders came around the desk, balled his fist, and bumped Luke's shoulder. "But I don't need to tell an old pro like you, do I?"

Luke left and found his way to King Street. As he drove near the overpass, a converted building came into view with a sign, *Redemption Hope Church*. He drove by once, went around the block and came back. He glanced at his wristwatch. Ten o'clock. What did pastors do at this hour on a Thursday?

He parked in front to keep an eye on the jeep.

Finding the main door locked, he almost left. Instead he knocked, feeling a little foolish. In a couple of minutes, Gordon Cushwell opened the door. The penetrating brown eyes Luke remembered spoke sincerity, as did the quick grin, the pastor flashed. "Hello, Luke. Glad to see you. Come in."

"Hope I'm not interrupting anything."

"Not a thing. Let's go back to my office. Our secretary only works Monday through Wednesday and all the men upstairs in the men's shelter work during the day, so it's the better part of wisdom to lock the front door." He peered outside. "I see you parked on the street. You should be okay this time of day."

"You're probably right about locking your door in this section of town." Luke glanced around the simple sanctuary as he followed the minister. Chairs in rows faced a low stage with drums and a keyboard. They passed doors with signs designating clothing and groceries.

The pastor's small room, in spite of being packed with office equipment, boxes of literature and shelves of books, seemed comfortable. The chair Cushman offered him was anything but chintzy. Luke sat down and ran his hands over the smooth leather arms to relieve the tightness in his shoulders.

"You like the chair, huh? A donation from a sweet elderly lady in town." Gordon smiled and poured Luke and himself a cup of coffee and sat behind his desk.

Luke sipped the hot coffee, strong like he preferred, and scanned the room. On a shelf, a military photo of Gordon in an army uniform caught his eye.

The pastor spoke. "I was glad we got to meet at the ice cream shop. I think a lot of Rachel. And it was nice to see Morgan again." The minister took a long sip of his coffee and studied Luke's face. "You're in love with her, aren't you?"

Luke's head shot up. "Who?"

"Rachel."

Luke grimaced and pretended to inspect the ceiling. "Was it so evident? I hardly looked at her twice."

"Afraid so. If you know people like I do. Maybe I should say like God shows me."

"What do you mean?"

"Love is from God. It's the most powerful force in the universe, and you can recognize it—in the face of a mother for her child, or a man's gaze or efforts not to notice, a woman he loves. And definitely in the face of a friend giving his life for another. Like Jesus' countenance from the cross."

The cords in Luke's neck tightened. Was the man going to start preaching?

Gordon continued as if he hadn't noticed Luke stiffening. "I heard about your fire last night. Cade called me. I sure am sorry, Luke. What happened? Did you suffer a big loss?"

So this was Cade's church? "We lost most of the tea harvest but not the building. Right now we're investigating how it happened."

The pastor set his coffee cup on the desk. "Where did you serve in the Middle East?"

"Wherever the Marine Corps deemed the hottest spot. You?"

A corner of Gordon's mouth quirked up. "The same, but with the Army."

Luke cleared his throat and tightened his fists. Where did he start?

Gordon leaned forward. "It's over but you still can't talk about it, can you?"

Luke relaxed his hands. "No, and it may be over, but I sometimes fight it again at night. You ever bothered with night sweats?

"Oh, yeah, I used to suffer those things. Big time." The pastor drained his cup. "More coffee?"

"No." Luke sat his empty cup on the edge of the desk, every muscle alert. "You mean you did fight this werewolf, but you're not now? I would be interested in the solution, if you've found one. In fact, it's really why I dropped by, and to find out about the Ava person."

The pastor's face perked up. "What about Ava? Her last name is Jenkins, by the way."

"Something Rachel said to me. I really wouldn't recognize her if I saw her."

The pastor stood up. "Come with me, I believe her picture is on our hall collage."

Luke followed Gordon back into the hall and to a large bulletin board filled with pictures and activities.

"There she is."

Luke stared at the pregnant young woman standing at a yard sale table. He turned to the pastor. "So, does her husband come here, too?"

"Actually, she's not married, Luke. And Rachel's friendship has been good for her. What exactly did Rachel tell you about her?"

Luke rocked back on his heels. "It doesn't make any sense. We, uh, were having a kind of heated discussion, and right as I was walking out the door, she said, 'What about Ava?' And I never did get around to asking her what she meant. But you mentioned her name at the ice cream shop."

Gordon appeared thoughtful. Then a light came

on in his dark eyes. "Wait a minute. Let me check something in my notes." He walked back into his office.

Luke glanced again at the bulletin board and squinted at a picture in the upper left corner. Cade, standing in front of a church bus. This was where he spent his weekends.

"I think I have it." Gordon came back, nodding his head. Ava told me, and I am sure she told Rachel, the name of her baby's father. In fact, I understand he does send money regularly, but the bad part is he didn't offer to marry her and he insisted she have an abortion. He broke up with her when she refused." They both still stared at Ava's picture. "Since you carry his same last name, perhaps Rachel thought you were aware of the situation."

The pastor's eyes now turned toward Luke. "Ava said a Dan Barrett is the father."

"Wh-at?" Acid boiled up in the pit of Luke's stomach.

"Is this a relative of yours perhaps?"

Luke stared at the picture a moment and gritted his teeth. He slammed a fist into his palm. "*My* name is Luke Daniel Barrett, but I promise you I am not the father of this child and I have no cousins."

"Whoa-a." The pastor folded his arms and glanced back at Ava's picture. "Something strange is going on here."

"I tell you, something *crazy* is going on." Luke's scowl shadowed his face. No wonder Rachel acted so strange. Did she really believe this guy was him?

"Come on back into the office, Luke. We'll get this figured out." Sitting on the edge of his desk, Gordon reached for his phone. "I think we can begin clearing it up with a simple phone call. Do you mind if I call Ava and ask her for a description of Dan Barrett?"

Luke gave him two thumbs up, and plopped into his chair, hardly able to breathe.

Three minutes later, Gordon replaced the receiver. "She says he's blond, a real cowboy and he owns a plantation somewhere. Sound like anyone you know?"

"Dakota Busby. I'll kill him for using my name."

Gordon walked around his desk and sat. "I hope you don't mean that literally, Luke. Who is this man?"

Luke lowered his face, unwilling to meet the gentle eyes of the pastor. "My ex-farm manager. The slime ball."

"So, you think Rachel thought you were the father? That's tough. But there's nothing like the truth to set things right." Gordon took a deep breath and leaned back in his chair. "In fact, I can help, at least with Ava—if you're sure he's her man."

Luke finally met the pastor's glance. "It's him. He's one of the few who know my middle name, but yeah, we'd better make sure. Reckon she's got a picture of him?" His breathing came easier now.

"I'll check it out. Is there a big rush on this? It's gone on now for, well, for almost nine months."

"No, I guess not, especially where she's concerned. We shouldn't upset her."

Meanwhile, he'd find the dirt bag and straighten him out.

"Good." Gordon rubbed his hands together and smiled. "Since we're on the way to getting that settled, let's get back to nighttime werewolves."

Tension oozed from Luke's body as he stared at the man. Whatever ministers were supposed to possess, this one had a good measure of it. He could trust him. "So how did you beat the syndrome?"

Gordon set up in his chair. "Luke, do you mind if we pray before we get into this?"

Luke bowed his head. "Go right ahead." He wasn't a heathen.

"Father, we ask Your help. Of ourselves, we can do nothing. In Jesus' name. Amen."

Luke grinned. "That's about the shortest prayer I've ever heard a minister pray. You don't waste time." He liked the man and experienced strange peace.

Gordon sat up straight and propped his arms on his desk. "I'm not going to mince words either, Luke, and I also don't want to patronize you or give you pat answers you already know. But I will tell you my experience.

"In my last battle in one of those places the news reporters aren't invited, my special ops team ran into a bloody fight. A terrorist group came over the hill and everything exploded in our faces. Before our backup showed up, with my buddies dying around me and thinking I would be next, I absolutely experienced something akin to a presence that settled around me. It was like an island of calm in the middle of hell. I was busy, and I shook it off and did what I had to do, but I never forgot it. It followed me home and I wrestled with it, kind of reminded me of a guy in the Bible named Jacob."

Luke's shoulders tightened again as he listened with every fiber of his being. The man survived a deadly battle but now had peace about the whole thing. There was hope.

Gordon grimaced and his eyes blazed. "For a time I suffered all sorts of recurring nightmares, what the docs call post-traumatic stress disorder. And nothing they gave me worked. One morning, at the end of my rope, and I'm sure my praying mother's sanity, I gave up. I said, 'God, I know You're real and You're after me. I've done a lot of bad stuff, but if Jesus can clean me up, I'm ready. I repent. I'm Your man and I'll even be Your special ops or whatever You want."

The pastor stopped and tapped his desk with his big fist. He smiled at Luke. "That was seven years ago. So here I am. No more night sweats." He paused, and cocked his chin. "But I do have a few day timers — like Ava's situation."

Luke's shoulders relaxed.

Gordon leaned forward in his chair, his cheerful brown eyes extending an invitation.

Luke cleared his throat. "I'll think about what you've shared, but I'm not sure I could live up to…"

"Hey, bub, you don't have to be perfect. You just decide to put yourself on the potter's wheel."

They both stood.

Gordon came around the desk and stared straight at Luke, man to man. "In fact, between you and me, when I look at Morgan Pennington, I think I might need another twirl on the wheel myself."

"You're kidding." Luke searched the man's face. *Morgan?* There couldn't be two more opposite poles on earth. *Thank God it's not Rachel.*

Luke followed the minister back into the sanctuary.

Gordon stopped and turned to him. "Luke, I'd like to pray with you about those night sweats. I understand how gruesome they can be. May I?"

"Yeah."

This is it. Time to decide.

Luke glanced around. The voice sounded a little

241

like Jessica's, but no one else was in the building.

Gordon led the way up to the small altar with its steps across the front.

"I'm going to kneel here, Luke, but you can stand, if you prefer." He knelt down on the bottom step, and Luke, stiff as a board, did the same. His heart pounded against his ribs as the strong voice of Gordon Cushwell rose up in the quiet building.

"Father, I bring Luke to You. He needs Your help. Make Yourself real to him and bless his sleep with peace."

A presence settled over Luke making his scalp tingle. This time he surrendered. Surprisingly, tight springs began to release all over his body.

The pastor hesitated, opened his eyes, and cast them toward Luke. "I feel led to pray specifically about forgiveness. Has this been a problem like it has been with most of us vets?"

Luke's words exploded out of him, "Yeah, I guess it has." Suddenly, the urge to weep overtook him as memories of Georgina's car wreck came into his mind, as well as the morning the doctors told him they could not save his eye. Bile rose in his throat as it always did with the memories but this time, a peace seemed to encase them, cover the raw edges. Shocked, Luke took a deep breath, put all doubts away, and listened as the pastor continued praying.

"Jesus, You said to pray, 'forgive us our trespasses as we forgive those who trespass against us.' Help Luke forgive others, You and himself for all that's happened to him and his family."

The pastor turned again to Luke. "Do you want to pray anything yourself right now?"

A long list of things.

Luke bowed deeper, all stiffness gone. He cleared the growing lump from his throat and prayed hesitantly, as if relearning how. "Lord Jesus, I am so sorry for...for drifting away from You, and doubting You and even blaming You for things that happened. Forgive me for thinking I could handle everything, anything, by myself." Rachel's lovely face flowed into his mind. "Forgive my anger and all the other things You know I've done. Put me on Your potter's wheel. You've got a lot of work to do."

A weight lifted off his shoulders, leaving his spirit light.

The pastor touched Luke's shoulder. They both stood. "Good place to start, my man. Good place and with a great potter."

As Luke strode to his car, he reveled in the peace and the presence of God flowing around him. He no longer wanted to escape, no matter how painful the potter's wheel might become. Like, if Rachel left as planned.

He drove back to Barrett Hall still enveloped in serenity. He parked in the garage and decided to trek around to the front porch, hoping to catch Rachel there after she put Kristina down for her nap. He had a lot to tell her and to apologize for. She'd been right about so much. As he walked, the grass of the lawn appeared greener, the flowers of the garden more brilliant. A harmony filled his inner being, and he started to whistle. An unfamiliar male voice from the front porch silenced his lips and stopped him in his tracks.

~*~

"Rachel, honey, I am deliriously happy to find

you. And you look wonderful."

Rachel stepped out onto the porch after answering the door, prepared to avoid a hug from Easton Watkins. But he surprised her by behaving well. "Hello, Easton."

He ran his fingers through his short honey hair. "Boy, I've got a ton to share with you. Can we go somewhere?" He glanced at the rockers and to his Thunderbird in the drive.

Rachel motioned toward the chairs. But neither sat.

No way would she get in the car with Easton.

"I was such a fool to break up with you. It's over with Janet. I let her think she broke the engagement so she's okay." He moved closer. "Rachel, I've come to the conclusion you're the best thing that ever happened to me."

She stared at him, wondering how to assimilate what he was telling her, and feeling nothing. That long ago spark had been extinguished by a much greater fire.

She shook the thought away and studied his strong, handsome face drawn tight with seriousness. He did appear different. Sincere? On the other hand, was this another of his lawyer acts, like those he used to convince juries?

Easton cleared his throat and spots of color appeared on his cheeks. "I need to tell you, I've experienced a spiritual renewal, Rachel. I'm not the same man you left in Ohio."

His voice even cracked. If this were an act, it was a good one.

He reached for her hand. She didn't resist. In his dark eyes something new instead of guile surprised her.

"I found the Lord, like you used to talk about, and I'm so sorry for never listening and living so selfishly."

Rachel was touched, but she pulled her hand away, disturbed. Was this some kind of sign she was supposed to get back in a courtship with Easton? She shook her head without realizing it.

Easton's voice rose a level. "Rachel, I'm serious. I'm even going to the little church on the 'quote' wrong side of town who does the soup kitchen. Remember?"

"Yes, I do, Easton. And I'm glad for you, if what you're telling me is true."

His face and eyes took on an earnestness Rachel had never observed in the two years she dated him. "It is the truth, Rachel. How do you think I talked your Aunt Ruby into giving me your address? She believes me."

He leaned closer.

Overcome, Rachel stood and walked to the edge of the porch in the shadow of a giant camellia bush, her thoughts in a jumble. Easton followed her and stood behind her, not touching her.

"I love you, Rachel. I want to marry you. I came to drive you home. I'm not leaving Charleston, until you come with me. I told the firm I'm out of there for as long it takes."

She turned to stare at him in amazement. What woman in her right mind could ignore such words? When he put his arms around her and drew her to him almost reverently, she stiffened, but didn't move away.

Lord, is this Your plan? This potter's wheel hurts so much. You know I love Luke.

Easton kissed her.

His lips were the wrong ones. She twisted around.

A movement behind the camellia bush surprised her. Her heart stopped as Luke turned and walked away. Tears began to fall down Rachel's cheeks.

Easton pressed her shoulders. "You and I can enjoy a wonderful life together, since I've gotten my priorities in order. There's a lot of good I hope to do with my law degree." He turned her about to face him. "Hey, what's this? Tears?" Easton tried to kiss them away.

She pushed from him. "No. Easton, I am happy for you but—"

"No buts. I have something for you. I planned to wait, but can't." He pulled a small black box from his pocket and opened it. A large diamond winked in the sunlight. He reached for her hand and slipped it on her finger.

"Easton, I cannot accept this." She pulled it off and handed it back.

He smiled. "I can wait. You only have what? Three or four more days here? A week? Cancel your plane tickets. I want to drive you home, and I won't even pressure you about this." He waved the box, and put it in his pocket. "Will you let me escort you home?"

"I don't think so." Rachel trembled and swiped at her cheeks. Finally, she said, "I appreciate your offer, Easton, but I really want to keep to my original plan. I need to finish up here. Alone. Do you mind?"

Easton whipped a business card out of his wallet and the pen in his breast pocket.

He scribbled a number on the back of the card. "I am staying in Charleston. Call me if you change your mind."

I won't change it.

But she took the card he pressed into her hand.

"Easton, why are you really here in Charleston?"

"Yep, you're right. I am killing two birds with one stone. There's a convention going on I'm attending, as well as taking a few days off—but your being here is what sealed my decision." He stepped back and gazed at her. "Do you believe anything I've told you, Rachel? You are different somehow—and more beautiful, I might add."

It's called survival mode.

~*~

Luke plodded around to the patio door and to the game room, his chest ready to explode with pain. He dropped in his chair and leaned his head back.

Too late. Was this the Potter's wheel? Or a test of faith?

After some time, he took a deep breath and looked around like someone who has come through a bombing raid. Strangely, everything was still intact. And yes, the Presence, was still with him. Peaceful thoughts fluttered across his mind. She wasn't gone yet. It wasn't over. Even on the Potter's wheel. He stood and walked to his room, changed into work clothes, and drove the jeep out on the plantation.

Chapter Twenty-three

Rachel's last Sunday in Charleston proved bittersweet. After church, Ava surprised her with a going-away dinner at her apartment. Rachel came into the living area and smiled. How could anyone eight-months pregnant keep everything so spotless and neat?

After lunch, while Ava put away the leftovers, Rachel walked to the mantle to examine a framed photo. Startled, she picked it up. What was Dakota Busby's likeness doing in Ava's apartment?

"This picture on the mantle, Ava, is it someone you know well?" she called toward the kitchen.

Ava appeared in the doorway, wiping her hands on a towel. "Can't you guess? It's my baby's father."

"But, didn't you say, his name was Dan Barrett?"

"Yes. It's him." Ava turned back into the kitchen.

Rachel almost dropped the keepsake. Shock, relief, and indignation battled in her heart.

Luke was not the father. Dakota stole his name. But how to tell Ava? *Help me, Father.*

She turned to the young woman as she came in the room. "Ava, come and sit down. I've something I must share with you."

They both sat on the sofa.

Rachel held up the photo. "This man's name is Dakota Busby."

"What?" Ava sank against the sofa cushion and laid her shaking hands over her bulging stomach.

Rachel peered down at her. "You okay?"

Ava shook her head. "You ask me if I'm okay, when I've just learned I don't even have the right *name* of my child's father." She looked at Rachel and tears gathered in her wide eyes. "Do you know this man?"

"Yes, I'm afraid I do, Ava. He is, he was, until recently, the farm manager at Barrett Hall and the owner is Luke Daniel Barrett."

Tears trailed down Ava's face. "Everything's been a lie." Her voice rang with emotion.

Rachel reached for a box of tissues, and patted Ava's arm. Her throat tightened. She didn't trust herself to speak for several moments.

"I believe God is going to work in all this, Ava, because He loves you and your baby so much." Rachel knew it to be true as she mouthed the words. "And no matter what Dakota told you," she pointed to the photo, "it doesn't change the fact this man is the father, right?"

"Yes. No question there. He's never denied it." Ava blew her nose. "Dakota did you say? I kinda like that name. Of course, this baby's gonna have a deceased father when I get through with him."

Rachel laid a hand on Ava's shoulder. "Perhaps, he was going to come clean with you, Ava, before the baby's birth. And one good thing, you said he's been sending you money regularly?"

Ava sniffed. "Oh, yes. And he's said he has the money in an account to pay the hospital."

"Well, I guess something his mother taught him is sticking in there somewhere. His mother is the housekeeper at Barrett Hall."

"She is? Well, I don't have any real folks I'm aware of. I was a foster child from a baby." Fresh tears began to flow. "And I don't ever want that to happen to this little tyke."

Rachel drove home with a prayer on her lips.

Father, how can I leave Charleston, not knowing for sure how things will work out for Ava and her baby?

The day of the Costume Ball Kristina burst into Rachel's room in tears. "It's gone. It's gone. My mother's diary. I couldn't find it nowhere upstairs."

Rachel pulled the child down beside her on the sofa and hugged her. "Don't worry, hon, I'm sure we will find it. And you are supposed to be taking a nap, young lady."

Rachel led Kristina back to her room. *Did Luke take the diary? Maybe to get Kristina ready for a new mother? Morgan Pennington.* The thought made her stomach churn. After promising Kristina she'd search for the diary, she read the child a story until she fell asleep.

Rachel was halfway back to her room when the Harvest Ball and the needed costume popped into her mind. She needed to search for a costume in the attic, and while there she'd also check for the lost diary.

As she stepped onto the faded runner of the upper floor, the heat and stale air enveloped her. She opened the attic door at the far end. The space appeared more organized. *Did Luke's trip earlier have anything to do with it?*

The heat stifled her until she pulled open a window. A cool, fresh breeze refreshed the room. She glanced out across the fields. *Where were Luke and Cade working today?* Surely he'd quit early to prepare for the ball.

She sighed and made her way through the sundry discarded chairs and boxes to find the trunk Kristina had opened on their first attic visit. Two dusty green steamer trunks set side by side. She bent to open the nearest one. The sheet covering a large painting beside her slipped to the floor. She turned, and her breath stopped in her throat.

Before her, almost life-size, stood a pirate in an elegant black coat, his lean face deeply tanned. A blood-red plume curled over the brim of his hat. He wore a ruffled silk shirt and shiny black boots up to his thighs. At his waist, in a sling of scarlet silk, hung a sword and two silver-mounted pistols. Cool, green eyes challenged her. The curling thin lips beckoned her. A shock of recognition traveled from her head to her toes. *Luke.*

Shaking, she pulled the trunk to the side and leaned down to read the engraving at the bottom of the frame. *Captain Lucas Bloodstone Barrett, 1730.*

She stared at the bronzed, arrogant face with its trim mustache. Luke's pirate ancestor. She closed her eyes and imagined a Spanish galleon bobbing on the waves, a smaller boat pulled up to the beach, a trunk of gold lugged across the sand and buried by a motley crew of buccaneers.

Rachel cast her daydreaming away and opened the larger green trunk. White ruffles popped out. She lifted the piece and discovered a long, creamy period dress with green ribbons cascading down the sides. Lovely. Rummaging deeper in the crate, she found a layered petticoat with the same green ribbons. The dress and under garment reminded her of southern belles she'd watched in movies. She stood up, wiped the perspiration from her upper lip, and, trembling with anticipation, held the dress to her body. It might fit her. And her green heels would match. What a memory she would make of her last night in Charleston. And why not?

She closed the trunk, laid the dress and petticoat on top, and opened the smaller green chest. This one she remembered holding Georgina's diary. But it was no longer there. She moved the dress and lifted the larger trunk lid again and systematically searched through its folded contents. Finally, she slid her hand down the sides. She encountered something smooth and soft, a thick packet of some sort. Curious, Rachel withdrew it. The clear, plastic bag held white powder. She cried out and dropped it like it was on fire. Drugs. Probably cocaine.

Ron had shown her pictures of confiscated contraband. She was staring at a sizeable fortune, if this package hit the streets. But who hid it in Barrett Hall's attic?

She glanced again at the painting. The familiar eyes of the pirate mocked her under his red-plumed hat. It was as though he held her bound—intending to convey a message she did not wish to understand.

Rachel's forebodings of the past months flashed through her mind and cut her heart like a sword. She dropped her face into her hands and pressed her burning eyes. Was Luke a twentieth-century pirate on the same coasts his cocky ancestor once plundered?

Everything fit. The easy access to the Caribbean and South America from Charleston, the planes in the wee hours, Luke's nighttime rides—and the plane he'd met. His telling her soon after her arrival the attic was "off limits." His visit to the attic days ago. And his persistent distrust of her, as if she might be an agent. Even his not appearing too worried after the fire, took on new significance. Nausea burned in the pit of her stomach. Why worry about a few thousand dollars' loss in tea if one possessed many thousands, even a million, in cocaine?

The whine of a jeep through the window interrupted Rachel's blazing thoughts. Luke. He must not find her in the attic.

Her eyes fell on the packet. What to do? She needed to report this, but meantime, she must hide the drugs somewhere safe from anyone who came to collect them.

The jeep grew louder, and squealed to a halt under the window.

Forcing her stiff limbs to move, Rachel grabbed the thick bag, dropped it behind the painting, and replaced the sheet covering the frame. She closed the lid of the trunk and pushed it away with her foot. She swept up the dress and petticoat and dashed to the door.

The open window gaped at her. She moved to close it but Luke strode toward the patio beneath her. She fell back against the wall, her heart pounding, and waited for him to enter the house. She eased the window down and slipped out into the hall.

She listened at the top of the staircase until the game room door slammed and sprinted to her room. Dropping the costume on the floor, Rachel fell across the bed.

Dear God, please don't let Luke be involved in smuggling drugs. But if he's not, who hid the package in the attic? Show me what to do.

Chapter Twenty-four

Rachel passed the rest of the afternoon in a surreal state. The discovery of the drugs consumed her mind. Grief sat like a ton of lead on her heart. It must be Luke. Who else had access to the attic, and regular night excursions? And who needed cash for a dream resort? Reality finally separated from imagination — and hope.

She tried to busy herself preparing for the trip home, but packed, and unpacked items she needed to use to dress for the Costume Ball a few hours away. One thought hammered in her mind. What should she to do about the drugs? Could she climb on the plane late the following evening and do nothing, let someone else discover the drugs? Never. It was not an option to walk away from Barrett Hall with the possible link and evidence in Ron's DEA investigation lying on the third floor. A tear slipped down her cheek. Ron gave his life trying to unravel the truth.

The dinner hour arrived early because of the ball and still Rachel had made no decision about the drugs. To her dismay, Luke came to sit at his usual place at the table. After the blessing, his eye flickered in her direction. Against her will, Rachel met his glance for an electrifying second. Neither spoke.

Jessica broke the tension. "Well, Luke, Rachel is set for the ball tonight. She found a costume in the attic without my help."

Rachel's eyes flew to Luke's face, but his expression did not change.

"And she's gonna let me see her all dressed up." Kristina glowed with anticipation.

"Good." Luke passed a platter of fried chicken toward Rachel. She dared not look at him again. She took small portions of everything and placed forkfuls in her mouth, with no idea how anything tasted. Voices buzzed around her.

When conversation stopped, Rachel raised her head to find Luke and Jessica staring at her. Heat rose in her cheeks. "I'm sorry, did you ask me something?"

Jessica's brows lifted, but a smile creased her face. "Luke asked if you need the car for the ball tonight."

"Oh, yes, please. I may not stay long."

Rachel was never more anxious for a meal to conclude. It proved a mammoth task to keep her mind on the talk, to answer polite questions about her departure and new job, and most of all to avoid meeting Luke's warm gaze.

Toward the end of the meal, she began to feel like an actor in a play. Everything was unreal. Had she, indeed, discovered a fortune in drugs in this house two floors above this elegant dinner scene? Nothing about Jessica's bright conversation, Luke's calm demeanor, or the beautiful table setting hinted of a crime being perpetrated—a crime that would send the guilty party to prison.

Her eyes burned toward Luke. Poor Kristina. And Jessica. She choked down a final bite of food.

Later, in her room, Rachel lay across her bed and tried to will away the burning behind her aching eyelids.

Father God, how can I report these drugs? Luke must be guilty.

A sharp rap at the door startled her.

"Rachel."

Luke's voice jolted her heart against her ribs. She sat up and drew her knees to her chest for support.

"Yes?"

"Please come back downstairs. I want to talk to you."

Rachel laid her head on her knees and searched for the right words. "Luke, I—can't."

"You sound pretty sure about it."

Something crushed and broken inside her laughed at the thought. Was she sure of anything?

"Yes, I'm positive." She wished she wasn't.

"Okay. If that's the way you want it. One last thing. Be careful, Rachel, when you drive to Pennington's. A storm may be heading up our coast." His voice exuded something she didn't recognize. Concern? Yes, but also *patience* in the king of short fuses?

"I don't plan to stay long. I'll be cautious, Luke."

His retreating steps faded down the hall. Why had he given up so easily? It was unlike him.

Indecision played kickball with sorrow in her heart. What should she do? Call Joseph? Tell Jessica? She might even try to contact James Sanders at the costume ball. She decided she would phone Joseph and get ready for the ball.

She opened her door, scanned up and down the hall, and slipped across to the sitting room. Luke should be dressing for the ball and Jessica probably catching the evening news in her room.

She would simply tell Joseph she had found the

drugs. Let him take it from there. The investigation could point to Luke—or exonerate him. But what hope was there of that? She took a deep breath and dialed the number. She let it ring fifteen times. *Where are you, Joseph?*

Finally, she replaced the receiver and walked back to her room, fighting a sense of helplessness. Tomorrow about this time she'd be stepping aboard her plane home. Should she try to talk to Jessica or James Sanders?

She gazed at the lovely dress hanging in front of her closet door. She'd try James Sanders at the ball first. Her last resort before going to Jessica. Or outright calling the DEA office in Charleston.

She bathed and dressed while her mind kept spinning around the drugs and Luke. She curled her dark hair to cascade to her shoulder on one side, pulled tight curls up on the other side, and pinned them with a green velvet bow. Last, she fastened on a thin gold necklace with its jade teardrop and matching earrings, a high school graduation present from her own mother given to Aunt Ruby for safekeeping before her mother passed.

Rachel glanced in the mirror and froze. A girl from another century stared at her with large, expressive blue-green eyes. Bouncy curls, which Jessica suggested, complemented the costume perfectly. She clasped the ruffles of the full skirt with its emerald bows and twirled around in the middle of the floor twice, enjoying the swishing sound and touch of the thick layered satin petticoats against her ankles. In the mirror, the short, puffy sleeves of the dress and scooped neckline revealed her soft tan. She closed her eyes for a moment and imagined a time when people lived quieter, more isolated lives, dependent on a ball a few times a year to fellowship with their distant neighbors and no one thought once about drugs and criminals.

The terrible reality of the hoard upstairs hit her again with such force her stomach roiled. She swallowed hard and stepped into the hall toward Kristina's room.

The child's eyes turned big and round. "You look like Cinderella going to the ball!"

Rachel smiled and swished over to the bed where Kristina perched amid her books. She gave the child a hug and read a story to her. Her plan was to arrive late at the ball and leave early.

Jessica peeked in. "Oh, my, Rachel. How lovely. I'm glad you're going. Let me go down with you."

"Okay, but first, let me step back into my room and get Penny and a light wrap."

"Oh, you're taking Penny?"

"Yes, I don't plan to stay long, and she'll be fine in the car with a new chew bone and the windows down. It's turned out much cooler than I expected. If I leave her, you people will be sorry. She might howl all evening."

Rachel returned with a light shawl draped on her arm and the little dog with its tail happily hitting both sides of the carrier. She walked down the steps with Jessica to the patio door. A sharp wind rattled the glass. Jessica touched a puffed sleeve of Rachel's dress. When she glanced at her, the woman smiled but sadness flickered across her face.

"Rachel, I would do about anything to keep you from walking on that plane tomorrow evening. You understand that, don't you?" A tremor laced Jessica's voice.

Rachel could not trust herself to speak. She held the carrier aside and hugged the elderly woman and pushed out the door and to the garage. The stiff cool breeze lifted her skirts. After considerable effort pressing her ballooning costume into the car, she drove the luxury car down the back road past Granny Eller's to Pennington Plantation.

Rachel decided to park behind the house so she could slip away early and return by the same route to Barrett Hall. She glanced up at a dark cloud coming in from the coast but lowered the windows anyway for Penny's air. She would not be staying long. The puppy settled down contentedly with the chew bone Rachel gave her.

Clasping her ruffled skirt against the brisk wind, she stepped along the well-lit garden path and emerged at the front steps of the plantation house. She made her way between costumed guests, most wearing masks, and entered the foyer.

Archer broke away from a group and strode toward her. His narrow mask concealed little of his handsome face. "Well, hello there, gorgeous."

He was dressed as a colonial planter in gray knee britches, long-tailed green coat, and white ruffled shirt. "Would you believe this came with a white powdered wig? And do we make a great match? Where in the world did you find the period dress?" Archer reached for her hand, twirled her around, and drew her close.

"Let me go, you rogue planter." She pushed him away.

Archer moved to greet other guests, and Rachel stepped aside and glanced into the next room. Where would she find James Sanders in this crowd, even if she'd recognize him in a costume?

A movement on the stairs drew her attention, as well as those around her. Morgan descended, quite aware, Rachel decided, of the entrance she generated. Her shining, blue silk gown, cut daringly low, cascaded with ruffles into an elegant bell about her ankles. A powdered platinum wig piled in thick gleaming curls on top of her head hid her blond hair and allowed a full view of gleaming sapphires at her neck and ears. A narrow silver mask covered over her eyes. She came straight to Rachel and Archer, a brittle smile on her rosy lips.

"Rachel, how charming. Georgina loved that dress, wore it to her last ball here."

Rachel's legs went weak. She gazed down at the dress aghast. Of course, it had belonged to Georgina, not Jessica, as she had assumed. She chewed her lower lip. How could she avoid running into Luke?

Someone called Morgan and Archer away to Rachel's relief. She started down the hall. A figure in a red-plumed hat and crimson-trimmed black coat emerged from the dining room. She gasped. The pirate from the painting at Barrett Hall stood in the doorway. His eagle eye skimmed the clusters of guests. A pistol and sword gleamed at his side above black boots. He clasped a cup of punch in his hand, but he wore no mask. Only an eye patch.

Rachel started to turn back. But the swooping gaze stopped on her. The blood drained from Luke's face, and the cup of drink shook in his hand.

He stormed toward her. "How did you come to choose that dress, Rachel?" His voice was low and raw.

Dear Lord, does he think I did this on purpose?

Before she could frame an answer, Morgan came

down the hallway. "Oh, Luke, there you are, we really must greet our guests." She barely glanced at Rachel and put her hand on Luke's arm. His lips thinned into a tight line and he turned and went with her.

Rachel walked away, her heart pounding with pain.

For the next hour as she searched for James Sanders, she managed to keep her distance from Luke and Morgan. But his black and crimson costume appeared around every corner. Finally, she glanced at her wristwatch and decided she would go back to Barrett Hall and call the solicitor the following morning. Or phone Joseph again. She went in search of Archer to take her leave. As she passed the stairs, she ran into Luke.

He grabbed her wrist and pulled her toward the patio entrance. Rachel balked at the doorway. The secluded back patio was the last place she should go with him.

"I'm not used to a woman who won't follow my lead." His voice sounded carefree as he drew her out the door with his firm grasp.

Rachel stumbled. "My shoe!"

Luke caught her in his arms and deposited her on the nearest bench. He laid down his plumed hat and retrieved her lost pump with a smile and bow to a couple passing in the hallway. He closed the door and came to kneel in front of her. His sword scraped the patio bricks. She gazed at his bent head and breathed in the zesty tang of his aftershave. When his warm hand touched her bare foot and slipped on the green satin slipper, she trembled. Was she dreaming this whole scene?

He stood smiling. "This reminds me of a story

Kristina wants to hear over and over. But that girl lost a shoe trying to return home before twelve. I don't think she was mad at the prince."

He wasn't a prince, he was a 20th century pirate. Rachel's heart cried out as she sat willing her emotions not to respond to Luke's easy-going manner, his husky voice, and his appreciative glances.

"But I'm not a prince," he continued, "and you're not a girl in a fairy tale, you're—"

She stood but he wrapped his arms around her before she could escape.

"You've the most beautiful woman here. And yes, this particular costume gave me a start, but I've managed to get over it."

"Luke—" she began, but he pressed her close and the breath left her body.

"Hush," he commanded softly. "Do you really think I'm going to let you climb on the plane tomorrow?"

Rachel stiffened.

He brushed her forehead with his lips and weakness threatened to engulf her. She placed her hands on his chest and pushed away from him with all her strength, only to bring her face closer to his. He gazed long and deep into her eyes.

"I really wish I understood what is going on in your pretty head, Rachel. This afternoon you were so strange, and I needed to talk with you. I had something important to tell you, but you wouldn't even give me a chance. What is it?" He released her and stood back. "Tonight I sense the same thing. It's more than what you've shared of your faith, and it's not Morgan standing between us, is it?" He hesitated and his brows knit together. "Does it have to do with the guy you kissed on the porch? Is it him? If so, why did you send him away? Surely, you realize by now I am not in love with Morgan, and I want to talk to you regarding my tardy faith."

Rachel tore her eyes away from his and blinked back moisture. Tardy faith? Morgan? Easton? Can we discuss drug smuggling? A sharp sword stabbed Rachel's heart and she averted her face. He did sound different, but it must be an act. "Luke, it's not any of those things, and I really can't discuss this anymore." Her voice came out as a whisper.

"Look at me, Rachel."

She gazed at him—his firm jaw, his blazing eye in the moonlight, and the black and red pirate costume covering his broad frame. Standing there in a dress from long ago, Rachel battled an ethereal quality threatening to envelope them. Luke's voice even sounded unlike him.

"If you're running away from something, believe me, it can't be done. What you run away from moves faster and no matter where you go, it will be there waiting for you when you arrive." He balled a fist and cupped it with his other hand. His voice reduced to a whisper. "Like my war nightmares."

What was he saying? But how could it matter when a stash of cocaine lay hidden in his attic? She almost smiled. Yes, she wanted to run and hide. She'd tried to escape the pain of Ron's death by coming south. And now, when she climbed on the plane tomorrow, she would be denying her love for a drug smuggler. A huge lump rose in her throat. "You may be right," she murmured, her voice breaking.

Before Luke could stop her, she turned and hurried through the patio door. In the cool recesses of the lady's room, she patted water on her burning eyes and willed away tears.

When calmness returned, she went back into the hall to find Archer and take her leave. Not wanting to run into Luke again, she asked the butler where she might find her host. The man bowed and told her to check the library. She entered the large, paneled room and her breath froze in her throat. Luke in his pirate costume and Morgan in her blue dress stood wrapped in each other's arms at the fireplace.

Rachel moved back, eased the door to and sank against it. Luke's denial regarding Morgan minutes before. His sincere demeanor. All an act. And she needn't worry about confronting him again soon.

She spent the next half hour easing around the grouped guests seeking James Sanders or Archer. But the two were nowhere to be found. She finally gave up and hurried out the front entrance and around the darkened garden path to her car. The wind whipped her bouffant skirt, almost unbalancing her, and twigs and leaves blew into her face, but she didn't slacken her pace.

Driving back to Barrett Hall, heated thoughts assailed her. So he didn't care a thing about Morgan? And he thought marijuana shouldn't be legalized but he stashed a fortune of cocaine in his attic.

A limb bounced off the hood of the car shocking Rachel from her thoughts and awakening Penny. What kind of southern wind was this? She squinted through the windshield, now laced with drops of rain, at trees bending toward her headlights. Rachel let the dachshund crawl out of the carrier and snuggle up against her as she drove more slowly, scanning for other debris on the unpaved road back to Barrett Hall.

She patted the small dog. "Well, little girl, after tomorrow, you will become a Yankee pet and you must forget your southern birth place."

A tear plopped down Rachel's cheek. She brushed it away.

As she passed the road to the dock, she glanced out the window and hit the brakes. A white yacht bobbed and pulled at its ropes in the choppy waters, almost hidden by the swaying swamp grass, but her headlights picked it up as it rose and fell in the waves. The boat had not been there when she drove by earlier. She struggled a moment with indecision. Should she try to investigate? Was this Luke's contact for the drugs? The scene in the library with Luke and Morgan flowed into her mind. The man didn't appear worried about anything. Perhaps his arrest would wake him up. Most important, maybe she could help uncover something Ron gave his life trying to investigate. The real reason she'd come to Charleston.

Taking a deep, shaky breath, she killed the headlights and motor, drew Penny in her arms and stepped out of the car. The damp wind whipped her skirts and almost knocked her over, but she soon found her footing.

"For you, Ron," she whispered, keeping to the shadows.

She pushed against the wind toward the dock, gripping her skirt with one hand and Penny with the other. If she only caught a glimpse of the boat's name, that would be something. If it had one. Ron told her drug smugglers often used unmarked boats to move drugs into the United States. Did Luke even own a yacht? If he did, he'd kept it a good secret. But, of course, he would do so if it were used for drug smuggling.

She stopped at the edge of the tall, billowing grass and scanned the sides of the boat for a name as scattered raindrops began to fall. Her lips tightened. The boat boasted no name or identifying mark.

Something moved behind her and she gasped. She turned around as fast as her unruly skirts allowed. Judge. She breathed a sigh of relief as the collie emerged from the bushes and came to her. Penny gave a warning bark.

A figure stepped from the shadows behind Kristina's dog. Rachel's heart jumped into her throat and every muscle in her body tensed for flight. A crimson-coated pirate emerged in the wind and rain, his red-plumed hat held down to keep the moisture out of his face. Luke. No wonder Judge had not barked.

She froze, unable to cry out or even think. It was like a dream. But it was all true. Luke was a pirate. A criminal with his own unmarked boat.

Judge came to sit beside her. He pressed his muzzle against her windswept skirt and whined.

Yes, he too loved a law breaker of the worst sort. And now, like Ron, she'd lost her chance to do anything.

Suddenly, strength flowed into Rachel's limbs. She whirled left toward a narrow path of escape, but her wet skirts hampered her. She managed three steps before strong arms closed around her and Penny and a heavy hand clamped over her mouth. She was lifted right out of her flimsy heels.

A scream tore at her throat. She struggled but held firmly onto Penny, growling in her arms. She finally ceased struggling, hopeless, wet and angry. Her captor, still gripping her waist, set her feet back on the ground, and leaned close to her ear. She smelled his hot, alcohol-reeking breath on her cheek. So much for Luke not drinking.

Chapter Twenty-five

"Don't make a sound if you want to live. You or the puppy."

Rachel moaned and almost dropped Penny at the gritty words. Dakota's voice—not Luke's! She relaxed in the firm arms holding her like a balloon with the air escaping. *Thank You, Father.*

A voice with a heavy Hispanic accent hissed from the yacht. "Who is de girl, Coda?"

Dakota swore under his breath. He dragged Rachel toward the boat where a dark man in oil skins glowered at them. Behind him another man aimed an automatic rifle.

"Who do you think she is?" Dakota pulled her close in his arms. "She's my woman."

"Well, get rid of her." The man's cold, flat voice, sent chills up Rachel's spine. "No passengers allowed."

"On second thought," he moved closer to the edge of the boat and leered at Rachel. "Perhaps we should dispose of her on our way."

Dakota stiffened behind Rachel. "No, let's don't worry with her. I can handle the problem. "Give me a few minutes." He spoke with a confident, coaxing voice.

"It's all I'll let you have—and you better take good care of her, you understand? And quick, if you don't want to be left. This wind and rain is real bothersome."

"Yeah."

The man cursed and disappeared inside the boat's cabin, but the guard kept the rifle pointed toward them.

Jerking Rachel away from the boat, Dakota whispered in her ear. "Those guys will kill you without blinking an eye, or worse, sell you in South America to the top bidder. Do you understand? So, for God's sake, be quiet, while I figure out what to do with you."

"Oh, Dakota, why are you—"

"Shut up!"

Rachel clamped her mouth shut as Dakota stomped toward the beach with her in tow, swearing under his breath when she stumbled in her bare feet or her long skirt caught on debris blowing about. Once he muttered, "What is this crazy weather up to?"

Her mind whirled with questions as she avoided rocks and driftwood scattered in their path. "Dakota, did you kiss Morgan Pennington tonight in the library?"

He glanced back at her and his mouth curved up in a mocking grin, "Yeah, if you're taking notes. Where were you? Behind the sofa?" He gave her arm a jerk. "Walk faster."

The small beach house appeared ahead. Dakota pulled a key from his pocket, unlocked the door, and pushed her in. You can scream all you like, but I don't advise it, my dear girl. No one can hear you with this choppy ocean tonight, unless it's those bad guys back yonder. And you sure enough don't want to alert them."

Rachel examined the flimsy boarding of the floor and cringed at the increasing roar of the waves. "Dakota, don't leave me here." Wet now from her head to her bare toes, she shivered with cold. Penny was also soaked. She sat the puppy down and it promptly shook itself, showering droplets on the wooden slats.

Suddenly Dakota reached for her and pulled her close. "Would you rather I took you with me? I've got a little stash to set me up pretty somewhere." His mouth was sickeningly near hers.

She twisted her face away. "Where are you going?"

"South. Way south where nobody cares who you are. I came back to pick up my last deposit I've kept for my future."

She stopped struggling. "Dakota, did you hide it somewhere?"

"Yep, right where Luke Barrett will get the blame if anything goes wrong."

The attic of Barrett Hall, of course.

Rachel's lips tightened. "I'd never go anywhere with you, Dakota, and what are you going to do about your son who might be born any day now?

"So you and the little lady got together? She'll do fine without me. I've left a small account for her."

A criminal, with a piece of a heart.

Her forehead creased. Could she reach that sliver of compassion in the man? Her words tumbled out. "Dakota, give yourself up. God can forgive—"

"Shut up. It's too late for that, and I've got to go." He pushed her away so hard she fell to the floor. Penny ran toward her, whining. He slammed the door shut. The key turned in the padlock.

She pulled herself up from the floor, ran to the door, and pushed on it with all her might. She shook it and banged with her fists. Until a splinter pierced her hand. She winced and sat down on the small bench against the wall to run her finger over the protrusion. It was impossible without light or tweezers to remove it. She picked up Penny and began to pray.

Father, I've been wrong about so many things. Please forgive my stubbornness and jumping to conclusions, and taking such foolish risks. Most of all, forgive me for totally misjudging Luke. He wanted to tell me something, and I gave him no chance.

He's not smuggling drugs. Her heart sang with each beat.

And no wonder she'd seen him around every corner at the ball. Dakota dressed like the pirate picture, too. He was the real pirate involved in drug trafficking. Did the man understand the criminal element he'd joined? Ron called drug dealers the worse kind of scum. She remembered the cold, hard accent of the man on the boat. Dakota probably saved her life. But why did he lack regard for his own unborn son?

Rachel sighed and leaned her head against the wall. She hugged Penny in her arms and was amazed at how much warmth her pet generated. "Well, little one, we will wait and pray and expect the Lord to intervene in this whole situation."

Penny licked her hands and whined.

Sometime later, the roar of the ocean now many times louder, roused Rachel from her prayer and weariness. She stifled a scream as the shack rocked and creaked

Water flowed across her feet and to her ankles. She gasped. Was the tide all the way up to the beach house?

The strange whistling sound of the wind penetrated through the rain pelting the roof. A deafening roar of the ocean covered all other sounds.

She jumped and almost dropped Penny.

The whole building groaned. A loud, splitting noise erupted, and the beach house moved from its foundations. Rachel screamed.

Father, help us!

~*~

Luke searched for Rachel at the ball and finally for the German import he'd lent her outside. It was gone. He didn't like the way the wind whirled the tree tops and the off and on again rain. Tropical storms started the same way. He found James Sanders.

The solicitor took him aside. "The DEA has a lot of guys out and about tonight, Luke. They think something's going to happen. And a sizable storm warning has also come in."

"Yeh, it's the reason I'm heading back. Rachel left earlier. Need to check on her."

Sanders nodded, a knowing gleam in his eye. "Don't let anything happen to Rachel York, Luke. And I'm about positive I'll see you later tonight." He tapped his cell phone in his breast pocket. "I'm waiting to get the word from Deeson."

"Hey, tell Morgan I had to go, will you?"

"Sure."

Luke sped down the narrow, storm-swept hard dirt road between Pennington and Barrett Hall, familiar with every twist and turn like the back of his hand. He drove so fast, he shot by the entrance to the dock about the time he glimpsed the car he loaned Rachel parked in the shadows. Slamming on the brakes, he braced as the Italian import slid several yards in a perfect arc and turned totally around facing the dock.

He jumped out in the pelting rain and sprinted to the automobile shrouded in darkness. His gut lurched when he found it empty. Something glinted in his car headlights beaming on the dock. He scrambled forward. His breath stopped in his throat. Rachel's green heel with its rhinestone strap. "Oh, my God, no."

He scanned the river bank up and down, while the wind whipped his costume. His red plumed hat sailed out over the churning waters. He found a new rope tied to the end of the dock in the rice grass. Someone had hacked it in two. A quick undocking.

He rushed to the car, clutching Rachel's shoe. At Barrett Hall he ran across the lawn through the rain. In the game room he picked up the phone and called James Sanders' cell phone.

"James, she's gone! I think—" His voice broke. "The smugglers may have kidnapped her."

"Who? Kidnapped who?"

Luke swallowed the bile in his throat. "Rachel." He stared at the soiled green heel lying on his desk where he'd dropped it. His stomach twisted into knots. "I found the car she drove and her green shoe on my dock."

"I'm calling the Coast Guard, old friend. You sit tight. They may be right on top of this already. I told you the DEA has all their boys out tonight."

Sitting was impossible for Luke. He slammed his fist on the desk, stood, and paced making wet tracks across the wooden floor, trying not to imagine what may have—what might *be* happening to Rachel.

God is this Your idea of the potter's wheel, tearing me to pieces? Oh Lord, protect her.

Cade opened the door. "Hey, boss, I heard you

racing up the drive and then saw your light."

Luke swiped his forehead and hair with his broad hand. "Cade, Cade, I'm afraid they've taken her. Rachel."

Cade bowed his head as Luke relayed the finding of the car and the muddy shoe, now sitting on the wide desk. They both stared at it.

Luke swung his face away and paced to the fireplace. He gripped the mantle and hung his head.

"I feel so helpless, Cade. In Iraq my weapon was my confidence. I could at least shoot anything moving. But if she's out in a drug lord's boat and they make it to the open sea, even the Coast Guard might not be able to—" He swallowed. "I should've never let her stay here this summer."

Cade frowned and squeezed a large hand into a fist. "They won't get far in this storm. They'd be crazy even to head out to sea." He walked over to where Luke stood, rigid with anger and fear. Cade recognized the stance. His voice softened. "Cap'n Luke there's someone much more interested in her safety than you and me. Why don't we talk to Him about her?"

They bowed their heads. Cade prayed a fervent prayer. Luke interceded next, almost as if he'd forgotten Cade was present. When they finished, Cade's face registered surprise as he scanned Luke's face.

A light knock sounded at the door. It opened.

Maggie stood there, twisting a handkerchief. "Mr. Luke, I knows you don't have much use for my mother, but she says she's got 'portant information about Miss York."

Luke and Cade glanced at each other, their eyes wide.

"Send her in." Luke said.

Granny Eller walked in. Water dripped from her rain bonnet and her slicker onto her shiny, wet army boots. Fire blazed from her eyes.

"I see'd that boat. And the girl didn't go on it. A pirate-looking fellow drug her and the puppy down toward the beach." She pushed the cover from her damp, gray hair. "I followed them fur as I was able 'fore the white man doubled back by hisself. Ya'll oughta check the beach shack. May God help her if it's washed away."

Luke dashed to the door. Cade sprinted a hairsbreadth behind him.

"The horses, Cade. We can't risk road blockages with the jeep."

Granny stomped her boot. "Well, ain't nobody gonna thank me fer this night's work?"

Maggie moved beside her mother as the two men hurried out the patio door. "Give 'em time, mama. We gotta pray they save Miss York. Now let's git you dried off and some hot tea in you."

Chapter Twenty-Six

The door of the hut split open from the hinges. Clutching Penny and dragging her swirling skirt, Rachel stumbled over the threshold. Her heart sank to her toes. Foaming water and broken tree limbs spread as far as she could fathom in the darkness. Where was the beach? Rain mixed with salt spray covered her face, choking her. She swiped at it and peeled clinging hair from her vision. Which way to go? Weakness rolled over her as she confronted the wild sea. Huge waves and white caps reared many feet into the air. She needed to get to higher ground!

She tried to hasten through the churning tidewater, but her long, soaked dress imprisoned her legs at every other step or caught on a floating limb. Fear threatened to overcome her as new waves washed over her, almost knocking her down.

"When you pass through the waters, I'll be with you." *Thank You, Father.*

A manmade rock cliff loomed ahead, barely discernible in the darkness and rain and Rachel pressed toward it, clutching Penny with one hand, and dragging her heavy skirt with the other. As she drew nearer, a flat area appeared midway above the formation, a shelf the waves did not reach. At the same moment a huge roar sounded behind her. A giant wall of murky water as high as she could see rose in the angry sea. She must wedge herself in between the low rocks and hold on for dear life or be washed out to sea.

What about Penny?

The wet and shivering miniature dachshund whined as if she discerned the eminent danger. Rachel made a fast decision. "You'll be okay, little girl," she shouted, and with one great stretch, she lifted the puppy up and half shoved, half tossed her onto the high ledge. Penny immediately hugged the inside wall of the shelf formation.

Rachel barely got her skirt and body lodged between two huge boulders when the roaring wave washed over her, filling her eyes, ears, and nose. The last sound that reached her was her pet's mournful howl on the safe ground above.

~*~

Luke on Haidez and Cade on his horse behind him galloped the fastest route to the shack, across fields, bushes, gulleys, and storm debris. The rain stopped on the way. The storm started moving northward. They broke out of the trees toward the ledge above the shack. Luke walked Haidez up to the edge and peered down for the beach hut. Only the foundation was left. His heart stopped in his chest. He jumped off Haidez and fell to his knees. "Father, please let her be alive somehow. Forgive me for ever thinking I didn't need You."

Cade, still mounted, bowed his head.

A mournful howl from somewhere below alerted Luke. He stumbled to his feet and pulled Haidez along behind him as he searched the cliff's edge. He scoured the embankment. Penny sat on a rock ledge below, emitting the sorrowful sounds.

"Penny." Luke stooped down and called.

The dachshund lifted her head, wagged her tail, and started barking. Luke took half a breath.

But where is...? A terrible thought bombarded Luke's mind. But when the tide receded, something white flashed between two large rocks. It moved. Joy flooded his heart.

"It's Rachel!" Luke reached for the thick rope on his saddle. He tied one end to the horn on Haidez's saddle and made a fast seat harness for himself with the other end and jammed his hands into gloves from his saddlebag.

Cade swung down from his horse to assist. Luke stepped to the edge of the ravine and Cade helped keep the rope taunt with Haidez bracing as Luke began rappelling down the rock wall.

He dropped down on Penny's ledge first. He picked up the small dog and tossed her up to the waiting hands above.

Cade caught the wet puppy, petted her and placed her on the ground "You gonna be fine, little doggy." He also spoke gently to the horse with all its muscles straining. Haidez snorted and dug his hooves into the damp ground as the saddle rope tightened when Luke proceeded down the cliff.

Luke reached Rachel and leaned down before touching her. He scanned her head, arms and upper body for wounds and saw only scratches. She moved and a prayer escaped his lips. "Thank You, Father, thank You."

~*~

Rachel coughed and opened her eyes. Luke bent

close to her with a thick rope around his torso and upper legs. She smelled his aftershave mingled with sweat. Did he utter a prayer?

Luke smiled at her. "Do you think anything is broken?" His voice was so husky she barely understood him.

His face held such tenderness and concern she trembled from more than the cold.

"Are you okay?" Luke asked again. This time his voice sounded like music to her ears.

She pushed up from between the rocks and moved her arms and legs and took a deep breath. "I don't think anything is broken. A little bruised." She glanced up at Cade and smiled at Penny barking and racing back and forth along the cliff edge. "Thank you for rescuing Penny, Luke but how will you get me up there?"

"I rappelled down and Cade, Haidez, and the good Lord will pull us both up." He pointed at her costume's once beautiful long bouffant skirt, now soaked and torn in several places. "But some of this has to go. Do you mind?"

She shook her head. He pulled a knife from his pocket and made a small cut at the waistline of the dress. He ripped off the top soaked layer of satin and one petticoat layer, the very stuff that had cushioned her from the rocks. She was glad to get rid of the weight.

Luke instructed her to put her arms around him and lock her hands behind his neck. His warmth flowed to her body as she pressed against him. He secured the rope about her waist and tied her to him, knotting it just right so it wouldn't pinch when they began the ascent. She slipped into a dream state as

Cade and Haidez slowly pulled them up the rock wall. With one arm around Rachel and one hand grasping the rope Luke used his feet to push them out from the wall and possible scrapes as they slowly rose. If she lived to be a hundred, she would never forget this rescue.

When they reached the top, Luke gently lowered Rachel to the ground. Haidez nickered and came to nudge his shoulder. Penny jumped toward Rachel and licked her face. Rachel tried to pet the puppy but her chilled limbs wouldn't move. The last thing she remembered was strong arms lifting her into Haidez's saddle.

~*~

Rachel awoke with the memory of horrible waves crashing around her and her heart pounding in her chest. Where was she? She opened her eyes. The blue canopy of her bed comforted her. Light poured in the French doors and danced atop her comforter. The clock on her nightstand clicked to one o'clock. In the afternoon? Shocked, she took a deep breath and sat up. Bruises on her arms surprised her. Memory rushed back. The costume ball, the boat, Dakota locking her in the shack and the terrible storm. Luke and his daring rescue from the cliff, the first words from his mouth sounding like a prayer. Had she imagined them? The whole thing appeared like a dream in the daylight.

She pushed out of bed with a groan as her sore muscles resisted. But she showered and dressed in jeans and a yellow shell, gently pulling the clothing over her bruises. Thank God, she only suffered blue places and a few scratches. Today was the day to fly home. Why did her heart not jump with joy? She checked her ticket. Only six hours remained of her working summer holiday. All she really wanted to do was to climb back on top of the bed and crash, but she lugged her suitcase from the closet instead, and forced herself to pack.

A half hour later her bedroom door gently opened. Jessica and Kristina peeped in.

"Rachel!" Kristina flew in and threw her arms around Rachel's waist. Rachel tried not to wince.

Jessica's tired eyes crinkled in a deep smile. "So glad you're up and about after your ordeal. How are you?

"Oh, I'm going to be fine. The Lord really helped me." *And Luke.* "Only a few bruises." Rachel laid her last blouse in the suitcase.

"We put you to bed a few hours before dawn, and, of course, we want to learn what happened to you. But let's get down to Maggie's brunch. I'm sure you're starved."

Rachel followed the two to the loggia and the wonderful smells of Maggie's cooking.

During the country brunch of ham, eggs, grits, cantaloupe and tasty biscuits, Jessica filled Rachel in once Kristina ran outside to play. "The Drug Enforcement Administration suspected a drug operation going on from the coastline for some time, but were not able to get proof. They asked Luke to work with them."

Okay to the late night excursions and his distrust. But where was he now?

"Of course, Luke told no one about all this, except Cade." Jessica sipped her tea and glanced at Rachel. "Last night the DEA along with the Coast Guard were busy doing surveillance along our coast during the costume ball. The storm actually assisted them. The drug dealer's boat couldn't get away like planned."

"How did Luke find me?"

"Oh, now that's a story in itself. Granny Eller came and told Luke about your capture by Dakota. It appears she was on a tromp just as the storm hit. I hope she doesn't suffer from being out in it." Jessica lowered her voice as footsteps approached down the hall. "They arrested Dakota and his partners. Poor Mrs. Busby. Dakota has really disappointed her. Let's hope he repents and turns state evidence. Luke said it might go easier for him if he does."

Maggie entered, removed the empty dishes and left.

Jessica picked up her cup, and leaned toward Rachel. "One bright spot for Mrs. Busby. She knows about Dakota's girlfriend and she's looking forward to taking care of her first grandbaby and its mother. You met the mother, I understand."

"Yes, and I'm so glad she'll be cared for." Rachel averted her eyes and tried to still her increased heartbeat. "Where…is Luke now?"

"He's tied up with the solicitor's office, or the DEA. I believe the authorities are at this moment arresting a number of folks involved in the operation." Jessica's voice lowered. "More local people are implicated than Dakota."

"But—who else?"

Jessica raised her brows and pursed her lips before dropping a bombshell. "Luke said Archer has been arrested and Morgan is devastated. I understand she's even gone to counseling with your Pastor Gordon. Don't quote me on any of this, Rachel. We'll be sure by the end of the day or at least by the time tomorrow's papers hit the street."

"But I'm leaving tonight."

"Why don't you call and reschedule your flight? I'm sure James Sanders will want to talk with you."

Suddenly, Rachel envisioned the possibility of Ron's tragedy being reopened, discussed, and linked to her coming to Charleston. It would be painful and hardly useful. "No, I hope it won't be necessary." Then a small cry escaped her lips. "Oh, Jessica, the drugs!"

Jessica's eyes widened. "What drugs?"

"I found some drugs on the third floor when I went to find a costume yesterday."

Pain gripped Rachel's heart. Jessica would guess she'd suspected Luke and hadn't thought enough of their friendship to confide in her.

The kind blue eyes stared at Rachel a moment. "And you told not a soul?"

"No, I'm sorry I didn't."

"You suspected someone in this house. Luke."

Rachel lowered her head. "I didn't want to, but I had a hard time imagining how else the drugs got there until Dakota admitted it when he dragged me down to the beach house."

"Of course, and Luke, if I may say so, has acted mighty strange."

Jessica smiled. "This should do Luke a world of good."

"What will?"

"Finding out you suspected him of drug smuggling. What did you plan to do about your discovery?"

Rachel sighed, remembering the hopeless calls to Joseph. But why mention Joseph? "Well, I planned to talk with James Sanders at the ball, but never found him."

"Rachel, where are the drugs now?"

"I don't know, unless they're still in the spot I hid them on the third floor."

Jessica stood. "Well, for heaven's sakes, let's go check."

They found the packet exactly in the place Rachel dropped it. Behind the pirate picture.

Jessica went downstairs to call James Sanders.

Rachel decided to complete her packing. She would stay with her earlier plans. Why not? The drugs were taken care of. And Luke? She certainly ought to thank him for rescuing her. Say goodbye. But she cringed at the thought of facing him after suspecting him. She was happy he was not smuggling drugs but the fact did not alter what he'd already shared with her regarding his lack of faith. And saying goodbye would be most painful. Perhaps she'd write a note.

At three o'clock she checked her bags for the third time and tried to stir up confidence about her decision to leave as planned. Jessica would be glad to drive her to the airport for her seven o'clock flight. But there was one loose end she'd love to tie up. Was this drug ring the same one Ron had been investigating?

But Ron was gone. Wasn't it time she let him go?

And Luke. He floated across each breath she inhaled no matter how hard she tried to put him from her mind. His gray face when she opened her eyes in the cleft of the rock, his strength and warmth during the unbelievable climb up the rock wall. But he'd scorned Christianity being important. She was making the right decision. She *would* get over him. These thoughts swirled back and forth through her head, challenged by a choir of emotions.

Finally, she threw the French doors open and walked onto the balcony and into bright sunshine.

Was the porch still off limits?

The fragrance and colors of the garden after last night's storm burst upon her senses. Again, the hollyhocks needed righting. She walked down the steps and lifted the stalks back into place, stamping around their base to firm them up.

Scouring the rest of the garden path, Rachel found and moved some broken limbs then stopped and took a deep breath. She would always be glad she came to Barrett Hall. She'd grown in so many ways. Granted, some of the ways were painful. She'd experienced what beginning love between a man and woman felt like, if only for a few glorious hours. It hurt to breathe remembering. Some never knew this kind of love at all. She was one of the fortunate ones.

Suddenly, she wanted to gaze at the ocean one more time. In bright sunlight. Her home lay far from any ocean, and she hated to take last night's angry sea as her final summer memory. She glanced at her wristwatch. Still almost four hours until her flight. She skipped up the steps and left a note for Jessica on her bed, and headed back down to the beach road.

She stood on the sand at the edge of the tide and stared at the now calm, gentle sea. Sea gulls cried over her head and swooped down to investigate the interloper. A breeze lifted her hair, and she licked the salty taste on her lips.

Climbing onto a warm rock, she drew her knees up and tried to memorize the scene before her. Had pirates once walked this shoreline? She could imagine a black-flagged galleon, its anchor thrown, bobbing in the waves. A rowboat lowered, full of rowdy, sword-jangling pirates. Pirates who dealt in gold, not drugs. She cocked her head. Her ears played tricks on her. What sounded like oars plopped on the waves down the beach.

Rachel turned. Luke rode Haidez up the beach at the edge of the water. Her heart pounded against her ribs. The glistening black stallion, mane and tail flying in the breeze, set each hoof gingerly into the bubbling surf. He lifted his sinewy legs high and snorted when flying spray touched his nose. Luke sat astride the magnificent horse immobile, straight, in complete command with one hand on the reins.

She tore her eyes away and tried to breathe. A deep ache raced across her mid drift. The two of them, coming through the surf, burned into her memory. Luke, a true descendent of pirates like those who had filled her thoughts, riding on a creature straight out of the Arabian nights.

But, thank You Lord, Luke is no pirate. All her doubts, her suspicions had been wrong. Heat singed her cheeks. What must he think of her? How could she face him?

She hugged her arms about her knees and waited for him. The time undoubtedly had gotten away from her. He must have come in search of her.

He turned Haidez out of the surf a few feet from her, swung off the stallion's back, and dropped the reins in the sand. "Cold?"

Rachel tried to still the hammering of her heart. She stood, thinking of running up the beach and back to the plantation but something about Luke's manner, his voice, his gaze, held her.

"No. I'm sorry you had to come searching for me."

She groped for words and watched, intrigued, as he walked closer and withdrew something from his shirt.

She gasped. Her green satin shoe.

"When I found this at the dock last night...." His voice sounded rough as sandpaper as he fingered her shoe. "It was like the war all over again."

Her eyes flew to his face with its eye patch.

"But I had a rifle to plunge into the bushes with, in search of those who destroyed the innocents in village after village."

Tears formed in Rachel's eyes.

"Last night I was afraid it was too late, even for revenge—I thought the scum escaped to the islands or South America—and took you with them or killed you."

Suddenly, Luke dropped the shoe and pulled her to him with such force the breath swooshed out of her lungs.

"Luke," she murmured, but he continued with his lips against her hair.

"I cannot tell you what a rage filled me. It turned to pain and hopelessness, but Cade came in and we prayed. I found myself praying like I once prayed. Cushwell would've been surprised. And right after we said amen, Granny Eller appeared and told us about Dakota dragging you down to the beach shack." He held her at arm's length. "It was the fastest answer to prayer I've experienced."

Tears ran down her cheeks. He bent and kissed them away. The tender expression on his faced amazed her. Gone was the arrogant, cynical, harshness so often evident.

"Pastor Gordon?"

"Yeah, I went to visit him. He told me I needed to

get on the potter's wheel."

Rachel smiled through her tears. *Thank You, Lord.*

She looked up at him. "Did Jessica tell you about the…drugs I found?"

"Yeah, and I can understand why you suspected me. I guess." He grinned.

Rachel breathed a sigh of relief. "Was this a big drug bust?"

"The biggest on the whole southeast coast. The DEA's been working on it for months. Of course, it's not over yet. I've been out with them today serving warrants. There's been some surprising revelations, even besides Archer—folks you wouldn't imagine being involved. We've got a lot of work to do if we keep this mess from happening again. Which reminds me—would you mind having a husband who helps the DEA for a while?"

"Oh, Luke." Rachel's knees turned to mush. *A husband?*

"I'm asking you to marry me. Say you will."

She nodded dreamily.

"Uh, huh. Say, 'I will marry you, Luke Barrett, tomorrow.'"

"I will marry you, Luke Barrett," she whispered, her cheek snuggled on his chest.

"Tomorrow," he coaxed.

She lifted her head and gazed into his handsome face. "No, I can't tomorrow. My dear Aunt Ruby and best friend Raven need to be here and that's too fast."

"If your Ruby were going to be here tomorrow would you marry me?"

Aunt Ruby arriving the next day? "There's no way Ruby might be here on such short notice." She stared at Luke. Why was he joking?

He responded by pressing her close, holding her head against his shoulder.

Luke's voice, strangely soft, caressed her, his breath feathered her hair. "If the DEA called her earlier today and convinced her they'd have a seat for her on the first plane, she could be here."

Rachel frowned. A tremor started in her knees. "Why would the DEA ask my aunt to travel to Charleston?" Her mouth went as dry as cotton and the tremor reached her spine.

"I'm going to turn you around, Rachel. I want you to see why."

Luke turned her with his arm still clasping her. His heart beat strong and steady against her quivering shoulders.

She opened her eyes wide. Two men walked toward them. One, she recognized immediately— Joseph.

The other? The tall, blond, bearded man— something about his walk, his carriage, his confidence rippled through Rachel like lightning. "Dearest God!" She burst from Luke's arms with a sob, ran the distance, and threw herself into her brother's outstretched arms.

"Hey, kitten. Take it easy. Didn't know you cared so much." Ron's husky, familiar voice blessed her.

Luke came up and Ron reached out a hand to him. "You must be Luke Barrett. I'm Ron York, Rachel's brother and this is Joseph, my partner."

"Yes, Deeson told me you'd be coming." They shook hands. Joseph nodded at Rachel, a real smile beamed across his face.

Ron fished around in a pocket and handed Rachel his handkerchief, and added with a grin, "I hope what

I just witnessed on the beach means this guy is going to take responsibility for your hankies from now on, sister."

She laughed through her tears and finally found her voice. "Ron, *where have you been?*"

"There's plenty of time for the whole story when Ruby gets here," he said easily. "For now let's say it was best for me to stay dead until a big net could be drawn which, by the way, we are still drawing, so mum's the word."

"Oh, Ron, I can't appreciate your line of reasoning." Rachel pressed the handkerchief to her eyes.

Ron gazed down on his sister's tear-stained face, chucked her under the chin, and said in a hoarse voice. "You can't imagine how it hurt me to think what this was putting you and dear Ruby through." He pressed his lips together. "But I also found out breaking this drug ring depended on certain scum folks thinking I was a goner, so I prayed and came to my decision. Somehow I was certain you and Ruby would be okay. Was I wrong?"

She sighed and hugged him again. "Oh, Ron. I don't want to even think about it anymore. I'm just glad you're back." Tears threatened to pour down her face again.

"And Rachel, we'll talk a lot about this later, but guess who else was involved in this gang? Lester, our wonderful, deceiving stepfather. Remember all his trips out of the country?'

Joseph cleared his throat and Ron stepped aside. Luke moved forward and placed a secure arm around Rachel's waist.

Ron glanced at Luke and winked. "Hey, I'll look

for you two back at the plantation in a little while." He and Joseph turned and walked to a vehicle parked beyond the dune.

Luke led Rachel down the beach where Haidez waited. "One other thing, Rachel, you remember the resort vision I shared with you, Kingdom by the Sea? A group of businessmen want to buy in, and I'm thinking seriously about it. It could keep the plantation solvent for many years, and also make our secluded coastline most unattractive to smugglers."

Rachel rejoiced at the excitement in his voice. "Luke, how wonderful."

"And, of course, we'll continue our tea production." He took her into his arms. "Can you plan a wedding in two weeks, you think?

"How about three?"

He drew her so close she could hardly breathe. When his lips touched hers, fire coursed through her until her bones started to melt.

Luke released her and held her at arm's length. His hands shook on her shoulders. "Now, Miss York, we best be getting back to the plantation before…

"Before what?"

"Before I start hating those three weeks." He kissed her again, helped her mount Haidez, and swung up behind her.

Rachel wanted to lift her hands and shout for joy. She'd come to Charleston to find the truth about Ron. God gave her brother back to her. But He also gave her the love of her life, Luke Daniel Barrett. Indeed, all things had worked together for her good. Far beyond her highest expectation.

Epilogue

Rachel sat on the window seat in the upstairs sitting room of Barrett Hall in the early morning of the last Saturday in September.

My wedding day.

Delicious aromas from the baking taking place in the kitchen below stairs made her hungry. She'd scarcely been able to eat breakfast. A panorama of activity spread out before her eyes on the lawn and garden paths below. A canopy, bridal arch, rows of chairs, and a reception tent found perfect locations with the help of the event director flying around below like a bumble bee instructing the four workers from the rental company. Rachel smiled.

The woman Jessica steered Rachel to for directing was a jewel. She understood how everything needed to be done for a garden ceremony.

A floral truck drove up with special flowers—the yellow trellis roses and ivy, her bride's sweetheart rose bouquet and the flowers for the bridesmaids and groomsmen. When she thought of the snowy gown and veil hanging on her wardrobe door, her heart threatened to burst. She gazed at the huge diamond on her left hand, sparkling in the sunlight, and shivered with amazement.

Three o'clock stretched a long way off. Jessica, Ruby, her college roommate Raven, Maggie, Mrs.

Busby, and Kristina were downstairs helping with the reception fixings. The wedding guests would enjoy an afternoon tea like seldom enjoyed, even in Charleston. Luke encouraged Rachel to plan as big as she liked. She enjoyed choosing a menu of assorted open-faced tiny sandwiches, traditional crumpets with whipped cream, strawberry scones, an array of fresh fruits and homemade pastries and cookies. Jessica helped her pick out marvelous sounding teas including China Rose Petal and Peach Ginger Twist. The women would not let her do a thing, in fact, insisted she not come downstairs until she descended in her bridal finery.

From her balcony, soon after dawn, she'd watched Luke gallop away on Haidez with Cade and a barking Gabriel not far behind. He wanted to do a last minute check on plantation matters before their honeymoon. She whispered a prayer for nothing to go wrong in Luke's absence. Cade and Luke's other farm overseers would make sure.

The door behind her opened. Who had found her hiding place?

"So here you are." Luke stood in the doorway in his army boots, Levis, and Marine tee, much like the first time she'd met him on the porch months earlier.

She opened her mouth to tell him a groom must not see a bride until the ceremony, but he whipped off his cowboy hat and Rachel almost fell from the window seat. "Your eye patch—"

"Gone. I wanted to surprise you, but I didn't want you to faint at the altar."

She stood and walked to him, stunned. "Oh, Luke, it looks so...normal. I can hardly tell." Tears gathered in her eyes. "How did it happen?" She moved closer and breathed deeply of the outdoor scents of fresh air, horses and leather clinging to him.

"I got a call from my old army doctor a few weeks ago. He told me I needed to come in and check on some advancements made with artificial eyes. So, here I am, *advanced*." He smiled and drew her into his arms. "How about we practice our kiss for this afternoon?"

He kissed her long and deep and her brain turned to mush. He bent for another, but she pushed him away. "Oh, get out of here, before I lose it entirely, you wolf."

He let her go, grinned, and reached into his pocket and extracted a slender black velvet box. He pressed it into her hand. "Another of my wedding presents. One of the family heirlooms."

She untied the satin ribbon and opened it. "Oh, Luke, they're beautiful." She picked up the single strand of pearls and touched them to her cheek.

~*~

At five minutes to three the wedding director knocked on Rachel's door. Ruby secured the final rosebud on Rachel's headpiece and hugged her, careful not to muss her dress.

Jessica stood in the hall when Rachel emerged in her gown of snowy satin and lace with Luke's strand of pearls at her neck. The woman blinked back tears. "What an answer to prayer this is, my dear," she whispered. "And how lovely you are."

Rachel lifted her elegant veil and kissed Jessica's cheek.

The director arranged Rachel's train at the top of the staircase. Kristina, decked out in a yellow organza dress with a tiara in her hair, came forward. The child, coaxed not to hug Rachel, could not hide the joy on her face. Rachel pulled a bud from her bouquet and gave it to Kristina before bending to kiss the top of her head.

Rachel glanced down the steps. Ron, who was to give Rachel away, stood at the bottom of the stairs in his gray tux, in earnest conversation with Raven. The sudden strains of the Wedding March from the keyboard installed on the plantation porch interrupted their talk. The two of them turned and gazed up at Kristina and Rachel ready to descend. Warm smiles lit Ron's and Raven's faces.

Cade, Luke's best man, stood at the front door, pleasure blazing on his face like sunshine.

Stunning in her pink maid of honor dress and flower tiara, Raven crossed the hall and took Cade's extended arm. The two strolled out the door toward the garden canopy.

Kristina descended the stairs, keeping the rose petals in her basket, hopefully, until she reached the carpeted pathway between the rows of chairs. The child was doing great.

Rachel thought her heart might burst as she made her way down the steps amid the photographer's flashing bulbs.

Ron gave a low whistle as she stopped before him. She pulled her veil aside long enough to accept his proffered kiss on her cheek. When the wedding music swelled to its loudest, she clasped his strong arm and they began their march. She floated as if on air out the front door, over the rose-strewn path toward the bridal arch. Intakes of breath rustled like a gentle breeze through fall leaves as she and Ron passed. The yellow roses and calla lilies in her bouquet and woven around the canopy and arch filled the air with their fragrance.

Luke stood waiting for her at the garden altar in his black tuxedo with its yellow boutonnière. She forgot to breathe when their eyes met. They moved in place before the minister. She glanced at Cade standing beside Luke in a gray tuxedo and yellow tie. He ducked his head but couldn't hide a grin a mile wide.

Pastor Gordon performed a marriage ceremony filled with scripture. Rachel only had eyes for Luke, and he for her as they pledged their vows to each other.

At the reception under the tent Rachel smiled at the housekeeper, Mrs. Busby, cuddling Ava's two-week-old son, Caleb. Ava sat beside them enjoying tea and sandwiches. Dakota turned state evidence, but he would still be in prison for quite some time. Meanwhile, Mrs. Busby rejoiced to learn about her little grandson and invited Ava and the baby to move in her cottage at Barrett Hall. She told everyone the boy was the spitting image of Dakota as a baby.

Luke's warm hand on her waist brought her eyes to his. Her knees went weak as he caressed her face with a look of pure love. "Can you ever forgive me for being stubborn and bullheaded and almost missing out on this wonderful day?"

Rachel lifted a piece of wedding cake toward his lips. "If you can forgive me for jumping to conclusions, also for hardheadedness, taking foolish risks, and not trusting you with the truth about Ron."

"Probably. But I plan to stretch it out over a lifetime, my sweet, and make sure you stay out of trouble." He pulled her away from the tent and toward the house.

In twenty minutes, they emerged, dressed in casual outfits, their luggage already packed in the car.

Rachel hugged a happy Kristina, Jessica, Ruby, Ron and Raven. Luke shook Cade's hand, and embraced him unashamedly. Cade opened the back car door for them. Amid a heavy shower of rice, Luke and Rachel piled into the automobile. Cade drove them toward Charleston, humming a happy tune.

In the back seat Rachel broke away from Luke's breathless kisses to glance out the window. "Where are we headed, Luke? You told me to pack cool, but also to include some evening wear."

"I guess you can find out now. We are taking a chartered boat to a secret island first and afterwards to *islands* plural. Remember our rendezvous on the top deck of Archer's boat? I want to spend a lot of moments like that with you."

Rachel laid her head on his shoulder and her heart swelled with love. She'd never experienced such happiness. Who would've dreamed a summer job down south would end up being an adventure of a lifetime, bring her brother back from the dead, and seal her forever to the love of her life? She lifted her face toward Luke's. "My cup runneth over."

Luke trailed kisses from her lips to her ear lobe. His warm breath and spicy scent caressed her. "And mine, my love."

Made in the USA
Middletown, DE
26 June 2017